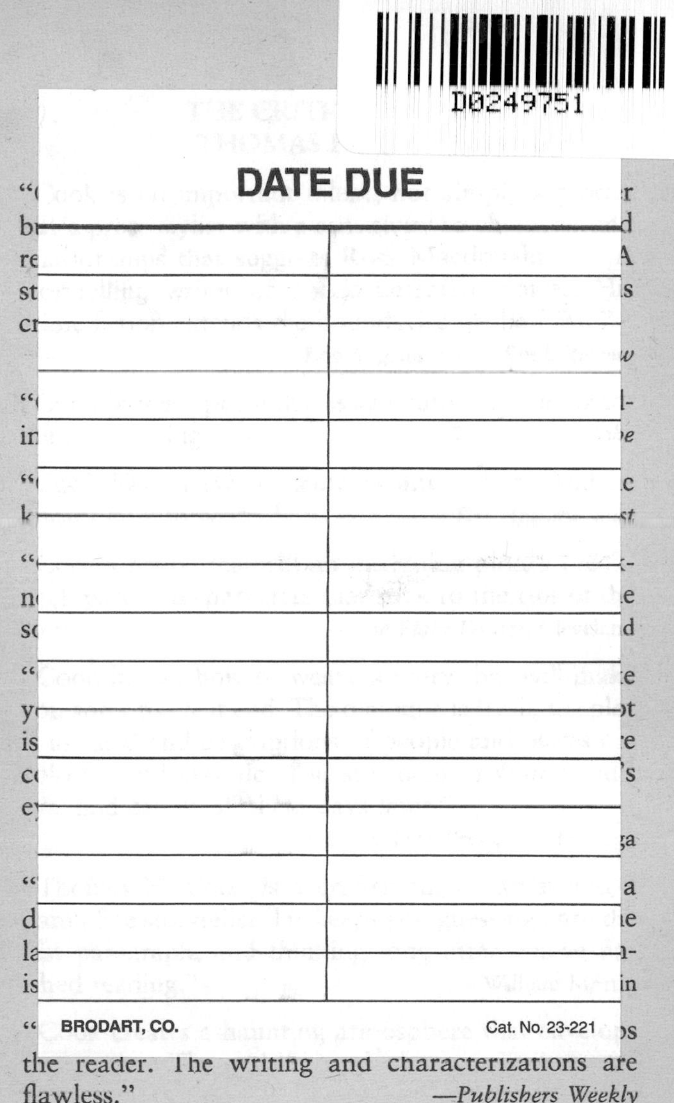

the reader. The writing and characterizations are flawless."
—*Publishers Weekly*

"Cook's night visions, seen through a lens darkly, are haunting."
—*The New York Times Book Review*

EXTRAORDINARY PRAISE FOR *MORTAL MEMORY*

"Cook builds a family portrait in which violence seems both impossible and inevitable. One of [*Mortal Memory*'s] greatest accomplishments is the way it defies expectations . . . surprising and devastating."

—*Chicago Tribune*

"Insightful . . . Unusually affecting."

—*Los Angeles Times Book Review*

"A waking nightmare . . . a creepy, beautifully paced book with a terrific twist. . . . Thomas H. Cook [is] a man of prodigious talent."

—*The Globe and Mail,* Toronto

"Riveting . . . Though you'll think you've solved the puzzle at least five times, I guarantee the ending will shock you."

—*The Plain Dealer,* Cleveland

"Impressive . . . Finely crafted psychological crimefare."

—*Kirkus Reviews*

"Cook writes of mental terror and suspense. His latest is as frightening as any ever written. . . . Cook's particular talent is that he haunts his readers, long after they have finished his work."

—*Ocala Star-Banner*

AND FOR THOMAS H. COOK AND HIS PREVIOUS NOVEL *EVIDENCE OF BLOOD*

"In such previous novels as *Sacrificial Ground* and *Blood Innocents*, Cook has shown himself to be a writer of poetic gifts, constantly pushing against the presumed limits of crime fiction. He has melded the classic puzzle mystery with more recent crime-writing, steeped in introspection and social realism, with impressive success. In company with writers as unlike himself as P. D. James and Ruth Rendell, Cook appears to set himself more demanding tasks each time out, testing his own gifts. In this fine new book, he has gone to the edge, and survived triumphantly."

—Charles Champlin, *Los Angeles Times Book Review*

"Thomas H. Cook is a master crime craftsman, and *Evidence of Blood* is blistering by the climax."

—*Booklist*

"A highly satisfying story, strong in color and atmosphere, intelligent and exacting."

—*The New York Times Book Review*

"Cook's splendidly written, continually surprising novel thoroughly rewards the reader. His pacing is taut, his characters and their stories memorable."

—*Publishers Weekly*

Also by Thomas H. Cook

Fiction

EVIDENCE OF BLOOD
THE CITY WHEN IT RAINS
NIGHT SECRETS
STREETS OF FIRE
FLESH AND BLOOD
SACRIFICIAL GROUND
THE ORCHIDS
TABERNACLE
ELENA
BLOOD INNOCENTS

Nonfiction

EARLY GRAVES
BLOOD ECHOES

Coming soon in hardcover from Bantam Books

BREAKHEART HILL

MORTAL MEMORY

THOMAS H. COOK

BANTAM BOOKS
NEW YORK • TORONTO • LONDON • SYDNEY • AUCKLAND

This edition contains the complete text of the original hardcover edition.
NOT ONE WORD HAS BEEN OMITTED.

MORTAL MEMORY

A Bantam Book/published by arrangement with G. P. Putnam's Sons

PUBLISHING HISTORY

Putnam's hardcover edition/April 1993

Bantam paperback edition/April 1994

Library of Congress Catalog Card Number: 92-43702.

ISBN 0-553-56532-X

Published simultaneously in the United States and Canada

Bantam Books are published by Bantam Books, a division of Bantam Doubleday Dell Publishing Group, Inc. Its trademark, consisting of the words "Bantam Books" and the portrayal of a rooster, is Registered in U.S. Patent and Trademark Office and in other countries. Marca Registrada. Bantam Books, 1540 Broadway, New York, New York 10036.

PRINTED IN THE UNITED STATES OF AMERICA

RAD 0 9 8 7 6 5 4 3

FOR

Maria Eugeina Caballero, David Delgado,
Carlo and Rachel Malka and
Pablo Martinez-Calleja in Madrid

AND FOR

Charles Radanovich and
Antonio Perez-Melero in New York.

ONE

This much I remembered from the beginning: the floral curtains in their second-floor bedroom pulled tightly together; Jamie's new basketball at the edge of the yard, glistening in the rain; Laura's plain white bra lying haphazardly in the grass behind the house, the rest of our clothes, drenched and motionless as they hung from the line above it.

And I remembered this: two men in a car, both in the front seat; the one behind the wheel younger, smaller, bareheaded; the other wearing a gray hat, breathing hard, smoking. It was the older one who first spoke, drawing his wire-rimmed glasses from his eyes, then wiping them with a white handkerchief as he shifted around to face me. Before Rebecca, I'd never been able to remember what he'd said to me, although, over the years, I'd imagined many different things, lines no doubt picked up from television or movies, but which had never struck me as exactly right.

Before Rebecca, I hadn't even been able to recall how long I'd actually stayed in the back seat of the car, although I'd always sensed that the light had altered during the time I'd remained there, a change which could have only come about slowly, as evening fell. I remembered a thickening gray as it gathered around the bare, autumnal trees. I even remembered shadows lengthening and growing darker as the hours passed, but given the thick cloud cover of that late afternoon, it couldn't have been real. Still, this false impression of shadows lengthening and growing dark lingered through the years, stubbornly remaining while other, vastly more important things, began to blur and fade.

More than anything, I remembered the rain. It had fallen steadily all that day, puddles growing larger and larger, streams tumbling like tiny mountain rapids along the slanting gutters of the suburban streets. It was a fall rain, cold and heavy, the sort that sinks into the bones, making them feel thick and soggy. All day, while I'd sat at my desk in school, I'd listened as it spattered against my classroom windows. Outside, it fell in great gray veils across the playground and the schoolyard, finally gathering in dark pools beneath the swings, the seesaws, the dripping monkey bars. It kept me in when I wanted to be let out, and I remember glancing longingly at the sodden softball field, the thick clouds that hung above it, the slender, wiry rain. Now, when I think of it, it strikes me that almost every impression I retained of that day had something to do with confinement.

That day: November 19, 1959.

The car I sat in as evening fell was dark blue and had a faintly sweet, yet dusty smell, probably caused by the cigarette and cigar smoke the upholstery had collected over the years. There was a chrome ornament on the hood, a bird with its wings spread, a common design in those days. I remember the bird because I focused on it from time to time, watching it rather than the men who sat silently in the front seat. It was very beautiful, or at least it seemed so at the time, a point of gleaming silver in the gloomy air, a vision of release, a creature taking flight. It seemed odd that it should be attached to anything, least of all to the flat metal hood of the car in which I sat while the rain thudded down upon it, throwing large drops of water onto the bird's uplifted, but unmoving wings.

The car itself rested in the driveway of my house. I don't know what kind of car it was, but I've always imagined it as a Ford or a Chevy. It had blackwall tires, and its interior was dark blue. Instead of the usual radio with small chrome dials, it had a strange metal box with a black microphone that dangled above the floorboard. I could sometimes hear static coming from the box, but I don't remember hearing a voice. As far as I recall, neither of the men in the front seat ever picked up the microphone. Instead, they seemed to sit rigidly in place, silent, heavy, like carved figures.

I sat mutely behind them, my short legs drawn up beneath me in the back seat of the car. Through the space between the garage and the eastern corner of the house, I could glimpse a small patch of the backyard. I could see the wooden fence my father had erected before I was born, and a portion of the metal swing set, which my brother and sister had outgrown, but which I still used at certain idle moments to entertain myself. Beyond it was the clothesline, sagging heavily with its burden of soggy clothes, and beneath them the white tangle of my sister's bra.

The house was made of plain red brick. It had a faintly Tudor design, two-storied, with a gabled roof and dark green exterior shutters that were purely ornamental. A straight cement walkway led to the front door. Two front doors, actually. One of glass with an aluminum frame, the other of wood, painted white with a brass knocker shaped in the figure of a hand holding a small metal sphere. I remember how gently the long fingers appeared to hold on to the ball, as if about to release it.

There were other ornate touches. Flowers, for example, which my mother had planted not only all around the house, but in two circular gardens on either side of the cement walkway. She grew roses, tulips, and azaleas of various colors, and I remember her stooped over them awkwardly, almost in a squat, dressed in a loose-fitting red housedress, poking at the ground with a small spade. She was thirty-seven, but in pictures she appeared considerably older. She was thin and blonde, and her face had many sharp angles. I remember her as being tall, but she was actually five foot four. Before Rebecca, I didn't remember the sound of her voice, except that it was rather high, or the touch of her hand, except that it seemed vague and hesitant, or anything at all of the heart that had beaten beneath the red housedress, not even the fact that, according to the coroner's report, it had weighed nearly fifteen hundred grams.

And so, through all the years that followed her death, my mother remained an insubstantial presence, a figure carved from beach sand, tentative and impermanent.

Her sister Edna was another story, and it was she who finally came to retrieve me from the car, the two men handing me over to her casually, without ever asking her to produce a single article of identification.

She would have had the proper identification, of course. She was a cautious, correct woman, and knowing what would be expected of her that day, she would have brought a driver's license or a library card along with her. But neither of the two men who sat in the front seat of the car bothered to ask her who she was. The young one simply said, "You must be the sister," then nodded toward me and added, "Okay, you can take him then."

And so it was my aunt who came to me that day. My father had always called her "the maiden aunt" or "the spinster," though I doubt that he meant anything cruel in using such phrases. She was forty-two years old and unmarried. It was as simple as that. Others might have felt differently, using the same words to point out that my aunt had failed in her central mission to attract and keep a man. But my father admired her solitude, I think, along with her capacity to endure a certain subtle scorn.

She was dressed in a thick cloth coat that day, her dark hair pulled back in a bun which seemed to hang like a swollen berry from beneath the curve of her broad-brimmed black rain hat.

The back door of the car swung open and I slid out of the seat and into her care. She didn't pull me into her arms, but took my hand instead, and then strode swiftly across the rain-soaked yard to her waiting car, jerking me along hastily, so that I nearly stumbled as I trotted along beside her.

Her car was an old green Packard, and as she hustled me into its front seat, I glanced toward my house, Jamie's basketball suddenly floating into my view like a tiny orange planet. As the car pulled away, I got up on my knees in the seat and turned to look out the rain-streaked window toward the house in which I'd lived all my life. There it stood, in all its forlorn and broken gloom. I suppose by then I knew more or less everything that had happened within its various rooms during the last few hours. But all that had gone before it, the long march we had all made to that day in November, remained beyond my scope.

"Face forward, Stevie," Aunt Edna commanded sternly. "Don't look back."

Before Rebecca, I never had.

But now, I think that memory is the consolation prize we get for each day's death, the place we go to edit and rewrite our lives, to give ourselves another chance. Perhaps, in the end, that was all any of us ever wanted, just another chance. My father, my mother, Laura, Jamie, all of us locked up together in that house on McDonald Drive. From the street, it didn't look like a prison, but I know now that it was one, and that although I didn't hear them at the time, the sounds of my childhood were sliding bars and clanging doors.

Perhaps Aunt Edna had already sensed all that, and fearing the worst, warned me never to look back.

She was a middle-aged woman the day she rushed me across the yard to her waiting car, but she seemed ancient to me. Once at her house, she fed me a light dinner of chicken and white rice. I sat at the table, nibbling at the food, stunned into silence by what I already knew. I remember that she looked at me for a long time, as if trying to find the right words. Then she gave up, and simply muttered, "I'll figure something out."

But she never did, and I think part of the reason for her failure ever to "figure something out" with regard to me was that in some way I scared her.

Without doubt, there were occasions during the short two months that I lived with her when she would gaze at me distantly, with an unmistakable apprehension, and I think that at those moments she was searching for the dark seed she thought must one day bloom in me, the ember that hadn't been entirely consumed in the burning ruin of my family, but which still floated in the smoky atmosphere, dense, acrid, waiting to ignite.

Once, late at night, I wandered downstairs and into the kitchen, took the long carving knife from its drawer and headed across the room to the bowl of apples that sat beside the old tin sink. I had only moved a few steps when I saw Aunt Edna step out of the darkness of the adjoining room. Her eyes were on the knife, rather than my face, and I could tell she was fighting a terrible impulse to snatch it from my hand.

"Put that back," she commanded.

"I was going to have an apple," I told her.

"It's too late to eat something," she said evenly. "It's bad for your stomach."

For a tense, trembling instant, we stared at each other, the long knife still held tightly in my fist, her eyes now shifting from its blade to my face.

"Put it back, Stevie," she repeated.

I obeyed immediately, of course, but I never forgot the look in Aunt Edna's eyes, the way she seemed to sniff some poisonous vapor in the air around me.

Years later, when I told my wife the story, she said only, "How macabre," and went back to her work. I know now that instead of such a light dismissal, she should have stopped me dead, stared at me and asked, "Was she right, Steven? Is it in you, too? What can we do to root it out?"

For years I believed that my mother should have demanded the same answers from my father, as if that one frank exchange might have saved us all.

My mother, Dorothy Coleman Farris, age thirty-seven.

During the brief time that I lived with Aunt Edna, she rarely mentioned my mother. When she did, she always referred to her as "poor Dottie," as if "poor" and "Dottie" were melded together in her mind, impossible to separate. There were even times when I suspected that Aunt Edna finally blamed my mother for everything that happened that day in 1959.

That was something my Uncle Quentin, the tall man in work clothes who picked me up at Aunt Edna's only two months after I arrived there, never did. Instead, he spoke fondly, and even a little comically, of my mother. And so, over the years, as his memories of her surfaced in one story or another, my mother began to emerge as a gentle and somewhat gullible person who, as a child, had always fallen for Quentin's tricks, believed his outrageous lies, and generally served as the butt of his harmless jokes. "Dottie always looked on the bright side," he told me once. Then added with a helpless shrug: "That was her downfall, you might say."

What did he mean by that?

He never said, and so I was left with only the vision of my mother as a person so ordinary she seemed featureless, bland, a bubble in a sea of bubbles.

Her school reports, which Aunt Edna had, and which were passed on to me when she died, revealed a similar figure to the one Quentin painted. There was a pattern of C's dotted from time to time with a

B or a B–, but nothing higher. Her fifth-grade teacher summed her up: "Dorothy is a very nice child, always kind and friendly. Her work is adequate, and she is always punctual. It is pleasant to teach her."

Nice. Pleasant. Punctual. Even at their best, these are not the towering virtues. They leave out courage and adventurousness. But more than anything, they leave out passion. There is nothing to suggest that anything ever moved my mother with great force. Perhaps, in the end, that's what Aunt Edna always meant by calling her "poor Dottie," that she was poor in spirit, that she had no inner will, that perhaps even on that November day, she'd gone to her death like a slave to her quarters, head bowed, arms hung, eyes scarcely noting the black tail of the lash.

But could any life have really been so spiritless and void? After all, at one point, this same "poor Dottie" met a boy named Billy Farris, tall with jet black hair, and when he asked her on a date, she accepted. Perhaps, on those evenings during the bright Indian summer of 1940, when they'd walked down to the old movie house on Timmons Street, or along the edges of the little stream that ran through the town's carefully tended park, perhaps on those quiet, humid nights, she'd found herself momentarily aglow with something strong, new, irresistible. Isn't it possible that there were moments early on, in the first blush of infatuation, when she had loved my father with the kind of love depicted in those little books they found beside her bed, tales of high romance in exotic places, Fiji, Paris, Istanbul? When his hand first brushed her breast, or drew slowly up her thigh, isn't it possible that even "poor Dottie" lost her breath?

Without Rebecca, I never would have known.

Even so, however, I would have known a little. I would have known that she married Billy Farris and later bore three children. And yet, despite such knowledge, I find that I still can't imagine her on those nights of conception, when Jamie and Laura and I were, in effect, born. I can't imagine her naked beneath a man, or over him, or beside him, as they move together on the bed.

She was on a bed that day, too, lying where he put her, her arms folded neatly over her chest, eyes closed, feet side by side, her stack of romance novels arranged neatly beside the bed, as if at any moment, she might roll over, pluck one from the floor, and immediately lose herself in the soap opera glamour of a beach romance.

It was Aunt Edna who identified her. From the back seat of the detective's plain, unmarked car, I saw two men in black rain slicks lead her down the walkway and into the house. A few minutes later I heard a hollow, wrenching sound come from inside the house. It wasn't so much a scream as a low, painful wail. It was then that the older detective turned and spoke to me, although, until recently, I could not remember what he said.

Aunt Edna was at the blue car a few minutes later, her jaw set, her lips so tightly closed that when the young detective asked if she was "the sister," she could only nod silently in response.

It would be many years before I saw what Aunt Edna saw that afternoon, my eyes lingering hypnotically on the body of my mother, how it was so carefully and respectfully laid out with perfect formality.

Other pictures showed that the same care had not been taken with my brother.

Jamie Edward Farris, age seventeen.

He was tall and lanky, with glistening black hair. In pictures, he appears rather thin, with a pale face and large, dark, nearly clownish lips. His eyes were a milky brown, like his mother's, with thin eyebrows, and short dark lashes. Like hers, Jamie's face gave the sense of having been composed of various parts selected from other faces, the eyes too dull and faded to go with the glossy black hair, the nose too flat to fit in with the high cheekbones and narrow forehead.

Jamie and I were typical "older" and "kid" brothers. We shared the same room, the same bunk beds. We often annoyed and frustrated each other. In the evening, we listened to music together, always records selected by Jamie, and sometimes played Chinese checkers on a bright tin board. From time to time, he would try to teach me things, the guitar on one occasion, and how to use a cue stick on another.

But despite all that, we were never really close. There was a sullenness in him, a sense of subdued explosion which kept me at arm's length. Wanting a room of his own, resentful that Laura had always had one, Jamie often made me feel unwelcome in his presence, as if I were an unwanted intrusion.

But even more than he resented me, Jamie resented my sister. "Laura gets her own room because she's a girl," he often sneered at those times when she would return home with some small school triumph. It was a maliciousness and envy of my sister which I didn't share and probably despised. In any event, I don't recall missing him a great deal after his death, certainly not in the way I missed Laura, longed for her and called her name at night.

Still, I do remember Jamie quite well. I remember that he often seemed listless, drowsy, the heavy lids drooping slowly as he sat at his desk, the head following not long after that, nodding almost all the way down to the open textbook before it bobbed up suddenly, and he began to study once again. More than anything, he seems to have been one of those people who feel estranged from their own existence. There were even times when he appeared to dangle above his own life, unable to touch ground, find direction, move in a way that he'd willed himself. Had he lived, I doubt that much would have come of him, for even as a boy, he seemed to have inherited that lethargy and lack of spirit that was so visible in the woman in the red housedress.

Even so, as I must add in a final qualification, he was not entirely inanimate. There were things that truly interested Jamie. He could spend long hours practicing his guitar, despite the fact that there was never any noticeable improvement in his ability to play it. He liked to fish, and he, Laura, and I would sometimes walk to the pond a half-mile or so from our house, cast our bait into the water and wait—usually for hours—before finally returning home with nothing. Even before Rebecca urged me back, I remembered those little fishing trips surprisingly well, the shade of the trees, the small boats that skirted across the nearly motionless water, the bell on the ice cream truck that made three rounds per afternoon, even when the driver knew that on this particular stop, there'd be no customers but the Farris kids.

What else of Jamie?

Only a few scattered items. I remember him rushing to hide something in his desk as I came unexpectedly into the room we shared. I remember him breaking a guitar string and cursing, then, his anger quickly spent, meticulously stringing another.

And finally, there is this, which I remember more vividly than anything else, perhaps because it occurred only two days before he died. I was riding my bike down the block toward home when I saw him standing by the mailbox at the edge of our yard. I waved as I sped by, but he did not wave back. Instead, he continued staring, a little anxiously, up the street. He was clearly waiting for the postman to arrive, but I never learned what he was expecting in the mail. Perhaps it was a letter from a sweetheart we never knew about, or some item from a mail-order house that came three days later. Perhaps it was no more than a signed photograph from a movie star.

Whatever it was, Jamie was waiting for it nervously, and it was there that my mind had chosen to leave him, a figure waiting, tall and gangly, his black hair tangled and unwashed, his languid, nearly lightless eyes fixed expectantly on the road ahead. Better there, than sprawled across the floor of our little room, his face a bubbly mass of shattered flesh, the side of his head blown away, and hanging in a red, glistening flap over his hunched shoulder.

And finally, there was Laura.

As the years passed, I continued to remember her best of all. I remembered her with every sense impression. I remembered the sweet smell of her hair, how soft her hands were when they touched my face, the taste of her skin when I kissed her. I remembered the edginess and restlessness that sometimes came into her voice, rebellion building in her like a wave.

Laura was sixteen. She had my father's black hair, as I do, but with features that were absolutely her own. Her eyes were dark brown, almost black when she walked beneath the shade, and her skin was a glowing white. Her lips were full and when she was cold, or when she cried, as she often did suddenly and explosively, for reasons I could not have fathomed, they turned a soft violet.

Even as a child, I recognized that there were powerful emotions in Laura. Something in her soul was always trembling. She seemed to stand on a ledge, looking down, at times with fear, at times with longing. Had she lived, I have sometimes thought, she might have ended up a teenage suicide. A great-aunt on her mother's side, Quentin later told me, had shot herself in a small cottage in Maine, and when he pulled a dusty family album from its ancestral shelf and pointed the woman out, the resemblance between the lost aunt and my sister was astonishingly deep. There was the same nervous tension in her eyes, the corners of the mouth drawn down along the same narrow lines, a certain stiffness and rigidity in the stance, as if rigor mortis were already setting in.

Remembering Laura now, the melancholy that at times consumed her, it's easy to see the ebb and flow of chemistry, to blame everything on the time of life she shared with my brother, he nearing the end of adolescence, she at its scorching core. But I believe that Laura suffered from more than a stage of development. There was something deeply wrong, askew, unbalanced. At night, she would often walk about the house, ghostly and forlorn, like some distraught maiden out of one of my mother's romance novels. To Jamie, it was an annoyance, and often, when he heard her footsteps in the hallway, he would yell at her harshly, demanding that she return to her room, then lean over the edge of his upper bunk, glance down at me, and rotate his index finger at the side of his head, whispering vehemently: "She's nuts."

Nuts, perhaps, to Jamie, but to me she was the most mysterious person in the world. The nightly rambling that irritated him, enchanted me. I sensed that there were secret regions in her, lost rooms, labyrinthine caverns. I know now that I was in love with my sister, and that the feelings I had for her, and even the way her memory still from time to time overwhelms me, that all of this was part of an early romantic attachment, a longing that I experienced as a natural adoration, something that all boys felt for their older sisters. I have since learned that it was no such thing, that the excitement which I felt in her presence, the way my breath stopped when I heard her pass my closed door, the way I stole glances even at her shadow on the wall, that all of this had its roots in the first inchoate gropings of desire.

I once said as much to Quentin. "I loved my sister," I told him. "Yes, of course you did," he said. "No, Uncle Quentin," I added pointedly, "I *loved* my sister." He waved his hand and laughed. "You were only nine years old, Steve," he said, then stood up and headed for the bathroom, something he always did when the conversation suddenly took a turn he didn't like.

But he knew.

I think he always knew that our house, the one with the dark green shutters and neat Tudor roof, held within its prim walls the most primitive and violent hopes, needs, and fears. And so he pulled me away from it, as if it were a whirling saw or an exposed electrical wire, snatched me away, and brought me north to the idyllic sterility of coastal Maine, to a landscape that seemed frozen in a rigid self-control.

"You have to keep a tight grip on everything," he once told me. "Remember what happens when you don't."

Remember, in other words, my father.

William Patrick Farris, age forty-four.

What I could never fathom was how much Laura loved him, how powerfully she was drawn to him, how much she craved his admiration. Often, in her nightly wanderings, she would move down the stairs to the small solarium which led off from the living room. My mother had placed a few plants there, mostly indistinguishable green vines, along with two white wicker chairs and a glass-topped table. I remember seeing the two of them together in that room, sitting silently opposite each other in the early hours, light gathering outside, while their eyes remained steady, their faces nearly motionless, as if after hours of struggle, they'd finally come to a grave understanding. At those moments, they seemed to share a peculiar exhaustion, their eyes glassy from lost sleep, their skin pale, muscles limp from too much strain.

Even as a young boy, watching them secretively from my place at the top of the stairs, I had felt a mysterious connection between them. Their voices at such moments were always soft, and when they touched each other, it was with an eerie grace.

Later, I imagined that it was at these dawn meetings that she must have revealed herself to him, told him all those secrets she would never have told me.

And so, even before I came to hate my father for what he did to my family, I had envied his relationship with Laura, the whispery conclave the two of them shared, a society that excluded and infuriated me. I wanted to know exactly what kind of power he had over her, break the code by which they spoke to each other, usurp his place in her esteem.

A few weeks before she died, I saw them together in the solarium for the last time. Laura was sitting on the floor, her back pressed against my father's long, thin legs, her hands resting loosely in her lap while he sat above her in the white wicker chair, gazing out into the early morning light. For once, she looked rested, almost serene, her eyes opening and closing slowly as if she were about to fall asleep.

As for the way my father looked at that moment, I can only say that I'd never seen a man who looked more troubled. It was as if the very thing that had brought Laura such peace that morning had filled my father with an all but unbearable anguish.

Perhaps, even then, he had sensed how she would end.

This way: lying on her back, faceup, her white arms stretched over her head, splattered with blood, two fingers and half the palm of the right hand blown away, as if she'd thrust it toward him at the moment he had fired.

Her legs spread wide apart as if in a vulgar pose, her white bathrobe pulled upward from her soiled bare feet, revealing her thighs and a thin line of white cotton panties.

Her chest blown open, ribs shattered like bits of porcelain, her flesh torn and mangled as if a bomb had gone off behind her heart.

Her mouth flung open, red and gaping, giving her face an attitude of grave surprise, one corner of the white towel she'd wrapped around her wet hair hanging limply, almost clownishly, over a single, blue, wide-open eye.

Along with Jamie and my mother, Laura died at

approximately four in the afternoon. It was almost two hours later that Mrs. Hamilton, a neighbor from across the street, saw my father walk out of the house, climb into the Ford station wagon, and drive away. He was wearing a black raincoat and an old floppy hat. He was not carrying anything, not so much as a small overnight bag.

During those long two hours in which he remained in the house, my father washed my mother's body, changed her into a pair of blue pajamas, and arranged her neatly on the bed. After that, he made a ham sandwich and ate it at the small table in the kitchen. I know it was his sandwich, because in the police photographs, there was a ring of raw onion on the side of the plate. No one but my father ate raw onion. He drank a cup of coffee, leaving both the plate and the cup in the sink as he always did, as if expecting them to be washed later, as normally they would have been.

He didn't pack anything, because he left with nothing; not so much as a pair of socks was missing from his closet.

He didn't reenter either Laura or Jamie's rooms. He made no attempt to clean up the frightful mess that had been made of them.

And yet, for no apparent reason, he remained in the house for a full two hours, alone, silent, surrounded by nothing but the bodies of his murdered wife and children.

What had he been waiting for?

When I became old enough to ponder that question seriously—I was probably around Laura's age, sixteen—I came up with a great many possibilities. He was waiting for some mysterious phone call. Or he was waiting to go to the airport at just the right time to catch some flight he'd booked weeks in advance. He was waiting to be picked up by gangsters, foreign agents, Communists. My own theory changed each time I considered the question.

Then, rather suddenly, on a spring day as I sat on a rock watching the waves, I arrived at the answer that had no doubt come to the police and Aunt Edna and Uncle Quentin long before, but which they'd kept to themselves, perhaps hoping that the question would never actually occur to me, that I would never seek its answer. But I did seek it, and it did come: He was waiting for me.

Once it had occurred to me, the answer was entirely obvious. Under ordinary circumstances, I would have been home from school by three-fifteen in the afternoon, just as Jamie and Laura would. But I'd gone to Bobby Fields's house instead, a play date my mother had known about all week, but of which my father knew nothing.

And so for nearly two hours my father had waited for me.

It's possible that he might have waited as long as necessary had not Mrs. Fields made two phone calls to the house on McDonald Drive. According to the statement she later gave police, she made the first call at around 5:30 P.M. When no one answered, she called again twenty minutes later. There was still no answer.

Five minutes or so after that last call, Mrs. Hamilton from across the street saw my father walk through the rain to the Ford station wagon, get in, and drive away.

A half hour later, Mrs. Fields decided, after a good deal of protest from Bobby and me, that she couldn't take me to the movies without getting parental permission first. She then drove directly to my house, and while Bobby and I remained in the back seat, she got out of the car and walked to the side entrance, which was nearest to the driveway, the one that led directly into the kitchen. She knocked at the door, glancing in as she did so, and saw a plate with a curl of raw onion and a coffee cup in the kitchen sink. Glancing idly to the left, she also saw a shotgun laid lengthwise across the small cutting board my mother kept in the corner beside the basement door.

I remember seeing her raise her hand to knock a second time, then stop, the hand motionless in the air, and turn back toward the car.

Before Rebecca, I remembered nothing else about that day except for the other car, the one with the two policemen in it, the older one turning toward me, drawing his glasses from his face, wiping the rain from the lenses with a white handkerchief, his lips parting to make a statement which, before Rebecca, time or shock had swept away.

TWO

Even now, when I return to my dead family, it's always by way of my father. It's as if he stands at the gate of my memory, the border guard of a dark frontier.

It was a border I rarely approached during the years that followed the murders, a frontier I almost never entered. It was the "terra incognito" of the medieval maps, the place where "there be dragons," as the ancient cartographers declared.

And so, over the years, I had not looked back. Because of that, everything had faded—Jamie, my mother, even Laura to some degree. Only my father had remained in stark relief, grim and unfathomable, the ultimate enigma.

Of all the questions Rebecca later asked about him, she never asked the easiest one, the one for which my life had provided two different answers: *What did your father do?*

Until I was nine, the answer came quickly, without that momentary twinge of dread or embarrassment that later accompanied it. I simply replied that my father owned a hardware store.

I could remember the store very well. It was on

Sycamore Street, and it had two large windows, which my father stuffed with anything that came to hand: hammers, saws, lengths of rope. In general, he stacked smaller items in the window to the right of the door, and larger ones, like enormous red toolboxes or shiny aluminum ladders, in the one to the left. He took no pains to make the windows attractive, or to display the goods in any particular way. He simply lumbered absently from the back of the store, his arms filled with anything he'd found in reach, and deposited it all neatly, but randomly, in the front windows. As far as I recall, the only regard he ever paid was to the seasons. From time to time he would shove a wheelbarrow into the fall window, the perfect tool for gathering leaves. In winter he would replace it with the snow blower that would remain in the window for the next four months. Beyond that, he seems to have had no theme in mind, no organizing principle.

Inside the store, the usual implements and materials hung from the walls, such things as rakes, shovels, and axes. Smaller items were gathered in wooden bins, nails, bolts, lengths of coiled wire and the like. The only thing I ever noticed in the store that seemed out of place was the single Rodger and Windsor racing bicycle which my father kept in the left rear corner of the shop, cordoned off from everything else, as if it were only for display. It was a fancy touring bicycle, imported from England, and each time the latest model was sold, my father would replace it, tediously assembling it himself in the basement of our house, then transporting it to the store in the back of his small brown delivery van.

The Rodger and Windsor was the only kind of bike my father ever stocked. It was always red, and it never appeared to matter that he sold no more than three or four of them during the entire year. The fact is, he seemed to love it, or at least to feel for it some kind of strange devotion.

More than anything, I think now, he loved the process of putting it together. It was a difficult and painstaking labor, and he worked at it for many hours without stopping. It was strange to see him alone in the basement, stooped over a disconnected wheel, meticulously tightening each spoke, then turning the wheel, and methodically tightening each of them again. As a working style, it was completely different from his usual habit, which was hasty and sloppy and impulsive, the way he arranged the windows of the store or tossed different-sized nails into a common bin, everything done offhandedly, without a thought.

The look on his face was different, too. Normally, it was rather expressionless, but when he worked on the Rodger and Windsor, it took on a wonderful intensity and concentration, as if he found something rapturous in the process of assembly. Perhaps in this, as in everything else, it was the building rather than the completion which attracted and sustained him.

In any event, I remember seeing him at work toward the end of October. The latest bike had arrived a week before, but he'd been occupied in trying to straighten out some entanglement with the Internal Revenue Service. The woman who'd done the store's books for several years had left a few weeks earlier, and without her, he'd been entirely at sea as he'd labored to give the IRS the information it had suddenly demanded. Normally, he would have set to work on the new Rodger and Windsor immediately, but because of the government paperwork, he'd been prevented from unpacking the bike for almost two weeks.

When he finally got to it, however, he went at it with the same persistence that he always applied to this task, working many hours at a time, always at night, with nothing but the single, naked bulb which hung above to help him make his hundreds of minute adjustments. I remember seeing him hunched over a length of bicycle chain, tapping at it with a small hammer, while his other hand caressed it with an eerie gentleness and affection. He was wearing his customary gray flannel shirt and trousers, and he had thrown the black sweater he often wore over the bike's chrome handlebars. It hung there like a dried animal skin while my father continued at his tapping, unaware that I stood not far away, poised, as he would be three weeks later, on the third step from the bottom.

For a long time, he didn't see me. Then, suddenly, he lifted his head and turned his eyes toward me, his gaze lingering on my face, but very dully, the way Jamie sometimes stared at his open textbook. For a time, his expression remained blank, the face of a mannequin in a shop window, colorless, with dim, unlighted eyes.

"Hi, Dad," I said.

He didn't answer at first, but after a moment, he smiled very softly, then said in a low, broken voice, "This is *all I want*."

This is all I want.

Neither that evening, as I went back upstairs, nor in the years to come, did I ever give the slightest thought to what he might have meant by that. And yet, almost without my realizing it, it had always suggested to me that on that particular October night, a full three weeks before the murders, my father had already determined that we were going to die, that he was going to remove everything that stood between him and whatever it was he wanted out of life.

What did your father do?

After that day in November, the question took on a completely different significance. After that day, he could no longer be defined by what he "did" for a living. He could no longer be reduced to the man in the hardware store on Sycamore Street. What he "did" was kill his family.

But as I'd watched Mrs. Fields walk to the kitchen door, knock, start to knock again, but grow rigid instead, then return to the car, I hadn't realized that the strained, tortured look on her face was the same one I would see from now on when I answered the question truthfully. What did your father do? He killed my mother, my sister, and my brother, then waited in the kitchen to kill me.

It was all in Mrs. Fields's face that afternoon, the world's response to my father, the dread and horror his image would conjure up forever.

I could see her eyes in the rearview mirror as she wheeled the car into her own driveway, tense, darting, as if desperately trying to avoid her own terrible conjectures. Bobby was bouncing playfully on the seat beside me, the rain blowing against the car window, pounding at it with huge gray drops. Mrs. Fields opened the back door and pulled him out, almost violently, so that he squealed "Mom," then ran into the house. I looked at her curiously, trying to determine if I'd done anything to cause the strain and alarm I could see in her face. She lifted her hand toward me, the painted red fingernails like little arrows of light in the shadowy interior of the car.

"Come out, Stevie," she said, still offering her hand.

I took it reluctantly, let it tug me out into the rain, then bolted for the front door of the house. Bobby was waiting for me down the hall. He motioned me into his room. He didn't bother to close the door, and so I could hear Mrs. Fields on the phone a few feet away. She was clearly distressed. She was calling for help.

For help, but not for the police. She called Mrs. Hamilton instead. I could hear her voice, hesitant, restrained, and although I can't be sure that I gathered the words in exactly, I know the kind of call it was:

"Hello, Jane? This is Mary Fields."

"Oh, hi, Mary."

"Jane, I was just over at Dottie Farris's house. Stevie is with me, and I was bringing him home. And well . . . I went to the door, the one at the kitchen, and I saw . . ."

It was only at that moment, Mrs. Hamilton would say later, that she remembered the three muffled booms that had swept through the sheeting rain that afternoon, the second rapidly following the first, the third coming several minutes later.

Several minutes.

What, during those several minutes, did Mrs. Hamilton, the gray, overweight wife of the town's only Presbyterian minister, think was going on across the street at 417 McDonald Drive?

Several minutes.

Later, when I began my search, I read those two words in the thick file which the Somerset, New

Jersey, Police Department finally allowed me to see: "Witness stated that although the second shot followed closely after the first, there was a duration of several minutes between the second and final shots."

And then this: "Witness stated that the television program *Queen for a Day* had just ended, and therefore estimates the time of the last shot at between 3:55 and 4:00 P.M. EST."

And so, all across the Eastern Seaboard, *Queen for a Day*, with its bilious host and tacky audience applause meter, had just ended when the last member of my family died.

What did your father do?

Years later, looking at a series of police photographs while two uniformed officers watched me warily from the other side of the room, I tried to reconstruct the grim choreography of my family's murder:

From them it seemed clear that Jamie had been the first to die. In the pictures, a set of bloody tracks lead from Jamie's room down the upstairs corridor to Laura's. She'd probably been near the window when she heard first the deafening roar which came from Jamie's room, then footsteps moving down the corridor, and last the sound of her own door as it opened toward her. Reflexively she turned toward it, and saw my father standing there, the barrel of his shotgun lowering toward her. Against its blast, she raised her hand, perhaps to shield her face, or perhaps in a pleading motion which he immediately refused.

From Laura's room, the tracks, still thick with blood, lead directly to the room opposite Laura's, the master bedroom, the one with the floral curtains. He must have found it empty, because my mother was not killed in that room. There were no spattered walls, no blood-soaked carpet for the police to photograph in that dimly lighted bedroom.

The tracks head back down the corridor, down the stairs, into the living room, and through it to the small solarium, where they move into it a little way, then turn and head out again. It is a line of trajectory which could only mean one thing. That my mother was trying to escape, but witlessly, never thinking of leaving the house, too passive even to make that final domestic break.

The tracks then move back through the living room, a little wider now, for he is searching for her desperately, taking longer steps, perhaps in fear, or rage. Certainly, he is moving faster.

The tracks are seen in the dining room next, then in the kitchen. Still, she eludes him. He wheels around, leaving a slender mark on the tile floor to indicate the fierceness of his turn, how for just an instant, he lifted almost entirely from the ground, whirling on the backs of his heels.

The tracks move again, toward the door that leads to the basement, then down the wooden stairs toward its flat cement floor. At the third step from the bottom, they stop.

Because of the hard rain which had been falling for hours by late that afternoon, water had seeped into the basement, a small lake gathering near the middle of the room. My mother passed through that puddle several times, her watery trail making a bizarre and illogical pattern on the cement floor. Perhaps she ran about, zigzagging in her terror, while he stood on the third step, laboring to bring her into his sights.

At last, she came to rest in a back corner, behind

the huge cardboard box in which she'd once stored our Christmas decorations. It was there that he raked her with a third and final blast.

All of this, then, was what my father did.

And in the years that followed, it was to this single horrendous act I had reduced him. All his life had collapsed into a single savage and explosive instant. I couldn't imagine his life before or after it. My father was frozen forever as he had stood upon that third step, his shoes still glistening brightly with my brother's and my sister's blood.

But there had been a life before that one murderous instant. Not a great life. Not a life of high achievement, or even noble failure. But a life nonetheless, the kind that most of us live, plain but sturdy, building day by day a structure that holds up.

My father, as I came to discover, was a country boy. Throughout all his early years, he lived on a small farm in rural New York. Each day, he did the chores common to children on a farm. He gathered eggs, milked cows, cleared the weeds that sprouted intransigently among the neatly proportioned rows of the family garden. In the summer he swam in the great blue lake several miles away. In the fall he went to a country school named for Daniel Webster where he learned to read and write sufficiently to carry out the basic tasks of life. Later, when he was fourteen, he transferred to the high school in the nearby town of Highfield. It was named for a local boy who'd died in the Spanish-American War, and my father graduated from it at somewhere near the middle of his class in June of 1931. In the class photograph, taken at the town ball field on graduation day, he is positioned on the back row, the fifth boy from the left, his black hair greased back, staring at the camera with an ordinary smile. Inside the high school yearbook for that same year, a slender volume made of cheap paper and bound in leatherette, and which I found in one of the boxes I inherited from Aunt Edna, he is said to have been a member of the baseball team. A picture shows him individually, dressed in a flat black suit and bow tie, his nickname printed underneath: *Town Crier*.

Town Crier. What had his classmates meant by that? Was there something in him that suggested warning and alarm, a sense of being startled from one's sleep? Had the faces of his classmates ever grown taut as they stared into my father's youthful eyes? When some of them later read of what he did, were there a few among them who had not been surprised?

I wondered about his parents, too. In photographs they are a sturdy, farming couple, plain in that way that makes plainness seem beautiful, noble, and even a little superior to more sophisticated and elaborate things. At night, when the lights were out, and they lay together in the darkness, had they ever voiced the slightest concern for some odd look or disturbing word they'd noticed in their only son?

During all his early years, my father lived with his parents on the same small farm. It was nestled in a grove of trees, with a broad expanse of field on either side. The house still stands, and only a few weeks before Rebecca, I visited it for the first time. Peter, my nine-year-old son, had spent the summer at a camp in upstate New York, and around the middle of August, Marie and I drove up to the camp to pick him up and bring him back home. I had a Volvo station wagon then, and we piled all his belongings into it and headed back toward Connecticut.

I hadn't intended to visit the little house where my father grew up, but on the way to the expressway I saw a small sign for Highfield. I recognized the name, although I'd never been there. My father's parents had died within a year of each other when he was only twenty-five, and evidently he'd never felt the need to visit the farm after that. I don't think he ever took my mother there, or Jamie or Laura. At his parents' death, it appeared to have dissolved from his mind.

But it hadn't dissolved from mine, and according to the sign, it was only twelve miles away. Even so, I continued straight ahead, expecting to turn onto the expressway well before I reached the town. It was Marie who stopped me, looking quizzically in my direction only a few seconds after we passed the sign.

"Highfield," she said finally, her eyes drifting over to me. "Isn't that the town your father came from?"

I nodded silently and kept driving.

"He was born there, right?"

"On a little farm right outside it."

"When did he leave?"

"When he graduated from high school, I think."

Marie turned back toward the road. She knew about my father, of course, and I think that something in him, his sudden, inexplicable murderousness, had always interested her. Early on, she'd asked a great many questions about what he was like, probing like an amateur, somewhat Freudian detective, looking for *the reason,* as if there were some twisted secret in his past, which, if unearthed, would bring everything to light.

"Wouldn't you like to see the house?" she asked after a moment.

"Why would I want to do that?"

"Because he was your father," she answered.

I glanced in her direction. "I think you're the one who wants to see it."

She shook her head. "No. You do." She smiled. "It's only natural. Why don't we drop by?"

I shrugged. "Okay," I said.

And so I didn't get on the expressway that afternoon, but headed toward Highfield, then drove through it, searching for the small road that Quentin had long ago described, a road that wound off to the right at the end of a stone wall.

The road came up shortly, looking like little more than a cattle trail through a green field. A narrow sign marked it with the words I'd seen on the letters my father had written to his parents during the brief time he'd lived in New York City: Lake Road.

I slowed as I neared the sign, stopped just before I got to it and looked at Marie. I remember very well the clipped, undramatic exchange that followed:

"Should I?"

"Why not? . . . It's just a house."

And so it was. Just a house, run-down a bit, but otherwise as I might have expected. The yard was neatly mowed, and a line of flowers had been planted along the small walkway which led to the front door. Two large trees kept the grounds heavily shaded. It had a gravel driveway, but no garage, and as I got out of the car, I could see an old wooden fence, weathered and dilapidated, which, I suppose, my father had helped build.

I left Marie and Peter in the car, walked up the small walkway to the house and knocked at the door. The woman who answered it was middle-aged, plump, her hair pinned up behind her head. She was wiping her hands with a dishcloth bordered with small red flowers.

"Hello," I said.

She nodded, neither friendly nor unfriendly, simply curious to know who I was.

"My name is Steven Farris," I told her.

"Uh-huh," she said.

"This is a little strange," I added, "but years ago my . . ." I choked briefly on the word, but nonetheless got it out. ". . . father lived here, in this house."

The woman smiled. "Oh," she said and, without another word, swung open the door. "I guess you'd like to see it then."

"Well, I don't want to disturb you."

"No, not at all," the woman said. She leaned out the door slightly. "That your family?" she asked, eyeing the people in the Volvo.

"Yes."

"They want to come in?"

"I guess so," I told her, then turned and waved Marie and Peter toward the house.

We were only there for a short time. Marie engaged the woman in conversation, the two of them finally heading up to the second floor, while Peter sat indifferently in the foyer, lost in one of his electronic games.

And so, for a moment, I was alone in my father's house. Not alone physically, of course, but alone in the way that I could look at it without distraction.

At first, I wandered into the living room, glancing at the old fireplace, the neatly arranged furniture, the varnished wooden floor. A great number of family photos hung from the walls, sons in uniform, daughters in communion dresses, and later, grown older now, these same boys and girls with strangers at their sides, children on their knees, the boys with moustaches or thinning hair, the girls with wrinkled eyes. Time went forward on the wall, and hair retreated even more, faces grew more slack. The children left their parents' knees to dress in uniforms and bridal gowns, choose strangers from a world of strangers, have children of their own.

"Steve, you want to look upstairs?"

It was Marie's voice. She was standing on the staircase, leaning over the rail. "His room must have been up here," she said.

I headed toward her, walking up the stairs, touring the house now as if it were a black museum, my father's room cordoned off as Washington's or Lincoln's might have been, all the furniture in place, but with an atmosphere altogether different, sinister and grave.

Marie was standing at the end of the short corridor, poised beside an open door, the woman standing beside her, smiling sweetly.

"This must have been it," Marie said. "There are only two bedrooms up here, and the other one's big, so it must have been for his parents."

It was the amateur detective at work again, and as I walked to where Marie stood like a guide waiting for a straggling tourist, I remember resenting how flippantly she had come to regard the story of my father, treating it more as a childhood tale, an imagined horror. Of course, I'd been partly to blame for that, answering her questions matter-of-factly, without emotion, like a reporter who'd covered the story, rather than a child who'd lived it. Perhaps, because of that, she'd come to think that the whole dark history meant little to me, that I no longer felt its grisly power.

And yet, for all that, Marie didn't go in my father's room, but remained outside, waiting in the corridor.

I have often wondered why. Was there something in that tiny room that warned her away, the ghost of the black-haired boy his friends called *Town Crier*?

In any event, I went in alone, stood on the circular hooked carpet at the center of the room, and turned slowly to take it in. I felt nothing. Everything that might have given me some sense of my father had long ago been removed. His bed was gone, along with whatever he might have tacked to the walls, maps or photographs or pennants. If he'd ever had a desk or chair, they were gone as well. In their place, the new owner had put a small worktable and wooden stool. The table was covered with spools of different-colored yarn, along with an assortment of needles and brass clips. "I make things for the crafts fairs we have up here," the woman said as she stepped up beside me. Then, glancing about the room, she added, "It makes a nice little work space, don't you think?" She smiled. "Very cozy."

She offered coffee and cake after we'd all gone back downstairs, but neither Marie nor I felt inclined to take her up on it. Instead, we thanked her for her generosity, returned to the car, and headed home, the old house growing small in my rearview mirror before it finally vanished behind a sudden curve.

It was dark by the time we reached Old Salsbury. Peter was asleep in the back seat. I took him up the stairs and laid him on his bed, then sat down beside him and ran my fingers through his hair. I had seen my father do the same to me, and certainly he'd done it to Laura and Jamie as well. There had been a gentleness in him, a guardianship and care. That murder might finally flow from such a source seemed inconceivable to me.

I left Peter to his sleep, and walked across the hallway to where Marie sat at her dressing table, applying her nightly oils and creams. I took off my clothes, placing everything neatly on the little wooden valet which stood on my side of the bed, and crawled beneath the covers. The sheets were very cool, as I prefer them, but later Marie drew in beside me, her body heating them, so that I pulled away from her, finally edging myself precariously toward the far side of the bed.

I rarely dream, or if I do, I rarely remember my dreams. But that night I had not so much a dream as what I would call a visitation. It was not a visit from my father. There was no shotgun-toting figure moving toward me from the depths of a smoky corridor, the subject of my childhood nightmares. In fact, there was no one in my dream at all. At least, no one but myself. And yet, it was so powerfully rendered, so elaborately detailed, that I could easily recall it the following morning.

In the dream, I awakened slowly, rather than the way I usually do, with a sudden start. It was a luxurious restfulness from what appeared to have been a state of great exhaustion. The dream gave no hint as to what had tired me so, but only that I had slept a long time, and was now rising with a natural and unhurried rhythm.

The room was very bright, but it was not my room, nor any room in which I'd ever been. It seemed a bit drab, but also strangely atmospheric, so that I felt completely at home in it, as if living there were my natural state. There was a large wooden bureau, the plain metal bed on which I had slept, and a sink. A pair of wrinkled towels hung over each side of the sink, and a slender full-length mirror hung from the wall beside it.

In my dream, I got to my feet languidly and walked toward the window. On the way, I glanced at the mirror. What I saw did not alarm me. I had about a three-day growth of beard, and I was wearing a white, sleeveless T-shirt and baggy brown trousers. I was barefoot, but I could see a pair of old shoes beneath the bed, one set of laces a little frayed, but otherwise in good repair.

At the window, I parted a pair of ragged white curtains and looked out. The sun was very bright, and I remember sensing that it was midday. Beyond the window, there was a large, dusty city, a conglomeration of rust-colored shingled roofs and distant church towers. In the streets below, I could see signs written in a foreign language, and hear men laughing in an outdoor tavern. Over their laughter, I could make out the sound of guitars, strummed softly by men I could not see, and the lilting cry of what I took for a wooden flute.

I awoke while still standing at the window. Nothing at all happened in the dream. And yet, it awakened me, not languidly, but with the usual sense of being startled. Dawn had not broken, and so I felt my way through the continuing darkness until I made it into the hallway. I switched on the light, walked past Peter's room, then down the stairs to the kitchen. There was a can of soda in the refrigerator, which I opened and poured into the huge mug Peter had given me the previous Christmas, porcelain with German figures on it, smiling milkmaids and old men in lederhosen.

I drank silently, the dream still lingering in my mind, as if it were an afterimage which needed only a bit more time to fade. But as the minutes passed, and I followed the first soda with a second, it still held its place in my mind, all its details fully intact, everything from the tiniest scratches I had seen on the old bureau to the notes I'd heard played on the flute I'd never seen.

I couldn't finish the second soda, and after a while, I walked back upstairs, crawled into bed again, twisted about uncomfortably for a few minutes, then returned to the kitchen. I switched on the light, and as I did so, my eyes caught on the half-filled mug I'd put in the sink. It sat near the drain, upright, but out of place, just as my father's unfinished cup of coffee had rested in nearly the same position on that November day, as if waiting still for Mrs. Fields to see it. It was then that it struck me that the dream had come from him, that it was a message —although still cryptic and unreadable—from my father.

What did your father do?

Even that night, after the visit to my father's house and the dream that followed it, even then, it was still someone else's question.

It was Bobby Fields's question when we met the first day of first grade, and to which I'd been able to give the simple reply that I would lose forever in only a few years: "He owns a hardware store."

It was Jerry Flynn's question when I was ten, and living in Maine, and when he asked it, he meant Uncle Quentin, whom he assumed to be my father.

It was Sally Peacock's question when I went out on my first date and had to explain, because there seemed no way to avoid it, that my father had left me years before and so, at the moment, I had no idea what he "did."

It was Marie's question that long night we first made love, and I told her in full and ghastly detail exactly what my father had done on that November day.

And at last, as it must always be with sons, it was my question, too.

THREE

The usual breakfast atrocities occurred the Monday morning after we brought Peter back from camp. Peter dropped or spilled nearly everything he touched, and Marie became increasingly exasperated with him, finally screaming at his back as he trudged, hunched and angry, out into the backyard.

Once he'd left, she turned her wrath on me, her eyes narrowing lethally, as if taking aim.

"Why don't you ever say anything to him?" she demanded harshly. "Why do I have to do all the yelling?"

"I don't care what he spills," I told her with a shrug. "It doesn't matter to me."

It was a reply which only concentrated her anger by focusing it on me.

"It's because you don't have to clean it up," she shot back. "If you had to clean it up, then you'd care."

I started to offer something in return, but she whirled around and strode out of the kitchen, tossing a wadded paper towel into the plastic garbage can beside the door.

It was typical of Marie to storm out of a room rather than engage in a longer confrontation. Even our first real argument had been a clipped and stifled affair, again with Marie leaving rapidly, this time from a car, but with the same air of unavoidable flight. Over the years I'd come to think of it as a way of avoiding some invisible line she feared to cross, a form of self-control.

I left around fifteen minutes later, waving to Peter as I headed for the car. He sat, slumped in a chair beside the pool, and as I went by, he waved back halfheartedly, then offered a knowing smile, as if we were allies in some war we waged against the central woman in our lives.

I backed slowly out of the driveway, glancing only briefly toward the house. I could see Marie at the window of our bedroom on the second floor. She'd thrown open the curtains and was standing in the full morning light, her arms folded tightly below her breasts, so that their round upper quarters were lifted and exposed beneath the partly open gown. It was a stance my mother would never have assumed, and I remember thinking, as I pulled out of the driveway, that for "poor Dottie" bedroom curtains were meant to be tightly closed. As for the woman poised behind them, a plain red housedress would do just fine.

There were other differences between Marie and my mother, as well, and on the way to my office that morning, I silently, and almost unconsciously, catalogued them.

Marie was stern and demanding, while my mother had suffered from a general lack of will, one so severe, I think, that it had even prevented her from disciplining her children. Thus, instead of ordering us to do things, help around the house, choose the proper clothes, keep our mouths shut when others were talking, she'd simply allowed us to find our own way through the maze, directionless and uninstructed.

Unlike Marie, who was self-assured and confident in her abilities and opinions, my mother had seemed to doubt her own adulthood, doubt even those of its prerogatives which my father had taken for granted and exercised with full authority.

My father.

The memory that suddenly returned him to me that morning, as I drove to work, appeared ordinary enough at first. It was clear and vivid, the setting laid out perfectly in my mind:

We had all been in the backyard, Laura and I tossing a ball back and forth while Jamie lounged in a small yard chair, leafing through some sort of sports magazine. As the minutes passed, the pitches became wilder and faster, with Laura lobbing the ball toward me at weird angles, or heaving it in a high and uncontrolled arc over all our heads.

Inevitably, one of her throws went way off, the ball crashing down onto Jamie's magazine, knocking it first into his lap, then onto the ground.

The ball startled and frightened him, and his sudden panic had no doubt embarrassed him as well, and so he leaped to his feet, angrily strode across the yard, grabbed Laura by the shoulders, and started screaming at her. She fought back, pushing him away violently and yelling into his face. I ran over to her, trying to get between the two, and started screaming just as loudly.

We were still going at it when we heard the door open at the back of the house and saw our father step out onto the small veranda which overlooked the backyard. He didn't say a word, but only stood, his hands holding firmly to the railing of the veranda, as he peered down at us.

All our attention was trained upon him, all our eyes lifted up, as if he were descending from the clouds. A complete silence fell over the backyard as the three of us stood in place, saying nothing, only watching him as he watched us during that brief, oddly delicious instant before he turned and walked away.

What had we felt at that moment?

As a child, it would have been impossible for me to say. But that morning, as I unexpectedly recalled this single incident with all the detail of something that had happened only minutes before, it seemed to me that I had felt the sweet and awesome luxury of a hand that stayed my hand. I had sensed my father's restraining firmness, and because of it, perhaps because of nothing more than his exercise of it, I had loved him deeply and inexpressibly. The solitary killer who'd crouched beneath that mask of paternal care and responsibility had never appeared to me. Instead, I'd glimpsed only that part of him that was beautiful and grave and unreachable, that figure of a father, steadfast and enduring, that all men wish to have and wish to be.

And so, it struck me that morning that my father's life had to have been a vast deception, a lie he'd lived in while he'd lived with us, harboring whatever resentment and bitterness it was that had finally boiled over on that day in November.

I was still thinking about him when I got to the office a few minutes later.

The architectural offices of Simpson and Lowe

were on the top floor of a five-story cubicle structure made of steel and tinted glass. It was a purely functional design, and no one but Mr. Lowe, the firm's sole surviving founder, ever liked it. Over the years the rest of us had either resented it or been embarrassed by it, thinking it a rather unimaginative structure, unlikely to impress prospective clients, especially those who might be interested in more innovative designs for their own projects.

But despite all our criticism, Mr. Lowe had remained firm in his commitment to it, stubbornly holding on out of loyalty to its aging pipes and circuits, its squeaky hinges and buckling tile. Wally had been arguing for years that we should move the whole operation to the new business center north of the city, but Mr. Lowe had always refused, shaking his head with that enormous dignity he still maintained despite the palsy that rocked his hands. "Don't abandon things," he once told Wally scoldingly at the end of one of these discussions. Then he rose and left the room, knowing that Wally remained behind to mutter against him resentfully, but wholly indifferent to anything he might say, as if all his malicious whisperings were nothing more than a light desert breeze.

Wally was already at his desk, meticulously going over the details for a new office building, when I arrived that morning.

"Another day at the venerable old firm," he said with a wink as I passed his desk.

I'd worked as an architect for Simpson and Lowe for almost fifteen years by then, and I realize now that it was no accident that I chose architecture as my profession, even though I had no great ability at geometry or drawing or any of the other skills the work requires. Rather, I chose it because it fulfilled an abiding need, appealed to one of the deeper strains of my character, my desperate need for order. For all its creativity, architecture is finally about predictability. It runs on what is known, rather than what is not. In a fully executed building, one knows with a comforting certainty exactly what the materials will do, their durabilities, the precise level of strain which each can bear and still hold on to its essential shape and function. It is a world which has no room for chance, which has doggedly eliminated the speculative and hypothetical from its principal calculations. Reality is its basis. It makes room for nothing else.

Before Rebecca, it was home.

I was working at my desk, when Wally appeared before me, a peculiar expression on his face.

"There's someone here to see you, Steve," he said. "Rebecca something. I lost the last name. I think I was in a daze."

"What are you talking about?"

"Go see for yourself."

She was in the small waiting room, seated on a dark red sofa, her face very serious as she rose. She put out her hand and I shook it as she introduced herself, her voice deep but not masculine, a fine, somber voice, though somewhat edgy, distant, intensely formal.

"My name is Rebecca Soltero," she said.

"Steve Farris. Did we have an appointment?"

"No, we didn't," Rebecca answered. "I believe in doing things face-to-face. That's why I didn't call or write you first."

She was very direct, a woman with a mission, though I had no idea what it was.

"What can I do for you?" I asked.

"I've come about your father."

She could not have said a stranger thing, nor one more utterly unexpected. It was as if he had suddenly materialized again, magically, in the form of a beautiful woman.

"My father?"

For an instant, I thought perhaps the police or the FBI, or some other agency, had actually begun to look for him again, had, in a moment of unconscious whimsy, assigned an alluring woman to track him down, bring him back, and make him pay, at last, for what he'd done to his family.

"But you must know that my father . . ."

"Yes. That's why I want to talk to you," Rebecca said. "I'd like to hear what you remember about him."

"Why?"

"I'm writing a book about men who've killed their families," she said.

It was strange, but until that moment, I'd never thought of my father as one of a type, a member of some definable human subcategory. Instead, he'd always come to me as a lone wolf, cut from the pack and set adrift by the awesome nature of his crime. I'd never seen anything in him that suggested a common thread, a link with the rest of us.

"I've already done a lot of work," Rebecca added, "particularly with one of the men who investigated the case." She stepped back slightly, as if to get a better view of me, or the room, or something else she might later want to describe. "You probably remember him," she said. "He remembers that you sat in the back seat of the car and that it was raining."

I could see the silver bird as the rain crashed down upon its outstretched wings.

"His name is Swenson," Rebecca went on, "and he remembers turning around and saying something to you."

At that instant, I remembered everything exactly as it had happened that day. I saw the black arms of the windshield wipers as they floated rhythmically over the rain-swept glass, the curling smoke that came from the other one's cigar, the big, white face as it turned toward me, Swenson's pudgy pink thumb gently rubbing the lenses beneath a slightly soiled white handkerchief, his voice low, wheezy: *One day you'll be all right again.*

"He had red hair," I blurted suddenly.

"It's more of an orange-white now," Rebecca said. "His health is not very good."

She described him briefly. Despite his illness, he was still large, she said, with very intense green eyes. He had a gentle manner, but she had sensed great reserves of fortitude and courage. She said that he'd looked long and hard for my father, had followed scores of leads, but that finally, after several years, he'd been told to let it drop, that there was no more money to pursue an unsolvable case. He'd retired not long after that, his health failing steadily, so that during her interview with him, he'd sat near an oxygen tank, taking quick breaths through a plastic mask. It was a condition that reminded me of Quentin's final days.

"My uncle died like that," I told her. "Some sort of respiratory thing."

"That would be Quentin Coleman, the man you lived with in Maine?"

"That's right."

Rebecca said, "I know it's sudden, the way I've just shown up here at your office, but I hope you don't mind." She paused, then added, "I'd like to talk to you for a longer time. It's up to you, of course."

"To tell you the truth, Miss Soltero," I said, "I don't know if I could be of much help to you. I was only nine years old when it happened."

"But you remember your father, don't you?"

"No, not much."

She looked at me very intently. "Are you sure?" she asked.

It was more than a question, and even at that moment I recognized that part of it was a challenge, and part an accusation, the notion that if I didn't help her unearth my father's crime, then I was, to some degree, a partner in it, his cowardly accomplice.

"Would you be willing to meet me again, Mr. Farris?" Rebecca asked directly.

She had drawn the line in the dust. Now it was up to me either to cross it or drift back, draw away from her, but even more critically, to draw away from my father, to close the door forever in his ghostly face. There was something in such a grave finality that I couldn't do.

"Well, I guess we could talk," I replied, "but I still don't think I'll be able to remember much."

Rebecca smiled quietly and put out her hand. "Thank you," she said. "I'll call you."

She left directly after that, and I went back to my desk and began working up a preliminary design for a small library in neighboring Massachusetts.

Within an hour the clouds had broken. From my

desk I watched the morning air steadily brighten until it reached a kind of sparkling purity at midday.

I ate my lunch in the park, watching the swans drift along the edges of the pond, until Wally suddenly plopped down beside me, stretched out his thick, stubby legs, and released a soft belch.

"Oops. Sorry, Stevie," he said. "It's the spaghetti. It always repeats on me." He patted his stomach and went on about other foods that had the same effect upon him—popcorn, melon, a vast assortment—until, near the end of a long list, he stopped, his eyes fixed on a figure he saw moving along the far edges of the pond. "Well, I'll be damned," he said wonderingly. "Christ, that's her, Steve."

"Who?"

"Hell, it's been ten years. I don't know her name right off."

"Who are you talking about?"

"That woman, there."

He nodded, and I glanced over in the direction he indicated. I could see a tall, thin woman as she strolled beside the water. She was wearing a plain, dark blue dress. Her hair had once been very dark, but was now streaked with gray. Her skin looked very pale, almost powdery, as if she were slowly disintegrating.

"Yolanda, that's it," Wally blurted. "Yolanda Dawes."

"Who is she?"

"You kidding me, Steve?" Wally asked unbelievingly. "Hell, man, she's the evil home-wrecker, the menace on the road."

"What are you talking about?"

"She's the broad that killed Marty Harmon."

I turned toward her as if she were a creature out

of myth, the scarlet woman of immemorial renown. She'd reached the far end of the pond by then, the bright midday light throwing a dazzling haze around her as she strolled along its smooth, rounded edge.

Wally had returned to deeper interests, plucking at his nails with a tiny clipper. "Even way back then, she never struck me as something to get all that worked up about," he said absently. "But she sure killed old Marty Harmon, just as sure as if she'd put a bullet in his head."

I hadn't thought of Marty in years, but it was not hard to conjure him up again. We'd come to work for Simpson and Lowe at nearly the same time, and although he was older than I, we'd both been novices at the firm. Because of that we'd socialized together, usually going out for an hour or so after work on Fridays, a custom that neither Marie nor Marty's wife had ever seemed to mind.

Marty's wife was named LeAnn. Before marrying Marty, she'd spent most of her life in Richmond, Virginia. They'd met while Marty was in the navy, married, then moved north, where Marty felt more comfortable. By the time he joined Simpson and Lowe, they'd had two children, a boy of eleven and a girl of nine. I don't recall their names, but only that they were both strikingly blond. By now their hair has darkened. In all likelihood, they have married, and have children of their own. Perhaps, had I kept in touch, I might have been of some assistance to them, since, like me, they were destined to grow up without a father.

As a fellow-worker and, to some extent, a friend, Marty was self-effacing, witty, and very kind. He was not a terribly ambitious man, and he might never have become a partner. But he was highly competent, great with detail, organizational and otherwise, and socially adept enough never to embarrass himself or anyone else by his behavior at office parties or other business functions.

Our favorite place was Harbor Lights, a little bar-restaurant on the outskirts of town. The interior was decked out like the inside of an old whaling boat, complete with oars, coils of thick gray rope, and a few rusty harpoons. For almost two years, we went there at least two Friday evenings out of each month. We talked business and office gossip, the usual end-of-the-week banality. Marty seemed to enjoy the time we spent together, loosening his tie, and sometimes even kicking off his black, perfectly polished shoes. We talked about sports a great deal, and sometimes about our families. Marie was pregnant by then, a child we later lost to miscarriage in its second month, and Marty sometimes fell into the role of the older, more experienced man, warning me of the changes that would inevitably come with fatherhood.

"But all the changes are worth it," he told me cheerfully, "because being a father, it's a different kind of love."

He was always reassuring, and even after the miscarriage he continued to talk about parenthood, clearly encouraging me to try again.

Then, without a word, our Friday meetings came to an end. At first I thought that, after two years, Marty and I had simply come to that point when there was nothing more to discuss and so had drifted in other directions.

I might have felt that way forever if LeAnn hadn't called me three months later. It was just past midnight on a Friday, and her voice was strained.

"Steve, have you seen Marty tonight?"

"No."

"You didn't meet him at that restaurant you go to?"

"No, LeAnn. Why?"

She didn't say. She never said. But something in the tone of her voice that night suggested to me that the snake which seems to lie coiled at the center of so many lives had suddenly struck out at her.

"LeAnn, has something happened?"

She didn't answer.

"LeAnn? Are you all right?"

"Yes," she said, then immediately hung up.

She'd lied, of course. She wasn't all right. She'd dropped from girlhood into womanhood as if through a scaffold floor. "Boys come to manhood through mastery," Rebecca would write years later, "girls come to womanhood through betrayal." So it was with LeAnn Harmon.

The following Monday, I found Marty already at the office when I arrived. He looked haggard, his shoulders slumped, as if under heavy weights, as he shambled toward me.

"LeAnn said she called you," he said. "What did you tell her?"

"What could I tell her, Marty?"

He nodded helplessly. "I should have mentioned something to you, Steve. I'm sorry you got pulled into it."

"I didn't know what to do."

"No, of course not," Marty said. "There's nothing you could have done."

He walked wearily to his desk, then pulled himself in behind it. He didn't speak to me again that day, and only rarely after that, as if I'd become a source of embarrassment to him, something he'd rather have been rid of.

For the next month, Marty worked steadily and well, but during those intervals when he wasn't completely engaged, he looked lost and distracted. At noon, he would wander into the small park across from the office and take his lunch alone. From the window beside my desk, I could see him on the little wooden bench beside the pond, dressed in dark pants and a white shirt, the sleeves rolled up to the elbow, the black-rimmed glasses like a mask over his eyes.

I talked to Marty for the last time about three weeks later. It was at our old haunt, Harbor Lights. I found him sitting alone at a booth near the back. He was smoking a cigarette, his other hand wrapped around a glass of scotch. The jacket of his suit lay in a disordered lump beside him, and he'd yanked his tie down and unbuttoned the top two buttons of his shirt.

"You know what the trouble with men like us is, Steve?" he asked. "We think we can handle anything." He leaned forward, squinting in my direction. "But there is a force, my friend," he said with a sudden vehemence. "There is a force that none of us can handle."

I never asked him what that force was, and after a while, he finished his drink, took a long draw on his last cigarette, then got to his feet and walked away, giving my arm a quick, comradely squeeze as he headed for the door.

There was a small hotel a few blocks from Harbor Lights. It had a neat mid-Atlantic design, all wood and white paint, with bright red shutters. The door had panes of inlaid glass and the sign which hung beside it showed a teenage boy in Colonial dress, red vest and tri-corner hat, a snare drum hanging at his side.

At 11:15 A.M. the following day, Marty checked into room 304 of that hotel. Twenty minutes later, he shot himself.

Marty was buried a few days later, and only a month after that, LeAnn returned to Richmond with her two blond children. I never saw any of them again.

"Yolanda Dawes," Wally said again, shaking his head, as he sat on the bench beside me. "Doesn't look like the black widow, does she?"

I glanced toward her again, my eyes lingering on the wistful, beguiling grace her body had assumed as she made her way along the water's edge.

Wally smiled. "That's the trouble with black widows, buddy," he said, "they never do." He grunted as he stood up, adding nothing else as the two of us walked back to work.

For the rest of the afternoon, I concentrated on the little library in Massachusetts, then left for home at around five-thirty.

When I arrived, Peter was shooting hoops into the basket I'd nailed to the garage door years before. He hardly noticed as I walked by, merely nodded briefly, fired a quick "Hi, Dad," and continued with the game. I could hear the ball thudding like an irregular pulse as I went on past the garage and up the stairway that led to the side entrance of the house, the one that opened onto the kitchen.

Marie was in her office down the hall, working at her computer and listening to Brahms's violin concerto, the only one he ever wrote, a work that Marie liked more than any other, obsessively buying each new rendition as soon as it was released.

"How'd it go today?" I asked.

She barely looked up from her keyboard. "Okay," she said idly. "You?"

"Fine," I told her, paused a moment, then added, "Nothing new."

In that brief pause, I'd thought of Rebecca, considered mentioning her visit to Marie, then decided not to. It had all been done in an instant, a choice made in favor of concealment, even though there'd been nothing to conceal. I realize now that it was a choice made out of a subtle yearning to have a secret in my life, something hidden, tucked away, a compartment where I could keep one treasure for myself alone. The fact that this "treasure" was a woman meant less to me at the time than that it was clandestine and mysterious, a secluded back street I wanted to walk down.

"Go change, then," Marie said, her eyes still fixed on the monitor. "We need to start dinner."

I headed upstairs to the bedroom, pulled off my suit and tie, and returned downstairs. Marie and Peter were already in the kitchen.

"Okay, let's get started," she said, handing me a wooden salad bowl.

Making dinner together was a ritual Marie had long ago established, a "family time" that was busy and productive, a moment when we had to "face" each other, as she said, without the distraction of a game or television. Over the years it had become routine, something I neither looked forward to nor dreaded, a fact of life like any other, open, aboveboard, beyond the allure of the unrevealed.

FOUR

The light in the bedroom was dark gray when I woke up the next morning. Marie had already gotten out of bed. I could see a little sliver of light under the door of the adjoining bathroom. I closed my eyes, heard the toilet flush, then, a few seconds later, the soft scrape of the bathroom door as she opened it.

"It's time, Steve," she said firmly.

I didn't open my eyes. I didn't want to open them. I wanted to sink back into my sleep, but a heaviness in my chest nudged me awake. It was as if someone were sitting on me, looking down.

"Steve, it's time."

Her voice was more insistent, and I knew that she'd keep at it until she saw me climb out of bed. I opened my eyes and glanced toward her. She stood at the bedroom window, a figure in silhouette, the curtains flung open behind her.

"Get up, Steve."

I pushed the covers aside and got to my feet.

Marie looked satisfied and headed for the door. On the way she said, "It's raining. Can you drive

Peter to school this morning? I have to see a client in Bridgeport."

I waved my hand. "Yeah, okay, I'll drop him off on my way to work."

Marie turned and left the room as I staggered toward the bathroom, then disappeared inside. I could hear her as she moved spiritedly along the corridor, then trotted down the short flight of stairs that led to the first floor.

My own pace was slower. The heaviness I'd felt in my chest had managed to creep into my arms and legs, drawing me downward like metal weights.

Peter was already at the table when I finally came downstairs a few minutes later. He'd poured himself a bowl of cereal and was staring at it without interest.

"Mom's already gone," he told me.

"She had to go to Bridgeport."

"So you're taking me?"

"Yeah."

Peter ate the rest of his cereal while I drank a quick cup of coffee, then went back upstairs. I finished dressing, carefully knotted my tie, gathered up the office materials I'd brought home the night before, and returned to the kitchen.

Peter was standing at the door that led from the kitchen to the driveway, tall for his age, and slender, as I had been, but with his mother's straight, determinedly erect posture. Behind him, I could see the rain as it drove down through the trees that bordered the driveway, and against its gray veil he appeared almost ghostly, his large round eyes blinking slowly, like an owl's.

It was a floating, disembodied look that reminded me suddenly of Jamie, of the strange vacancy that had sometimes come into his face, lingered a moment, then dissolved into the pinched and irritated expression that was more usual with him. I remembered that during the last months of his life, those oddly resentful features had hardened into a mask of teenage hostility and sullenness, a face my father had finally aimed at directly, then reduced to a pulpy, glistening mass.

I glanced away from Peter, as if expecting to see his face explode as Jamie's had, then motioned him out the door, following along behind at a cautious distance, my shoulders hunched against the rain.

In the car, Peter sat silently, staring straight ahead, his face no longer locked in that strange innocence and helpless doom I had suddenly associated with my murdered brother. I looked at him and smiled.

"Everything going okay at school?" I asked.

He nodded.

"Good," I told him.

Glancing toward him from time to time as I drove toward his school, I could easily remember him as a little boy, warm and glowing, his hair even lighter, a silver sheen. In the mornings he'd had the habit of crawling into bed with Marie and me, inching his head under my arm, then glancing up with a bright, sometimes toothless, smile.

Strangely, that remembered smile brought Jamie back again, and I recalled the only bit of conversation I'd ever been able to recall between him and my father. We'd all been heading through an indistinct countryside, toward somewhere I don't remember. My father was at the wheel, I in the middle, and Jamie pressed up against the passenger door. We'd been riding together silently, as we usually did, when suddenly my father had turned to Jamie. "You don't smile much," he said.

Jamie's eyes shot over to him resentfully. "What did you say?"

My father appeared to regret having brought the subject up. "Nothing," he muttered, returning his eyes to the road.

But Jamie wouldn't let it go. "What did you say?" he repeated.

"Just that you don't smile much," my father answered.

Jamie gave him that familiar pinched, irritated look. "I smile," he said curtly, as if my father had accused him of something he felt obliged to deny.

"Good," my father answered quickly, then let the subject drop.

But not before he'd briefly leveled his two light blue eyes on my brother, aiming them steadily at his face.

I shuddered, and my hands curled tightly around the steering wheel, as if to bring my body back to the present. It was a tactic that worked so well, I sensed that I'd used it before, but unconsciously, to prevent the emergence of such brief memories, rather than to return from them.

Once at the school, Peter got out quickly, with a child's enthusiasm, opening the door before I'd come to a full stop, then dashing through the rain to where a group of other boys huddled together beneath an aluminum awning. The bell was ringing as I pulled away.

I drove slowly toward my office. The rain grew somewhat lighter, but to the south I could see a line of clouds, low and heavy with rain. It struck me that the clouds lay between Old Salsbury and Bridgeport, and that Marie was probably driving under their low canopy at that very moment. It was then that I remembered that we'd not really said good-bye that morning. I'd heard the scrape of the bathroom door as it opened, then her voice telling me to get up, repeating it when I didn't. After that, nothing.

Marie Olivia Farris. Age, thirty-nine.

I'd met her during my last year in college. I was living in New York then, a small flat in the East Village. At night I worked as a waiter in a restaurant in Little Italy. It was frequented by a well-heeled assortment of mobsters and mid-level show people, whom the owner, Mr. Pinaldi, liked to identify. "You know who you're serving, don't you?" he'd sometimes ask fiercely as I passed with a full tray.

Often I did know, but that particular night I didn't have the slightest idea and told him so.

Mr. Pinaldi looked at me as if I'd just walked out of the Amazon, knew nothing of the civilized world. "The one with the bright red tie, that's Joey Santucci," he said in a vehement whisper. "He's a button man for the Brendizzi gang. He whacks people, kid. He blows them away."

My eyes had reflexively shot toward the customer.

Joey Santucci was sitting at a round table, with two women on either side, one middle-aged, like Joey, the other much younger, and a large man who was dressed in a dark suit. The older woman was overweight, with flabby arms, and had an enormous white flower in her hair. She had a smoker's voice, hard and gravelly, and I took her for some old whorehouse madam Santucci had met years before. The second woman sat directly across from Santucci. She was no more than a girl, really, with dark brown hair and an olive complexion. She did not laugh when the others did, and at times, she cast disdainful glances toward the older woman, though always reserving the fiercer and more contemptuous ones for the man with the bright red tie. She was already halfway through her shrimp cocktail when I heard her call him "Dad."

There was nothing to distinguish any of them, and I probably would have forgotten them immediately if it hadn't happened.

It was very late, and the restaurant was nearly empty. I had just stepped up to take their dessert orders when he came through the door, a short, small-boned, wiry little man with a thin moustache. He had dark, gleaming eyes, quick and feral beneath the slouchy gray hat. He opened the door very wide as he came in, and a whirl of snow swept in behind him, then lay melting on the checkered tile floor as he moved smoothly to the bar.

I watched him as he propped his elbow up on the bar, then glanced back toward me.

"I'll just have a dish of chocolate ice cream," the young one said.

I wrote the order on my pad, a quick squiggle of lines, then glanced back toward the bar.

The little man slid off the stool and now stood beside it, brushing snow from the shoulders of his overcoat as Sandy, the bartender that night, leaned toward him. I saw the little man's mouth twitch, then Sandy nod, turn around, and pull a bottle of scotch from the shelf.

A voice drew my attention from him.

"Just an espresso," the older woman said.

The man pulled himself up on one of the barstools, but did not actually appear to be sitting on it.

Rather, he seemed to be floating on a cushion of air, his body tilting right and left, while he drew his eyes over to the mirror behind the bar, then focused them with a dire intensity on the reflection of the man in the red tie.

"Bring me a brandy," Joey Santucci said.

I glanced down at the pad, scribbled the order quickly, then looked back toward the bar. The little man had wheeled around on the stool, facing me silently, his hands deep in the pockets of the snow-flecked overcoat. His eyes moved from Santucci to the man in the dark suit, the one who had ordered nothing after dinner, and whom I took for Santucci's bodyguard.

I turned, walked around the table, and headed back toward the kitchen. I could see the man at the bar spin slowly around as I passed him, his eyes trained on the mirror again, the four seated figures he could see very clearly in the glass.

Louie snapped the dessert order from my hand as I came through the double doors. He was grumbling angrily.

"That bunch at table six ever going to leave?"

"I don't know."

"Chocolate ice cream. That fat cow ordered dessert?"

"The espresso is for her."

Normally I would have dropped the liquor order on my way to the kitchen, but I had not done that, I realized suddenly, because something had warned me away, had unnerved me.

"Well, go get the drink, Steve," Louie said sharply. "I'll have the dessert ready by the time you get back."

I stepped toward the door, following Louie's instructions. I walked slowly, haltingly, the air growing thick around me. I made it all the way to the door, then pressed my face up against the little square of glass that looked out onto the dining room. I could not move any farther.

"What's the matter, Steve?" Louie asked after a moment.

I didn't answer. Through the small square window, I could see the man at the bar, his hands still deep in his overcoat pockets, the untouched drink resting before him, its amber reflection winking in the mirror, the now motionless eyes trained determinedly on the oblivious, unthinking family.

"Steve?"

I didn't look back at Louie. I felt the words form in my mouth, but I'm not sure I ever actually said them: "He's going to kill them."

I began to tremble. I could feel myself trembling. It was a sensation of helplessness, of being something small and delicate before a line of black, rumbling clouds. To the left, I could see the little man as he brought one hand from his coat, stretched his fingers slowly, then returned it to the pocket. A few feet away, the young girl fiddled with her napkin, looking out of sorts, while her mother toyed coquettishly with her husband's bright red tie.

"Steve, what's the matter?"

It wasn't Louie's voice this time, but a young woman named Marie who'd only come to work a few days before. She had reddish-brown hair, very straight, and her eyes were deep-set and dreamy, exactly the kind that in movies the leading man always yearns to kiss.

"What's the matter?" she asked.

I didn't look at her. I kept my eyes trained on the little man at the bar. "He's going to . . ."

"Who?"

"I . . ."

She saw the order slip quivering in my hand, snatched it from me, then burst through the door and out into the dining room, striding boldly up to the bar, where Sandy took it from her, reaching thoughtlessly over the little man's untouched glass.

I was still standing rigidly by the door when she came back into the kitchen. The little man had drunk the scotch in one quick gulp and was heading for the door. A few feet away, Joey Santucci gave his wife a kiss while his teenage daughter looked on sourly.

I felt myself collapse, as if every muscle had suddenly been ripped from its mooring. I was actually sliding helplessly toward the floor when Marie grabbed me by the arm, drew me over to the small bench beside the cutting table, and lowered me into it.

"You want me to call a doctor, Steve?" she asked urgently.

"No."

"Are you sure?"

I nodded. "I'm sorry. It was just something that reminded me of . . ." I couldn't keep back the words. ". . . of my father."

It was hours later, nearing dawn, and we were in bed in her apartment on MacDougal Street before I finally got the whole story out. I cried and cried, and so she held me through all that sleepless, gorgeous night.

And twenty years later, she'd walked out of our bedroom and down the stairs, and neither of us had thought to say good-bye.

* * *

I'd been at my desk for no more than an hour when the phone rang.

"Mr. Farris?"

"Yes."

"Rebecca Soltero. I was wondering if you might be able to meet me for lunch today."

"Well, it would have to be a short lunch," I said. "And near the office."

"That would be fine," Rebecca said. "I'd just like to get a few biographical details before we do the other type of interview."

She meant the kind, of course, that would return me to my father.

"All right," I said. "There's a small café on Linden, just down the block from my office. It's called Plimpton's."

"Yes, I saw it yesterday," Rebecca said. "What time?"

"I can meet you at twelve-thirty," I told her.

She was already waiting for me when I arrived an hour or so later. She was wearing a long dark skirt with matching jacket and a white blouse. Her earrings were plain gold hoops. She wore no other jewelry.

I nodded crisply as I sat down. "I wasn't expecting to hear from you quite so soon," I said cautiously.

She nodded. "I know," she said, "but I'm at that point where I need a little background information." She took a small notebook from her jacket pocket. "Information about you, I mean," she added. "Biographical details, that sort of thing."

"And the other interviews," I said, "they'll be focused on my father?"

"Along with your family," Rebecca said. "I'd like to have portraits of each of them."

"How many interviews do you expect to need?"

"It depends on how much you remember," Rebecca answered.

"Well, how long are you planning to stay in Old Salsbury?"

She looked at me very determinedly. "I live in Boston," she said, "but I'll stay here as long as I need to." Her eyes returned to the notebook. "I know that you lived with your aunt in Somerset for a while after the murders," she began. "How long?"

"Two months."

"And that's when your uncle came to get you?"

"Yes."

As I spoke, I remembered the morning Quentin arrived at Aunt Edna's house, the old truck shuddering to a stop in her gravel driveway. I'd been stacking dominoes on the carpet in the living room, and when I looked up I saw Aunt Edna part the translucent blue curtains which hung over her large picture window, release a weary sigh, and shake her head, as if the sight of him alone was enough to exasperate her.

He entered the house seconds later, a large man with a round belly and thick legs. He was wearing rubber boots which rose almost to his thighs, and a gray, broad-billed cap that looked like the type worn by locomotive engineers.

He hardly noticed Aunt Edna, but strode powerfully over to me, jerked me into his arms, and said, "Well, Stevie, ready to live a man's life now, are you?"

From the corner of my eye, I could see Aunt Edna looking at both of us crossly, her arms folded over her chest. "Put him down, Quentin," she said sternly, "and come on into the kitchen. We have things to talk about."

They'd talked about me, as I told Rebecca over lunch that day, a conversation I'd heard from just behind the closed door:

"As I said on the phone, it's not working out here, Quentin," Aunt Edna said. "That's the long and the short of it."

"I told you I'd take him, Edna," Quentin told her. "I know you don't want him."

"Well, it's not exactly that I don't . . ."

"Besides," Uncle Quentin interrupted, "he's better off with a man."

There was a brief silence after that, but finally I heard my aunt say, "All right, take him."

And he had, the two of us rattling for hours along well-traveled roads before turning onto the more deserted one that led out to Quentin's house by the sea.

"He was an older man, wasn't he?" Rebecca asked.

"Late fifties."

But he'd seemed much older to me, his hair entirely gray, his face heavily furrowed with deep wrinkles about his eyes and the corners of his mouth.

"Did you get along well, the two of you?" Rebecca asked.

We had, but he had brooked no whining, no grieving, no self-pity. The past was past in his book, and only a fool or a coward dwelled upon its scattered ruins.

"He tried his best to do things with me," I told Rebecca, "things a father would have done."

And so we had camped out from time to time, and fished in the local ponds. In the summer, he took me swimming, snoozing on the shore while I bounced about in the water.

The problem was his health. My first impression of him had been that he was vigorous and robust. But actually, he was rather frail. In the winter, he suffered from long, dreadful colds, and seemed particularly susceptible to digestive problems. He called whiskey his "medicine" and drank as much as he liked as often as he liked, though in all the years we lived together, I never saw him drunk.

I don't think I ever really knew him, as I admitted to Rebecca, but I did remember one incident when I was twelve, something which made me think that there was something deeply wrong with Quentin, something which seethed just below the surface.

It happened on a fall day, with the sky very low, hanging like a flat gray ceiling above my head. I'd been working on the front porch, mending some of the lobster cages which Quentin had hauled in the day before. It was tedious, uncomplicated work, no more than a matter of hammering in a few loose nails. I'd finished up within an hour or so, and after that I wandered around the house to the backyard. Years before, Quentin had built a small wooden shed there, a ramshackle structure which he used partly as a work space, partly as a storehouse for his fishing supplies. In the fall, he went there to mend his nets, and he'd gathered a huge pile of them together in the corner.

The shed had a few small windows, and that afternoon I absently walked over to one of them and glanced in. Quentin was sitting on a stubby wooden bench, working to separate two tangled nets. His face seemed very taut and impatient, and I noticed that his fingers were trembling. His face had taken on a reddish tint around the cheeks and his eyes appeared to glisten slightly, as if he were about to cry. Suddenly he threw the nets down, then picked them up again and began to sling them about, whipping them violently at the shed's skeletal supporting beams. I could see small puffs of dust come from the posts as the nets bit into them and hear the hard slap of the cord as it whipped about furiously.

In a moment, he stopped, then collapsed, exhausted, onto the spindly wooden stool he'd been sitting on before it all began. His head dropped slightly, and he wiped his mouth with his hand. His shoulders were lifting high and rhythmically, so I knew it had taken almost all his breath to groan the single word he said into the dusty interior of the shed.

"It was a woman's name," I told Rebecca.

She glanced up from her notebook, her face very still, intense, searching. "A woman's name?"

"Yes," I said. "But I have no idea who she was."

She seemed to consider the story a moment, turning it over in her mind. Then she sat back slightly, as if to regain her focus.

"When did you leave Maine?" she asked.

"Not until I went to college. Aunt Edna had sold the house on McDonald Drive and put the money in an account for me. That's what I used to pay for college."

"And after college, you never lived in Maine again?"

"Only for a little while. I went back to take care of Quentin. He was dying by then."

Old and frail and drinking far too much, he'd needed me to stay with him during the last weeks of his life, and so, directly after leaving college, I'd returned to the little house by the sea.

Quentin hadn't died quickly. It had taken a long time. Nor had he approached death gracefully. Instead, a bitterness and rancor had slowly overwhelmed him, filling his days with mean-spirited discourses on the inadequacies of life.

For nearly three months, I listened as he lay out on the back porch, staring fiercely at the sea, while fuming against and damning to hell almost everyone he'd ever known. He railed against his own parents, against Edna, against a host of double-dealing business partners. One by one the names passed his lips carried on a curse. Except one.

"He never said anything bad about my father," I said to Rebecca. "Not a single word."

Rebecca looked surprised.

"As a matter of fact," I added, "the only thing he ever said about my father was sort of complimentary."

"Complimentary?"

"One night, he was really having a bad time," I went on. "He was railing about things, as usual. But all of a sudden he stopped. Then he looked at me, and he whispered, 'Ah, your father, Stevie, he really took it by the balls.' "

Rebecca said nothing, but I could see something moving behind her eyes.

I shrugged. "He died ten days later," I added. "I never knew exactly what he meant."

Rebecca lowered her eyes toward her notebook, wrote something there, and then looked up at me. "Did he ever mention the woman again?" she asked. "The name he said in the shed that afternoon?"

I shook my head. "No," I answered, then smiled lightly. "I guess she'll always be a mystery."

Rebecca did not return my smile. "Like a lot of things," she said, but with a curious unease and sense of strain, as if it were a fate she was still unwilling to accept.

FIVE

It was nearly a week before I heard from Rebecca again, and I remember that the days passed slowly, like soldiers in a gray line. During that interval, I often thought about the life my family had lived on McDonald Drive. I recalled how, when I was very small, Laura had taken me out to the swings and played with me for hours. My father had often sat in a small wrought-iron chair and watched us. "Don't swing him too high," he would caution at those times when Laura's natural energy would get the better of her and she'd send me hurtling skyward, my feet soaring into the summer air.

There were other memories, too. I could recall my mother piddling about in the garage, moving small boxes from one place to another. She seemed always to be hunting for something small and inconsequential that eluded her again and again, a pruning fork or a spool of thread. Jamie would joke about it from time to time. "Everything she touches disappears," he once said with a mocking grin.

There'd been a fireplace in the living room, and I remembered the sounds the fire made in the winter, along with the rhythmic thump of the axe when my father chopped wood beneath the large maple tree in the backyard.

Smells returned. Laura's nail polish, the raincoat that Jamie often hung wet in the closet we were forced to share, my mother's cooking, always bland and unaccented, the smell, I often thought, of little more than boiling water. And last, my father's hands, the strange odor that always came from them, and which, one night during that week before Rebecca called again, I actually mentioned to Marie.

"Like soil," I said suddenly, as we sat at the dinner table one evening. The words had come from nowhere but my own mind. We'd not been talking about my father, or anything even remotely connected to him.

"What are you talking about, Steve?" Marie asked.

I felt embarrassed, surprised by the level of my own distraction.

"I was thinking about my father," I explained quickly. "The odor of his hands."

"Why were you thinking about that?"

It was the perfect chance to tell her about Rebecca, her book, the meetings I'd had, the ones I expected to have in the future. And yet, I found that I couldn't do it.

"I don't know," I told her. "Sometimes, things just pop into my head. This time, it was my father." I shrugged. "No reason."

And so, it had begun.

It was a Thursday afternoon, and I was at the drafting table in my office at Simpson and Lowe when Rebecca called to arrange another meeting.

"It's Rebecca Soltero," she said.

"Yes, I know."

"I was wondering if you might have an evening free this week?"

"Most of my evenings are free," I told her.

She didn't seem surprised to hear it. "Well, we could meet tonight, if you want."

"All right."

"Where?"

I suggested a small restaurant north of town. In the past I'd gone there alone in the late afternoon, simply to sit in the generally quiet atmosphere and have a drink before going home. At times I would do a little work, perhaps add a line or two to the drawing of the "dream house" I had been elaborating and modifying for years, and vaguely hoped to build one day. It was a house of floating levels and dreamy, translucent walls, of rooms that melted into other rooms. It was impractical and unrealizable, a structure bereft of all those mundane pillars and supporting beams without which it could not hope to stand.

She arrived promptly, carrying a black briefcase, and wearing a dark red silk blouse and a long black skirt. She'd added a bolero jacket, also black, unnecessary in the unusual warmth of that long Indian summer, but worn, I think, in order to conceal or diminish the more obvious contours of her body.

"Thanks for meeting me again, Mr. Farris," she said as she sat down.

"Steve," I said. "It's no trouble." I glanced about the room. "It's a nice place, don't you think?"

It was a garden restaurant, made of glass and hung with vines. Small fountains sprouted here and there among the foliage.

"A sort of Garden of Eden effect," I added.

"Yes, it's fine," Rebecca answered briskly.

The waitress stepped over, a young woman named Gail, with whom Wally claimed to have had a brief affair, though he probably hadn't. I ordered a beer on tap, Rebecca a glass of red wine. Gail glanced at Rebecca, then at me. She grinned knowingly, as if privy to a secret.

"When do you have to be home?" Rebecca asked after Gail stepped away.

"Home?"

"You're married, aren't you? With a son?"

I nodded. "A family man," I said, then added, "My son is nine years old. His name is Peter."

"And your wife's name?"

"Marie."

Rebecca smiled quietly, but with a certain quickness that made it clear that she had only a passing, casual interest in my present family, that her entire focus was on the other one that had been destroyed.

The drinks came promptly, and I lifted my glass casually for the customary toast. She raised hers as well, but when I moved to touch my glass to hers, she drew it away quickly, almost in an act of self-defense, and took a quick sip.

"I've been working on the book for three years," she said, after returning the glass to the table.

I nodded silently, watching the steady gaze of her eyes. They were dark eyes, sensual, but not dreamy, and there was nothing in the least sultry about them. They were the eyes of an explorer, searching, determined, curiously ruthless. I imagined them in the face of Pizarro or Cortés.

"I finally settled on five cases," she went on. "At this point I've finished four of them." She opened the black briefcase she'd placed on the table between us and drew out a large manila envelope. "I thought you might like to see the ones I've already studied."

"See them?"

"Well, I brought photographs of the men, and the victims," Rebecca explained. "I've also written short summaries of each crime. You can read them if you like."

She hesitated, her hand poised to open the envelope, her eyes leveled upon me, sensing the chilly dread that had suddenly gripped me as my eyes fell upon the yellow envelope.

"Of course, if you'd rather not do any of this . . ."

I rushed to assure her that she didn't need to be delicate with me. "No, no, I think I should know about the others," I told her.

She took a smaller envelope from the larger one, opened it, and pulled out a short stack of photographs. The one on top was in black and white, and it showed a tall, slender man as he leaned idly against the fender of a dusty pickup truck.

"This is the first man I studied," Rebecca said. "Harold Wayne Fuller. Age, thirty-seven."

That was all she said as she turned the photograph toward me.

In the picture, Fuller was dressed in loose-fitting trousers and a plain white shirt, its sleeves rolled up beyond the elbows. He wore a dark-colored baseball cap with the initials "AB" on the front, and a slender baseball bat dangled from his right hand.

"He was a steelworker in Birmingham, Alabama," Rebecca said, "a union leader, very respected by the men he worked with. As a young man, he played professional baseball for a few years, but a knee injury finally made him quit."

Her tone was very matter-of-fact, even a little rushed, as if this were a task she was anxious to get through.

"He had been married to his wife, Elizabeth, for fourteen years," she continued. "They had two daughters, ages twelve and thirteen. Both girls attended the local school, and both were good students. No one at the school had noticed any signs of emotional disturbance in either one."

She stopped, watching me as I continued to stare at the picture.

The face of Harold Wayne Fuller was the face of Everyman. It was plain and flat and impossible to read. There was no sign of dementia or murderous intent, of anything lurking beneath the surface, tightening the fingers around the baseball bat.

Rebecca let my eyes linger on the photo a while longer, then drew it away to expose the one that lay beneath it.

"This is the couple together," she said.

The second photograph showed Fuller and his wife on their wedding day, a picture taken outside a large gray public building, probably by a stranger, and which showed them smiling brightly, Fuller in a baggy double-breasted suit, his arm draped over his wife's nearly bare shoulders.

"Fuller married Elizabeth in the summer of 1952," Rebecca added. "She had their first daughter, Emily Jane, the following year."

Once again Rebecca drew the photograph away to reveal the one beneath it.

"This is Emily Jane," she said. "Age, nine."

In the small, black-and-white picture, Emily Jane Fuller was standing beside the same dusty pickup truck which had been captured in the first picture, the baseball bat her father had been holding now leaning against the truck's closed door, her father no doubt behind the camera now, aiming it steadily at his daughter.

After a few seconds, Rebecca slid the picture away, bringing a fourth photograph into view.

"A second daughter, Phyllis Beatrice, called 'Bootsie,' was born a year later," she said.

In the fourth photograph, "Bootsie" stood in a nondescript living room, dressed in a cowboy skirt and blouse, her long hair partly concealed by a large, western hat.

"Bootsie belonged to the same square-dancing club her mother attended," Rebecca said. "They seem to have been very close."

I let my eyes rest on the picture for a time, then glanced up toward Rebecca.

"Did he kill them all?" I asked.

Rebecca nodded. "With the baseball bat," she said. "The police still have it stored in their evidence locker."

"They kept everything they took from my house, too," I said. "I don't even know exactly what they took. I just know that they never gave anything back."

"No, of course not," Rebecca said. "The case is still open."

I dismissed the thought of it. "Open? That's just a formality. They can't ever officially close an unsolved murder case. There's no statute of limitations on murder. But they're never going to find my father. It's been thirty-five years since he did it."

Rebecca said nothing. She took a second, small envelope from the larger one and handed it to me. It was identical to the first, and as I drew it from her hand, I heard her call the man's name and age, though without expression, as if doing an inventory.

"Gerald Ward Stringer. Age, forty-one."

The second set of pictures was arranged in exactly the same order as the first, more or less chronologically.

"The summation of the case is under the photographs," Rebecca said.

I nodded, my eyes already settling on the first picture.

Gerald Ward Stringer sat in a recliner, shirtless, legs stretched out, his bare feet aimed at the camera, his belly pouring over his beltless trousers. He was nearly bald, a shiny star of light gleaming on his forehead, the result no doubt of the reflected flash that had been used to take the picture. He was smiling, very broadly, the happy fat man in his cluttered lair. The room in which he sat was paneled in pinewood. A few mounted animal heads hung from the walls that surrounded him, and I could see a rack of hunting rifles hung between a deer and a fox. A safari hat, one side of its bill turned up raffishly, dangled from one of the deer's upturned antlers.

Rebecca gave her narration as I leafed through the photos.

"The murders occurred six months after this picture was taken," she said. "Stringer killed Mary Faye, his wife of nine years, and his three sons: Eddie, four. Tyrone, six. And Jimmy Dale, seven."

She waited a moment, then added softly, "With a rifle, as you've probably already figured out."

As if realizing that I didn't want to read the summations she'd written, she continued on, relating the details of the case, describing what had actually happened on February 11, 1967. As she did so, I found that I could see it all quite graphically in my mind.

Gerald Ward Stringer had come home from one of a string of small, very successful bakeries that he owned in Des Moines, Iowa, at the usual time of seven-thirty. He'd gone to work at five o'clock that morning, and he was, as he later told police in a description of himself that was eloquently simple, "a very tired man."

Mary Faye worked as an office clerk at a local brewery, and she had been at work all day, too. When Stringer arrived home, he found her sleeping on the sofa in the den, one leg hanging over the side, her right foot almost touching the floor, her body in the exact position in which the police would find her several hours later, and which Stringer described as looking "sort of like a big towel that somebody had just thrown onto the couch."

The children, all three of them, were in the basement. Tyrone and Jimmy Dale were playing at the miniature pool table they'd gotten for Christmas two months before, while Eddie played with a set of Tinker Toys on the large square of outdoor carpet which covered the basement's otherwise cold, cement floor.

For nearly an hour, Stringer sat in the den only a few feet from his sleeping wife. From time to time during that fateful hour, Miss Zena Crawford, the woman who rented the small apartment over the Stringers' two-car garage, looked down from her window and glanced into the Stringer family house. From her position over the garage, she had a commanding view of the den and kitchen. In the den, she saw Gerald Ward Stringer as he sat silently in the big recliner. He sat upright, his hands in his lap, rather than the usual reclining position in which she'd glimpsed him at other times.

At 8:20 P.M., Miss Crawford heard Tyrone calling to his mother, asking her to unlock the door that separated the basement from the upper floor of the house. She looked out the window and saw both Tyrone and Jimmy Dale at the basement window, the one which looked out at just above ground level, and which was situated almost directly below the window in the den. She glanced up and saw Mrs. Stringer rustle slightly on the sofa, as if the voices of her children were awakening her.

Having seen nothing that alarmed her, Miss Crawford turned from the window, took a couple of steps toward her small kitchen, then heard a shot. She returned to her window, glanced down, and noticed that the blinds in the Stringers' den had been lowered. She looked down at the small basement window just in time to see Tyrone and Jimmy Dale as they turned away from her, back toward the basement's interior darkness, as if in answer to someone's call. They lingered at the window for an instant, then shrank away from it. Seconds after the two boys had left the window, Miss Crawford heard three shots.

Rebecca paused a moment after she'd finished her narrative. She was watching me closely, no doubt because this particular crime resembled my father's a bit more closely than the first. It had been committed with a firearm, and three of the murders had taken place in a basement, which, on the surface, appeared to resemble the sort of place in which my mother, too, had died.

"Do you have any questions?" she asked tentatively as she returned the pictures to their envelope.

"No."

Rebecca pulled out a third envelope.

"Herbert Malcolm Parks," she said. "Age, forty-three."

She said nothing else, now clearly preferring that I read the summaries she'd attached to the photos rather than listen to her own narration of the events.

The summary was neatly typed on plain white paper, and it was very succinct, giving the details briefly and without the slightest literary adornment.

Herbert Parks was a real estate agent in San Francisco. On June 12, 1964, he'd suddenly been stricken by an upset stomach while sitting at his downtown office. After complaining of the pain to several fellow agents, he'd driven to his home in Mill Valley, and there murdered his wife, Wenonah, age thirty-eight, and his two daughters, Frederica, twelve, and Constance, seven. Mrs. Parks had been shot once in the back of the head. The two girls had been forced to drink orange soda in which their father had dissolved several rat control pellets which contained cyanide. All three bodies had been stacked one on top of the other in the walk-in closet off the master bedroom.

The murders had occurred at approximately two-thirty in the afternoon, and as a result, there was no Miss Crawford to glance out her window and see something strange going on at the house next door.

Nonetheless, there were witnesses of a type. George McFadden, an electrical lineman perched high above the street only a few yards from the house, saw Parks's dark gray Mercedes pull into the driveway at approximately two that afternoon. According to McFadden, Parks had not gotten out of the car right away, but had remained behind the wheel, "as if waiting for some kind of signal" before entering the house.

A few minutes later, two young girls had come from the house, both of them moving toward the car. The smaller one, who must have been Constance, darted enthusiastically toward her father, while the larger one, Frederica, held back. Parks had already gotten out by the time they reached him, and, once again according to McFadden, he took each of them into his arms, hugged them for a long time, then, hand in hand, his shoulders slightly hunched, led them back into the house.

No one else saw or heard anything after that.

After reading the summation, I turned to the photographs. Arranged once again in the established order, the first picture showed Herbert Parks in a dark double-breasted suit. It was a professional photograph, done at a studio, and the smaller marks and blotches which must have been on his face had been air-brushed into oblivion. He had gray hair at the temples, but otherwise jet black, and for the purposes of the photo he appeared to have pulled a single curl down so that it dangled, slightly greased in fifties matinee-idol style, near the center of his forehead.

There were only two other photographs. The first, just under the studio picture of Herbert Parks, showed his wife posed beside the same dark Mercedes which George McFadden saw pull into the driveway on the afternoon of June 12, 1964. She was wearing a light blue blouse, its ends tied in a knot across her waist, a pair of jeans, rolled up to mid-calf, and white tennis shoes. She was holding a water hose and a red plastic pail, and seemed to be pretending to wash the car.

The last picture was from the family's personal

Christmas card of the year before. Both Herbert and Wenonah Parks were in the photograph, but the focus of the picture, its heart and soul, was the two little girls they held in their arms. Constance was clearly laughing, but Frederica seemed to stare pensively toward the lens, her tiny mouth firmly set in place, not so much frowning, as refusing to smile, her eyes oddly vacant, her arms wrapped tightly around Wenonah's slender neck.

Rebecca noticed how my eyes lingered upon her, then spoke:

"He put her on top."

"You mean, in the closet?"

"Yes. She was larger than Constance, but he stacked her on top, and folded her hands over her chest. The others were just sprawled across the closet floor."

I remembered how my father had done something odd as well, how he'd washed my mother's body and arranged it carefully on the bed while leaving Laura and Jamie to lie in their ugly, smelly pools of coagulating blood. And as I remembered it, my eyes drifted back to Frederica, and suddenly I thought I knew why she had clung so desperately to her mother in the Christmas card photo, why she had, as George McFadden had mentioned, "held back" from running heedlessly to her father on the day he had assigned to kill her.

"It was because she knew," I said, almost to myself, but loud enough for Rebecca to hear me.

She looked at me curiously. "Knew what?"

"That it was coming," I told her, "that her father was going to kill them." I looked at her pointedly. "There must always be someone who knows what's about to happen, don't you think? Not everyone can be entirely in the dark."

"Why not?" Rebecca asked.

"Because so much is going on," I said. "In the family, I mean. Surely someone has to sense it."

Rebecca looked at me squarely. "Did you?"

"No."

"Did Laura or Jamie?"

It was odd to hear their names again, to hear them spoken of as if they once had actually existed, had lived and observed the life around them, rather than simply as the faceless victims of my father's crime.

I shook my head slowly. "I don't think so."

"And your mother?"

It was strange, but at that moment, I suddenly suspected that somehow, through all the mists that must have clouded and thwarted and befuddled her, "poor Dottie" must have known that my father was approaching some dreadful line, and that if he crossed it, he might kill us all.

"She might have known," I said quietly.

"What makes you think so?"

A memory invaded me, and I recalled how often she'd gone off to her bedroom, closed the door and remained there for hours, as if locking herself away from him, from us, from whatever it was she could feel heating the air inside the little mock Tudor house on McDonald Drive.

"She spent a lot of time in the bedroom," I told Rebecca.

Even as I said it, I wondered what dreadful possibilities my mother might have envisioned while she lay alone on her bed. In her mind, had she ever seen him coming up the stairs, the shotgun in his hand?

And if she had glimpsed such a thing, had she ever considered packing us into the car and taking us away before it was too late?

"But if she did suspect something," I said, "she didn't do anything about it."

Except to let us drift, I thought with a sudden bitterness, let us slide into destruction because she was unable to summon up even enough will to throw off her red housedress, gather us into the station wagon, and take us away from him.

As all of this swept over me, I found that I suddenly blamed my mother as much as, maybe even more than, I blamed my father. The cool rancor and cruelty of my next remark amazed me.

"My mother was very weak," I said. "She was a nothing. She could have left him, but she didn't."

"Had he ever been violent with her?" Rebecca asked.

"No."

"With any of you?"

"No, never," I said. "He would sometimes get irritated. Especially with Jamie. But he never raised his hand against any of us."

To my surprise, Rebecca didn't ask any more questions. Instead, she simply handed me another envelope.

"This is the last one," she said.

I took the envelope from her and read it quietly.

Hollis Donald Townsend. Age, forty-four.

On July 12, 1961, Hollis Townsend, a certified public accountant and avid foreign-stamp collector who lived and worked in Phoenix, Arizona, returned with his family from a two-week vacation at Yellowstone National Park. A neighbor, Sally Miller, who came out to welcome them back, placed the time at

3:35 P.M. For the next few minutes, while Hollis Townsend unpacked the car, she spoke to his wife, Mary Townsend, thirty-seven. During this brief time, as she later told police, the Townsend children, Karen, five, and Sheila, eight, had played with the family dog, a large collie named Samson.

Nearly nine hours later, at around midnight, Mrs. Miller was awakened by a single shot, followed rapidly by two others. She rose, walked to her window, glanced out, and saw Hollis Townsend as he stepped out of the house, turned left, and headed for the garage. He had a large suitcase, one which appeared to be very heavy, since Townsend needed both hands to drag, rather than carry, it across the lawn. He was dressed in the same beige trousers and short-sleeved knit shirt he'd been wearing earlier in the day, an indication that he had not gone to bed, although, as Mrs. Miller told police, all the lights in the house had been off for more than two hours.

What had he done in that darkness?

Rebecca's summation gave a short but graphic answer. For one thing, he'd written several letters, all of which he'd eventually thrown into the kitchen wastebasket. The letters, written in Townsend's pinched script, alluded to an "inadequacy" which he had to face, the inadequacy, as he put it, "of life, of what I can't find in it somehow."

At some other point during the night, Townsend had poured gasoline in every room in the house, drenching carpets and furniture, and leaving a trail which began in the kitchen, then led through the rooms on the ground floor before heading up the stairs to where his family lay sleeping obliviously. At the last moment, however, he had not lit a match, but had simply dragged his enormous suitcase out across the lawn, leaving the house intact behind him, the bodies of his wife and two children still lying in their own beds.

Each had been shot one time. Karen and Sheila had been shot in the back of the head, Mary through the forehead, presumably because, unlike her daughters, she slept on her back rather than her stomach.

Only two photographs were attached. The first showed Hollis Townsend beside the family swimming pool. He was wearing only a bathing suit, and he appeared to be beating his breasts comically, in a mocking imitation of Tarzan.

The second photograph was of Mary Townsend. She was kneeling down, her arms around her small daughters. It was a picture that had undoubtedly been taken during the family vacation at Yellowstone. Old Faithful, the park's most famous geyser, could be seen exploding from a cloud of steam behind them.

Without comment, I returned the summation and photographs to their envelope and handed it to Rebecca. She took them from my hand, placed them in her briefcase.

"I think that's enough for tonight," she said abruptly.

I was surprised. "I have more time," I told her.

She began to gather her things together. "I'd rather start fresh next time," she said. "The questions I want to ask you would take a long time to answer, and I'd rather not go into them now." She closed the briefcase and started to rise.

I touched her hand. "Why my father?" I asked. "Why did you pick him?"

She drew her hand away from mine, leaned back slightly, and gave me her reasons so smoothly and matter-of-factly that she seemed to be quoting a long passage she'd written beforehand.

"Well, all the cases you've read about have a few things in common," she said. "None of them had serious money problems. None of them had medical problems. None of them had lovers. There were no 'other women' in their lives. All of them committed their murders in their family homes. All of them had planned the murders beforehand. Nothing about them was sudden or impulsive. These were not acts of rage. The killings were quick and clean."

She paused, as if waiting for a question, then went on when I simply watched her silently.

"And last, these men all tried to escape," she said. "They didn't kill themselves, as some family murderers do. They tried to get away instead, to escape. None of them succeeded, except, of course, your father."

As if in a sudden vision, I saw him. Through the rain, his hat pulled down, water dripping from its sagging brim, I saw my father move toward the family car, saw him as Mrs. Hamilton must have seen him, her eyes peering toward the street from behind the blue curtains that hung from her living room window.

"Yes, he did succeed in that," I said. I smiled ironically. "He would be an old man now."

Rebecca nodded, a small green leaf brushing against the side of her face.

"An old man," I repeated, though without emphasis, a simple mathematical determination. The others swam into my mind, Fuller, Stringer, and the rest.

"What are you looking for in these men?" I asked.

The question appeared to sink into her face like a dye.

"I want to find out what it was in life that they couldn't bear," she said.

"And because of that, killed their families?"

"Yes."

I looked at her, puzzled. "And you think that in each of them it was the same thing?"

She peered closely into my eyes, as if trying to gauge what my response might be to her next remark. "The same thing," she said finally, "in almost every man."

I was still going over that peculiar remark when I got home a few minutes later. It was still early, and Peter was in the small family room watching some sort of situation comedy on television.

"Where's your mother?" I asked him as I strolled into the room.

"In her office."

"Did you have dinner?"

"She fixed one of those cheese things."

I walked out of the room, down a short corridor, and opened the door to Marie's office. She looked up, startled.

"Please don't do that, Steve," she said.

"Do what?"

"Come in like that. Through the door all of a sudden."

I laughed mockingly. "What do you think I am, Marie, some crazed axe murderer?"

She did not seem amused. She went back to her work without saying anything else.

I remained at the door, looking at her. She was typing something at her computer, something that was probably businesslike, but uninspired, a bid for the job in Bridgeport, I supposed, a banal proposal for interior design. I compared it to the project upon which Rebecca had embarked, a far more profound investigation of a far deeper interior. Marie's work seemed small and inconsequential compared to that, scarcely more than the busywork of a life that had settled for too little, a life that had been lived . . . like mine.

Without warning, an odd sense of desolation suddenly overwhelmed me, and I left Marie to her work, walked to the kitchen, snatched the cheese thing from the refrigerator, and ate it pleasurelessly at the dining room table.

When I'd finished, I returned to the family room. Peter was still watching television, and for a few minutes I watched along with him, an action picture of some sort, all car chases and shattering glass.

He went to bed at ten, without speaking, a slender figure in red pajamas padding up the carpeted stairs to a room he had come to consider as his private domain, and which his mother and I had been forbidden to enter without permission.

I remained in the family room, my mind in a kind of featureless limbo until Rebecca's final remark came back into my mind, and I began to think over the cases she'd written about. I saw Harold Fuller leaning on his baseball bat, Gerald Stringer sitting rigidly upright in his big recliner, Herbert Parks slowly walking his two daughters hand-in-hand back into the house, Hollis Townsend beating his breasts beside the bright blue pool. What was it in any of these men that so fascinated her?

Finally, inevitably, I thought about my father, too, asking the same questions I thought Rebecca must be asking: Who was he? Why did he do it? From what dark, volcanic core had so much murder come?

At that early stage, I couldn't have answered any of these questions. Still, I felt the urge to pursue them, to press on toward finding some kind of solution to the mystery of my father's crime. Certainly, part of that urge came from Rebecca, but part of it also came from me, the need to touch the center of something, to reach the final depth . . . no matter where it lay.

SIX

"Steve, it's seven-thirty."

It was Marie calling from downstairs.

I got up slowly, showered, and dressed.

Marie and Peter were seated at the breakfast table. Peter was chattering on about some atrocity his teacher had committed against another student. As he talked, Marie watched him quietly, nodding from time to time as she chewed a final bit of toast.

When Peter had finished, we all fell silent, and after a moment, I found myself remembering those other family breakfasts I'd had so long ago at the little oval-shaped Formica table on McDonald Drive. Often, we'd all fallen silent, too, sitting for long stretches in a gloomy quiet. But it was not a moment like that which came back to me. Instead it was one of those rare occasions when my father and Laura, normally so withdrawn from the rest of us, had talked quite openly at the breakfast table, chatting with a rare spiritedness and candor, as if they were alone.

Laura had begun it, talking about some report she'd been working on in her geography class. It had had to do with an Oriental country. I don't remember the particular place, but only that my sister had spoken almost mystically about the beauty of the land, the strangeness of the people, all those bizarre landscapes and customs which would have fascinated any sixteen-year-old girl as high-strung and curious as Laura.

In any event, she'd finished by saying that she intended to go there at some point in her life, an ambition, as I noticed, which had spontaneously and very powerfully appealed to my father. As much as I ever saw his love pour out to her, I saw it at that moment in the little kitchen. It was a look of unqualified admiration, but a look that also seemed a kind of plea that she hold forever to this longing for distant things and lost, mysterious places.

Jamie saw it, too, however, and something in it infuriated him.

"You're never going anywhere," he sneered at Laura. "Who do you think you are, some kind of princess?"

Laura glared at him angrily. "Oh, shut up, Jamie," she snapped.

"Just big ideas, that's all," Jamie fired back. "You're not going anywhere."

"I said, shut up, Jamie," Laura screamed, "just shut up."

It continued in this way for some time, both Jamie and Laura growing hotter by the minute, my mother lamely attempting to quell the riot, but with her usual lack of force.

I don't know exactly at what point I became aware that my father had left the room. I hadn't seen him rise, walk around the table, and disappear into some other part of the house. It was as if he'd simply vanished.

The battle continued in his absence, growing more furious and abusive by the moment. My mother left after a time, coughing slightly, as if escaping from a smoke-filled room. I remained in my seat, of course, watching the battle like a child, fascinated by the flames. I was still there when it died away suddenly, and both Laura and Jamie moved out into the open air, Jamie to the basketball hoop, Laura to a chair in the backyard.

Later, coming from the upstairs bathroom, I glimpsed my mother as she lay on her back in the bed, one hand at her side, the other balanced palm up on her forehead, as if she were wiping a line of sweat from her brow.

A terrible silence had descended upon the house by then, one which no one seemed willing to break, as if this sullen, unhappy peace was the only kind of quiet we could know. I remember that in order not to break it, I had actually tiptoed down the stairs.

I was near the bottom of them when I saw my father sitting alone in the solarium. His legs stretched out before him, his arms hanging limply at his sides, he no longer looked like that commanding figure who'd once stepped out onto the balcony and brought all of us to attention.

At that point I might have thought him broken, I suppose, a pitiful shell in gray work clothes, but suddenly he looked over at me, and the man I saw was not weak, nor timid, nor lacking in resolve. Rather, he seemed to smolder with a strangely building purpose, the eyes small, intense, deeply engaged, the jaw firmly set. It was a face I'd seen in old cowboy movies, a man about to draw.

Now, as I sat in the silence of my own kitchen, my eyes moving slowly from Peter to Marie, I wondered if it was at that precise moment that my father had decided that he would bear no more, that he would kill us all.

"These men," Rebecca would later write, "shouldered all they had been taught to shoulder, until their shoulders broke."

Until their shoulders broke, and they reached for the pistol, the baseball bat, the pellets encrusted with cyanide. Until their shoulders broke, and they stood on the third step and followed the little watery footprints as they led toward the empty cardboard box . . . and fired.

Or was it only the slow wearing away she wanted to explore, the long descent toward that explosive second when the shoulders cracked and the savagery began?

"What are you thinking about, Steve?"

I glanced toward Marie. "What?"

"You looked like you were thinking about something."

"Just something at work," I said.

Marie took me at my word and didn't press the matter. She went back to her breakfast, and after finishing it, walked upstairs to finish dressing.

I walked to my car and drove to work. Wally was leaning against my desk when I arrived. He handed me a note.

"Phone message," he said with a leering grin.

I glanced at the message: "Call Rebecca," and then a number.

"Thanks," I said to Wally, as I pocketed the note and slid in behind my desk.

Wally continued to stare at me knowingly. "So, is she a nice woman, Steve?" he asked with a quick wink.

"Very," I told him, but without emphasis, in the same way I might have said it of a business acquaintance.

Wally grinned. "Glad to hear it," he said, then walked away.

I dialed the number, and Rebecca answered the phone right away. "Hello."

"It's me."

"Who?"

"Steve Farris."

"Oh, Steve, thanks for calling," she said. "Listen, I was wondering if we might meet again this Friday."

For the first time, I felt the pull of her voice as something alluring.

"I suppose so."

"The same place? Around five?"

"Okay."

Rebecca thanked me, then hung up. I went back to my work, but even as I continued sketching the design for the Massachusetts library, I felt both Rebecca and the task she had set herself lingering in the air around me. It gave a peculiar energy to my thoughts, a direction that hadn't been there before. It was as if, before Rebecca, a space had existed in my mind, empty and featureless, but which I had always felt as an odd, persistent ache. And so, as the days passed, and I went through the routine of work and home, I looked forward to my meeting with Rebecca as a wounded man might have looked forward to the first soothing touch of a doctor or a nurse.

I was relieved to see her when she arrived that Friday afternoon.

She was wearing a white blouse and dark green

skirt that fell nearly to the floor. I noticed the skirt most: "It's very beautiful."

"Thank you," Rebecca said. She was just that crisp and dismissive, a mode of behavior that her beauty had no doubt taught her, to be distant, restrained, to slap the hand long before it made its first uncertain movement toward her. She opened her briefcase and reached for something inside it, speaking at the same time, though with her eyes averted, focused on the papers her long brown fingers were riffling through.

"I brought a few pictures," she said.

"Pictures of the murders?" I asked.

A certain wariness came into her face, as if she didn't want to rush me into a terrain that she knew I would find horrible.

"I have those pictures, too," she said, "but they're not for today."

I watched her as she placed the pictures in a small stack at her right hand. It was obvious that she'd already arranged them in the order she thought appropriate. She shifted slightly in her seat, and I could hear the sound of her body as it rustled against her dark green skirt. It was a soft but highly detailed sound, crisp and distinct, like the crunch of bare feet moving softly over leaves.

She plucked the first picture from the stack and moved it slowly toward me. It was of my father when he was in his late teens. He was standing at the bus station in Highfield, dressed in blue jeans and a plaid shirt, his traveling case dangling from his hand.

"That must have been taken the day he left home," I said.

"He went to New York, didn't he?" Rebecca asked.

"Yes."

"Do you know anything about how he came to make that decision?"

At the time, I didn't. But I've learned a great deal since then. There was a box of letters and other papers which he left behind. Aunt Edna had stored them in her attic, and when she died, they came to me. For years they moldered in our basement, but when I finally began to look through them, I discovered, among other things, the world my father had confronted in his youth.

The Depression had been in full swing, of course, so that by the time he'd graduated from high school, he'd had few prospects in a town like Highfield. Because of that he'd gone to New York City, looking for work along with thousands of others, and had ended up in a dingy rooming house on Great Jones Street.

After Rebecca, when I finally visited that place, I found a plain, six-story brick building that had long ago been converted into a drafty, dilapidated warehouse. My father's room had been on the top floor, little more than a converted attic which he'd shared with several other men, a grim hall without a stove or a refrigerator, where the beds were hardly more than bunks, thin mattresses on wire springs.

From the room's dusty window, I could see the same brick street my father must have seen. The man who let me do it, standing in the doorway, watching me suspiciously as he puffed at a stubby black cigar, must have thought it odd that a son would wish to do such a thing, retrace, at such distance, the journey of his father. But he was willing to let me in anyway, escorting me up the stairs, and opening the long-closed door to a musty, unlighted room.

I didn't know exactly what part of the room my father had used as his small space. The beds had been removed years before, leaving only a bare floor and a scattering of loose boards. A great many names had been carved on the wooden walls and supporting beams, and for a while I looked for my father's name among them. I found J. C. Paxton and Monty Cochran and Leo Krantz and a host of other solitary males, but there was no sign of William P. Farris, or Bill Farris, or even W.P.F.

He'd lived there for nearly a year. Each night, from his small window, he'd seen the men in the street below, brooding by their open fires, tossing wooden slats into the flames while they grumbled about the state of things.

Dutifully he'd written home once a week, the letters preserved by his parents, then passed down to him, and finally, because of Mrs. Fields's second phone call, the one that made him quickly pull on his coat and hat and head for the waiting station wagon, also passed on to me.

They weren't chatty letters, and they suggested that my father hadn't felt much excitement about being in New York. They were informative, but little else. In them he mentioned the attic on Great Jones Street, but not that he shared it with a crowd of other itinerants. He talked about the weather, but only in the most general terms, days described as cold or hot, rainy or clear. The word "pleasant" recurred, as did the word "nasty," but all the more detailed descriptions were left out.

Left out too was the sense of limited horizons that must surely have overwhelmed him from time to time. He'd been a boy of only nineteen, alone in an enormous city, living in a dreary attic with nearly a dozen other people, men probably older than he, broken and displaced men, fleeing shattered homes. At night, he must have listened to their tales of bad luck and betrayal, perhaps from his own dark bunk, too young and inexperienced to join in the talk or to be treated as an equal.

Since Rebecca, I've often imagined him in such a posture, lying faceup on his grimy mattress, his pale blue eyes fixed on the ceiling, the murmur of voices curling around him while he tried to calculate his next move, a man locked in a grim and airless solitude.

But that day months before, as I stared quietly at the photograph Rebecca had placed before me, I saw only an empty-faced young man, a face without a past, almost a fictional character, one whom murder had created.

"I never heard my father talk about New York," I said. "I never heard him talk very much about Highfield, either."

Rebecca didn't press me for more. Instead, she drew the photograph away and revealed the one beneath it, a picture of my mother as she stood beside a low stone wall. She was dressed in a light-colored skirt and blouse, her hair shining in a bright summer light.

"She looks about eighteen," I said.

"Do you know anything about her youth?" Rebecca asked.

"I can't even imagine her as young," I said. "She always seemed so old to me." I thought a moment, then added, "I think she was probably a very depressed person. Clinically depressed."

"Why do you think that?"

"She never seemed to have any energy. There

was something faded in her, like she needed someone to brush the dust off her shoulders."

Rebecca nodded toward the photograph. "She seems to have a lot of energy in this picture," she said. "She looks quite vivid."

I looked at the photograph again. My mother was smiling very cheerfully at the camera. She seemed not only young, but free, lighthearted, happy. There was a flirtatiousness in the way she leaned back against the stone wall, in the girlish tilt of her head, in the "come hither" look she offered to the camera.

"Who took this picture?" I asked.

"I don't know," Rebecca answered. "They were among the pictures the police took from your house on McDonald Drive. No one ever claimed them, and so Swenson let me go through them. Most of them had dates and locations written on the back, but this one didn't." She shrugged. "I don't know why."

My mother's face appeared to beam toward me, her joy sweeping out like a wave. "I think I know why," I said quietly. "It was because she knew exactly where and when it had been taken, and knew that she'd never forget that particular moment."

Rebecca said nothing. Instead she waited for me to continue, to call up some other memory of my mother.

"I don't have anything else to say about her," I said after a while. "She never talked about her youth. She never seemed to want to talk about it."

"Why not?"

"Well, maybe she didn't want to be reminded of it," I said, though without much certainty, mere conjecture. "Maybe she didn't like to compare it to what her life became."

"Which was?"

"Drudgery," I said without hesitation, returning now to the woman of my most recent memories, the one in the red housedress, who piddled in the flower garden and lost herself in romance novels.

Rebecca nodded quickly, then slid the photograph to the side, revealing the one just under it.

It had been taken the day my father married my mother and it showed the two of them outside a small church. My mother stood beneath his arm, smiling brightly. My father seemed to be drawing her closely to his side, smiling, too.

Rebecca tapped my mother's face gently. "Did he talk about her?" she asked.

I shrugged. "Not to me."

I was still looking vacantly at the same picture when Rebecca slid another one up beside it, the one taken years later, which showed my mother on the bed, her face and body neatly scrubbed, hands folded, dead.

I realized, of course, that it was the contrast Rebecca wanted, perhaps for the initial shock of it, or perhaps for something deeper, the sense that for "these men" and their murdered families, life had been a long descent from some initial happiness to a murderous despair.

I looked at both pictures for a long time, shifting my concentration from one to the other before finally glancing up at Rebecca.

"What do you expect me to say?" I asked.

She didn't answer.

I tapped the picture of my father and mother on their wedding day. "They seem happy together, don't they?"

Rebecca nodded, then looked at me significantly. "Did you know that your mother was pregnant the day she got married?"

My eyes shot over to Rebecca. I was astonished. "She was?" I asked, unbelievingly.

"According to the records, Jamie was born on October 7, 1942, only seven months after your parents were married," Rebecca told me. "He weighed nearly nine pounds, so he couldn't have been premature."

I looked at the wedding photograph again, my eyes concentrating on my mother, the "poor Dottie" of Aunt Edna's vision, and yet a woman who, in her youth, had done at least this one daring thing. She had slept with a man who was not yet her husband, an act that had seemed beyond the reach of the woman I remembered.

"We never know them, do we?" I said. "Our parents."

"It depends on what they're willing to reveal," Rebecca answered.

I glanced at the photograph, this time settling on the tall, commanding figure of my father. He was dressed in his army uniform, the green garrison cap cocked raffishly to the right. "He must have been on leave," I said, unable to think of any other comment.

"Do you have his army records?"

"I don't know," I answered. "Are they important?"

"Well, I like to have a basic chronology of each man's life," Rebecca answered.

"I'll look for it," I told her, though unemphatically, my eyes still set firmly on my father's beaming face, on how happy he seemed. "He doesn't seem to mind the idea that he's about to be a father," I said.

"No, he probably didn't mind that at all," Rebecca said. "These men rarely do."

I could see "these men" more fully now. I could see them in their game rooms and their basements, in their trucks and station wagons, standing in their driveways and out beside their glittering blue swimming pools, men with baseball bats and rifles, who later killed their families in inconceivable acts of annihilating violence. Step by step, they were becoming less abstract to me, less headlines glimpsed in newspapers than faces emerging slowly from a pale white cloud.

I shook my head as I studied my father's smiling face on his wedding day. "I would never have guessed that my father would have ended up as one of 'these men,' as you always call them," I said.

For a moment I stared at the two pictures together, the wedding photo, and next to it my mother's motionless body, imagining the slow crawl of time that divided them, the invisible span of days and months and years that stretched from the smiling bride to the immobile corpse so neatly laid out behind the closed bedroom curtains. Suddenly, I saw my mother alive again, squatting by the little flower garden in the early evening, digging at the ground with her rusty spade as my father's brown van pulled into the driveway.

Often during those last weeks, he had not gotten out of the van immediately, but had remained inside, sitting behind the wheel, watching my mother silently while he smoked a cigarette, his light blue eyes piercing through the curling fog as they settled frozenly on my mother like the cross hairs of a telescopic sight.

"I can't imagine why he did it, Rebecca," I said.

She looked at me pointedly, but said nothing.

"But I think he knew why," I added.

I told about the time I'd gone down into the basement not long before the murders and found my father at work on the bicycle. I described his body clothed in gray flannel, his hands working steadily at the bicycle until they'd stopped abruptly, and he'd looked up at me, his eyes eerily motionless and sad, but utterly clear at the same time. I told her about standing on the third step, watching my father silently until he'd finally noticed me, lifted his eyes and held me in his gaze for a long moment before telling me cryptically that "this" was all he wanted.

Rebecca did not write any of it down in the little pad she'd placed at her right hand. She merely listened attentively until I repeated my inevitable conclusion.

"I think my father was very conscious that there was something missing in his life," I told her. I recalled his face again, the way he'd looked that night, the unreadable sadness I'd glimpsed in his eyes.

Once again my eyes swept down to the photograph, my father's face shining toward me from the picture taken on his wedding day. There was no doubt of his happiness on that day, of the delight he'd felt. He had the look of a man who believed that he'd accomplished something.

"Something missing," I repeated as I glanced back up at her again. "Which made him want to kill us all."

Rebecca's next question surprised me. "Why do you think he didn't kill you, Steve?"

"I think he intended to," I told her, "but that he got scared off by the phone calls."

"The ones Mrs. Fields made," Rebecca said. She took a pen out of her briefcase and held it over the blank page of her notebook. "So you don't think he spared you because he had some special feeling for you?" she asked. "Or maybe even because you were his youngest son."

"Well, he killed his oldest son," I said, "so why wouldn't he have killed me?" I shook my head. "No, I don't think he intentionally spared me. I think that if I'd come home on time that afternoon, he'd have killed me just like he killed the others."

She paused a moment before asking her next question. "What's your most vivid memory of your father?"

I hesitated before answering, though not in an attempt to keep her in suspense, but only because, at first, I wasn't sure. Finally, I said, "I remember how much my sister loved him."

Rebecca's eyes softened, as if this gentle answer had reached her unexpectedly.

"I don't know what she saw in my father," I added. "He always seemed so ordinary to me."

The word "ordinary" appeared to surprise her.

"I mean, he didn't have any special skills," I explained. "He wasn't a great talker, or anything like that. The only thing that ever really interested him was those bicycles of his."

Rebecca looked at me curiously. "Bicycles?"

I nodded. "He imported very expensive racing bikes from England. Special ones. Rodger and Windsor. They were always red, he sold them in that little hardware store he owned. It was like some kind of obsession. He would assemble them himself, and he was always down in the basement doing that."

"Down in the basement? Would your sister sometimes go down there?"

I'd never thought of it before, but Rebecca's question brought it all back.

"Yes, she would," I said. "I'd sometimes hear them talking together."

Even at that moment, with Rebecca sitting across from me as evening fell outside the glass windows, I could hear those voices as if they were still lifting toward me, rising like smoke through the floor. They were soft voices, almost in whispers, secretive, intimate.

"Do you have any idea what they talked about?" Rebecca asked.

"I don't think Laura ever told me."

I let my mind drift back. I could see Laura moving across the living room, her bare feet padding across the beige carpet, her long dark hair flowing down her back as she headed for the door that led down the stairs to the basement. I could hear my father's hammer tapping just below me, then the sound of Laura's feet as she walked down the stairs. It was at that point, as I remembered, that the tapping had always stopped. Stopped entirely, and never started again until Laura had come back up the stairs. The memory produced a faintly alarming realization.

"She was the only one in the family who could draw him away from that obsession he had with bicycles," I said. "I guess you could say she was the only person who had any real power over him."

"What kind of power?"

"I don't know."

"Well, there arc only a few kinds," Rebecca said, ticking them off one by one. "There's money, of course, and love. Kinship. Desire." Rebecca stared at me intently. "And duty. These men are always dutiful."

I nodded. "Yes," I said. "My father was dutiful."

As I spoke, I saw him join the ranks of these other men. Like them, he'd been dutiful down to the last second. For a moment, I envisioned him as a ghostly, scooped-out man in gray flannels, trudging wearily up the aisle of the hardware store, his arms laden with tools or boxes of nails. I wondered how often during that long walk up the same dusty aisle he'd searched for some way out of his vast responsibilities, a pathway through the bramble, before he'd settled upon murder. I imagined him making another choice, to live and let us live, going on, year after year, growing old and gray and bent as he sat behind the wheel of the brown van. I imagined my mother aging into a crippled husk, unable to bend any longer over her desolate little flower garden. I saw Jamie fattening into middle age, Laura drying into a parched doll. Had my father seen all that, too? Had he glimpsed the whole dark game, seen it play out move by move in a process so unbearable that he'd finally settled on murder as a way to break the rules?

"Very dutiful," I repeated. "Despite the way life is."

"The way life is?" Rebecca repeated, as if puzzled by the phrase.

"You know, the way people live," I said. "Going to work every day. Sticking to the same job. Coming home at the same time. Day after day, the same rooms, the same faces."

Rebecca began to write in her notebook. I watched her hand, the slender fingers wrapped delicately around the dark shaft of the pen. I'd heard the strange contempt which had risen into my voice as I'd described the mundane nature of everyday life, and as I watched Rebecca's pen skirt across the open page of her notebook, I felt that somehow I had exposed myself. It was an uneasy and unsettling feeling, and for an instant I regretted that I'd ever agreed to talk to her.

"You know, sometimes I'm not really sure I can go on with this," I said.

She looked at me squarely. "You can stop whenever you want."

But I knew that I couldn't in the least do that. I knew that I'd become enamored of a mystery, that I wanted to feel the edgy tension and exhilaration of closing in upon a dangerous and undiscovered thing.

For a moment, I let my eyes linger on her as she wrote, her head bent forward slightly, the long dark hair falling nearly to her pen. When she looked up again, I thought I saw a subtle recognition in her face, an uneasiness that made me glance away, my eyes fleeing toward the large glass window to my left and the darkening landscape beyond it. Far away, I could see night descending over the distant hills. It seemed to fall helplessly, out of control, to spin and tumble as it fell.

SEVEN

Night had fully fallen by the time I got home. Marie and Peter were in the kitchen, both of them working at the evening's dinner, Marie chopping onions, Peter shaping hamburger patties.

She stopped as I came through the door and looked at me closely. "You look tired," she said.

"There's a lot of work at the office," I told her.

"Are you going to be staying late often?"

"Maybe."

She nodded, then returned to the cutting board. "I finished the bid this afternoon."

"Bid?"

She glanced at me, puzzled. "The Bridgeport bid," she said, "the one I've been working on so long."

"Oh, right," I said. "You think you'll get the contract?"

She shrugged. "Maybe. You never know."

I began to set the table, one of the "family time" jobs that had fallen to me. Peter continued slapping at the raw meat, making a game of it.

"Do it right," I told him, a little sharply.

Marie looked at me, surprised by the edginess in my voice. "Are you okay, Steve?"

I nodded. "Yeah, why?"

She didn't answer. Instead, she returned to her work. "I thought it might be nice to visit my parents tomorrow," she said after a moment. "We haven't seen them in several weeks."

I nodded. "It's fine with me."

"So you don't have to go in to work tomorrow?"

"No."

Marie smiled. "Good," she said, "we'll have a nice day in the country, then."

Peter finished making the hamburger patties and handed them to Marie.

"Good job, Peter," she said lightly, as she took them from him.

We ate dinner shortly after that, then Peter went to the den to watch television while Marie and I cleaned up the kitchen.

"What exactly are you working on now?" she asked.

"A library for a little town in Massachusetts," I answered.

She looked surprised. "And that's what kept you at the office tonight?"

"Yeah," I said. "Mr. Lowe has a personal interest in the project. It's for his hometown, and so I want it to be right before he sees it."

The real reason for my being late in coming home swam into my mind, and I saw Rebecca's face staring at me questioningly. I remembered the request she'd made for more information about my father's life, the chronology she was trying to construct, her interest in his army records.

"Do you remember when Aunt Edna died, and we went to her house, and found that box of papers that had belonged to my father?"

Marie nodded.

"You took it out of the car when we got back," I reminded her. "Do you remember what you did with it?"

"It's in the basement," Marie answered. "I wrote 'Somerset' on the side of it. I think it's on the top shelf." She looked at me curiously. "Why?"

"I thought I might look through it," I answered. "I never have."

Marie smiled half-mockingly. "You're not gearing up for a midlife crisis, are you, Steve?" she asked. "You know, trying to get in touch with yourself, going back over things?" The smile broadened. "Reliving your 'significant life experiences,' that sort of thing?"

I shook my head. "No, I don't think so. I'm just curious about what's in the box."

My answer appeared to satisfy her. She turned to another subject, something about Peter wanting to try out for the school basketball team, and not long after that she joined him in the den. I could hear them laughing together at whatever it was they were watching.

I walked down the corridor to the stairs that led to the basement. The box was exactly where Marie had said it would be, on the top shelf, the word SOMERSET marked in large, block letters. I dragged it down and carried it back upstairs to my own small office.

I put the box on my desk and opened it. Inside, I could see a disordered mound of papers. They were all that remained of my father, a scattering of letters, documents, a few photographs. I doubted that there could be anything among them that Rebecca would find useful.

I started to reach for the first of the papers when I glanced up and saw Marie at my office door.

She was looking at the box. "Well, you sure didn't waste any time finding it," she said.

"It was where you said it would be."

She smiled. "Peter wants you to come into the den."

"Why?"

"So we can all watch his favorite show together."

I didn't move.

"You got home very late tonight," Marie added. "I think he sort of missed you." She stretched her hand toward me. "Come on," she said softly.

I rose slowly, reluctantly, and went with her. We walked down the corridor together. In the family room, I watched television with my wife and son, talking occasionally, laughing when they laughed, but only out of duty. The force that had once compelled me to such small acts of devotion was already losing speed.

We left the house at around ten the next morning. The drive north toward the Massachusetts border was along winding, country roads. Peter sat in the back, working with a portable video game, while Marie leaned against the door on the passenger side, the window open, the rush of air continually blowing through the red highlights in her hair.

Was she beautiful?

Marie would insist that I say no. She would insist that I admit that it was beauty which formed the grim core of what happened in the end, her own beauty either faded or familiar, Rebecca's either new or in full bloom. She would insist that it was desire which drove me forward, desire alone, since, as she would say to me that final night, "It was never love . . ."

We arrived at her parents' small country house only an hour or so after leaving Old Salsbury. It was a medium-sized, wooden house, painted white, with a large, wraparound porch. In his retirement, Carl had taken up furniture making, and in typical style, had overdone the labor, making far more plain wooden rocking chairs than were strictly needed. As I pulled into the unpaved driveway, I could see several of them on the front porch or scattered randomly about the lawn, rocking eerily when a strong burst of wind swept down from the mountains.

For all the abundance of empty chairs, Carl was sitting on the front steps of the house when we pulled up. Marie had called her mother earlier that morning and let Amelia know that we were coming, but from the pleasantly surprised look on Carl's face, I realized that she'd never gotten around to telling him to expect us.

He rose slowly, pulling himself up by one of the wooden banisters which bordered the stairs, then waved broadly as we all got out of the car. He was a tall man, with narrow shoulders and long, thin legs. He wore a pair of light brown flannel work pants and a short-sleeved checkered shirt. From a distance he appeared to have a thick head of snowy white hair, but up close, his pink scalp easily showed through it. I'd first met him only a month or so after meeting Marie, the two of us driving up from New York City. He'd tried his best to be lighthearted that evening, but even then, he'd had the aging factory worker's sense of the bulkiness of things, their ironclad inflexibility.

Marie made it to him first, pressing herself into his arms, then kissing him lightly on the cheek.

"Hi, Dad," she said.

He held her tightly for a moment, as old people sometimes do, never knowing which embrace will be the last. Then he turned to me and shook my hand with his firm, industrial grip.

"How you doing, Steve?" he asked.

"Fine."

It was Peter's turn then, and Carl all but yanked him from the ground.

"You got a girlfriend yet?" he demanded.

Peter had not had time to answer before Amelia's voice came booming toward us from above.

"Don't ask personal questions, Carl," she snapped, but in a friendly, joking tone. She shook her head with comic exasperation. "What am I going to do with him?"

She was a tall, slender woman, with thin arms and a somewhat hawkish face. She seemed to hop down the stairs toward us, nervous and bird-like. Once at the bottom of them, she swept Peter into her arms, then Marie. Finally she turned to me, gave me a quick, no-nonsense hug, then firmly pushed me away.

In her youth, Amelia had been a great beauty, locally renowned, and I assumed that the glancing, cautious way she had always embraced and separated from me was a holdover from those bygone days when her slightest touch had given too strong a signal to the breathless men who'd flocked around her. According to Carl, these same men, old now, with shaking heads, still spoke of her in the social club downtown. "They still can't get over that I had her every night," he'd once told me with a wry, self-satisfied grin, then added significantly, "And she was just eighteen years old, Steve. Can you imagine that?"

Now she was seventy-one, still tall and dignified, like her daughter, but with withered skin, iron-gray hair, and hasty, nervous eyes that glanced about restlessly, as if trying to get a glimpse of where it had all gone.

We followed her into the house, all of us climbing up the stairs toward the open front door. Carl brought up the rear, pulling himself up by means of the old wooden rail.

Marie and her mother disappeared into the back of the house while Carl and I sat down in the front room. I looked at him silently, smiling amiably, as I watched him ease himself down into the overstuffed chair by the piano. A mild heart attack had shaken him three years before, and only last summer he'd fallen in the garden behind the house, and, unable to get up, had wallowed in the tomato plants for nearly ten minutes before Amelia had finally spotted him and come running to his side.

Now, as I watched him, he seemed to age almost by the minute, his hair whitening, his skin wrinkling, his long legs drawing up under the cuffs of his trousers.

For a moment he remained silent, then he nodded idly toward the piano.

"You don't play, do you, Steve?" he asked, a question he had asked me several times before, always forgetting my answer.

"No," I said.

"Amy used to play," Carl said. He drew in a

deep breath and let it out in a quick, exhausted rush, as if the burden of holding in his breath were becoming too much for him. "She played for the Knights of Columbus," he went on. "At a dance one night when Jimmy Doyle didn't show up." He winked boyishly. "She wasn't that good, but she gave it a good try."

I smiled.

"All you can ask, right?" Carl added. "To give it a good try."

"I suppose so."

"It's the same for life," Carl said. "You can't do more than give it a good try."

I nodded softly, letting my eyes drift away, hoping that with that gesture I could avoid giving Carl any further encouragement toward sharing his philosophy. In the past few years, as old age had overtaken him, he'd become increasingly homespun and folksy, dotting his conversation with empty truisms that annoyed Marie, but which Amelia seemed hardly to notice.

"I wouldn't say Amy was at a professional level," Carl went on. "But she was pretty good." He pulled a red handkerchief from the back pocket of his trousers and began to wipe his face, his eyes drifting over the room.

It was a room that Amelia dominated entirely, pictures of her lined up on top of the piano or hanging from the walls, all of them taken much earlier, in the days of her youthful glory. She'd been her father's favorite, and probably her mother's, too, and she'd grown up beneath the gaze of a thousand desperately admiring eyes. From that spawning pool of frantically beseeching men, she'd selected a factory worker named Carl. It had been a choice which had baffled, disturbed, and finally embittered her parents. In the end, they'd entirely rejected Carl, an experience he'd never forgotten. "My wife's parents froze me out," he told me that first weekend when Marie brought me to his home. "My wife was so pretty, you see. They thought that was her ticket to a brighter future, you know? Then, poor thing, she got tied up with me."

It was precisely that brighter future that seemed to shine from the photographs which cluttered and overwhelmed the room, all of them taken during Amelia's glory days, first as a little girl in her father's arms, later as an adolescent growing toward a stunning womanhood, and finally as a young woman posing by the lake on that single, breathless day her beauty reached its frail, already fading peak.

I drew my eyes away from that last picture and toward the woman herself as Amelia suddenly came back into the room. She was carrying a large picnic basket, and Marie and Peter were standing just behind her, both of them holding a few lightweight folding chairs.

"We thought we'd go on a picnic," Amelia said. Her eyes swept over to Carl. "What do you think, hon? Just a short walk over to the spring?"

Carl nodded. "Yeah. I'm up for that," he said, already pulling himself to his feet.

I looked at Marie. She was smiling at Carl with great cheerfulness and affection, which were still on her face when she turned to me.

"Okay with you, Steve?" she asked.

"Sure."

The spring was small, and it flowed in gentle curves through a glade of trees. It was no more than a short walk from the house, but Carl's pace was slow and halting, so it was almost twenty minutes later when we reached the shady embankment Amelia had already designated for the picnic.

By that time it was early afternoon, the sun still high and very bright in a cloudless blue. Amelia and Marie spread a large checkered cloth over the grass and began to take the various sandwich meats and breads out of the basket. Peter opened the folding chairs and after a while we were all seated comfortably by the water.

"It's pretty here, don't you think?" Amelia asked, though to no one in particular.

Marie nodded, her eyes on me. "Dad and I used to fish in this little stream."

Carl chuckled. "You never caught anything though, did you, Marie?"

Marie shook her head. "How could I? All I had was that little plastic pole, remember? The one you bought at the dime store downtown?"

"He bought you that for Christmas one year," Amelia added, "and you had to wait several months for the ice to break before you could use it." She glanced at Carl. "I told you it would drive her crazy giving her a thing like that in the winter, a thing she couldn't play with right away."

Carl laughed again as he glanced toward Marie. "It did just about drive you crazy, too," he said. "We went fishing the first day the ice broke up." He shivered. "It was cold as hell."

In my mind, I could see them by the little spring, the winter thaw barely a few days old, a snowy border on both sides of the stream, the trees bare and creaking in the frozen breeze as they dipped their hooks into the icy, fishless water.

"You really kept at it, though," Carl said to Marie admiringly. "We must have stayed out here a couple hours. You just wouldn't go back in." He looked at Amelia. "How old was she that year, Amy?"

"Six," Amelia answered, almost wistfully. "She was six years old."

I looked over at Peter, remembered him at six years old, a little boy with reddish cheeks and gleaming eyes. It was the year I'd taken him to the state fair in Danbury, taken pictures of him as he was led about on a small, spotted pony, fed him hot dogs and cotton candy until he'd finally puked behind a huge green circus tent.

I laughed suddenly at the thought of it.

Marie looked at me, a smile playing on her lips. "What are you laughing about, Steve?"

"I was just remembering the first time we took Peter to the Danbury Fair."

I could see the whole day playing through Marie's memory, sweet, almost delectable, even down to the last unsavory moment. "He threw up," she said, "behind this big tent."

Peter grimaced. "I did?"

Carl waved his hand. "Everybody throws up," he said. He leaned back in his chair and lifted his face upward slightly, as if trying to get some sun.

"Careful there, hon," Amelia warned. "Don't tip back too far."

Carl waved his hand as he leaned back a bit farther. "A man's got to take a risk, right, Steve?" he said as he pressed himself back farther, Amelia watching him steadily, growing tense until he bolted forward suddenly and caught her eyes in his.

"Scared you, didn't I?" he joked.

Amelia's face relaxed. "He's always trying to get at me," she said, her eyes now on me. She began a story about some other occasion when Carl had "gotten her," as she put it, then followed with another.

While she spoke, I felt my mind drift away, drift along the shaded stream, as if skating lightly across the glassy surface of the water. I could hear Amelia's voice, as well as the laughter of the others as she continued with her tale. I heard names and places, dates, weather reports, ages. I could even feel the overall warmth of the moment we were all sharing, its calmness, pleasure, and serenity.

And yet, I could also feel myself moving away from it, down the softly winding stream, its twin banks gliding smoothly along either side, as if I were being carried on a small canoe. Overhead, I could see the flow of the trees as they passed above me, flowing like another stream, this one suspended surreally above my head. Slowly, almost without my realizing it, the stream became a sleek blue road, winding through a maze of suburban streets, neat lines of houses flowing past on both sides, until, in the distance, I could see the mock Tudor house at 417 McDonald Drive. It was silent, and not at all threatening, and as I continued to drift toward it in my mind, I could feel a grave attraction for it, an excitement at drawing near it, as if it were a place of assignation.

A burst of laughter brought me back, loud and wrenching as a sudden gunshot. I blinked quickly and stared around me. Everyone was laughing—Marie, Peter, Carl. Everyone but Amelia, who, as I noticed, was staring directly toward me with steady, evaluating eyes.

"Where were you, Steve?" she asked.

I shrugged. "I don't know."

She didn't seem to believe me. Her eyes remained very still, her face framed by the swirling circular maelstrom of her old straw hat. "Just in some other world, I guess," she said, in a strangely cool and brooding voice.

I nodded, but added nothing else.

Amelia returned her attention to the others. Carl was telling some story about Marie as a little girl, and a few feet away Peter was listening very attentively, as if surprised by the fact that his mother had ever been a child.

I listened attentively too, though from time to time my eye would return to the spring, follow a leaf as it flowed through the dappled shade until it disappeared around the nearest bend.

Toward the end of the afternoon, we repacked the picnic basket, gathered up the folding chairs, and returned to the house. Carl and Amelia walked in the lead, arm in arm, chatting quietly on the way. I could not make out any of what they were saying to each other, but from the quiet glances they exchanged it seemed one of those intimate, deeply familiar conversations one sometimes sees in older people, the sense of completedness, of everything having passed the trial stage.

Marie walked along beside me, her arm in mine, her head pressed lightly against my shoulder. She seemed contented, happy with how the day had gone, with the choices she'd made in her life so far, with me as her husband, with Peter as her son. It was the kind of satisfaction that seemed complete in itself, rather than the product of a thinly disguised resignation.

As we neared the house, Peter shot ahead, running through the tall grass, his blond hair glistening in the sunlight. I felt Marie press her head more firmly against my shoulder.

I glanced down at her.

She was staring up at me affectionately, as if marveling at her own contentment. Then she lifted her face toward me and kissed me on the mouth. Bathed in such sweetness and familiarity, the product of such a long and enduring love, it should have been the single most thrilling kiss I had ever known.

Toward evening, Carl made a fire in the old hearth, and we all sat around it, talking quietly. Marie sat beside me on the sofa, her feet balled up beneath her, her shoulder pressed up snugly against mine. Peter slept next to her, his head resting delicately in her lap.

"Everything going okay at work, Steve?" Carl asked idly, by then puffing on the white meerschaum pipe Marie had given him the preceding Christmas.

"Yeah," I said.

"He'll probably be made a partner soon," Marie said.

Carl looked at her. "How about your business?"

"It's fine," Marie told him. "I put in a bid for a job in Bridgeport last week."

I glanced over toward Amelia. She was rocking softly in one of the chairs Carl had made, but her eyes seemed not to move at all as she stared at me.

"So I guess everything's okay, then?" she asked.

I nodded. "Yes, it is."

I expected her to smile, or give some sign of satisfaction, but she didn't. She turned toward the fire instead, and held her eyes there, the light playing on her face in the way of old romantic movies.

We left an hour later, Peter piling groggily into the back seat while Marie and I said good-bye. Carl hugged each of us in turn, then stepped back to allow Amelia to do the same.

"Nice seeing you again," she said easily, then glanced over at me. "Be good, Steve," she told me in a voice that seemed stern and full of warning.

Marie sat close to me on the drive home, breathing softly as we drove through the dark countryside. Once back in Old Salsbury, we led Peter to his room, and watched, amused and smiling, as he collapsed onto his bed.

Later, in bed ourselves, Marie inched toward me, stroking me slowly. We made love sweetly and well, with that correctness of pace and expertise that only custom can attain. After that, Marie moved quietly into a restful sleep.

Toward dawn I felt her awaken slightly. She lifted her head in the early light, smiled, kissed my chest, then lowered her head down on it again and closed her eyes. While I waited for the morning, I stroked her hair.

So it was never love, as she would say to me that last night, it was never love . . . that was missing.

Marie was still sleeping in the morning when I got up and headed downstairs to my office. It was smaller than Marie's, since I'd always done most of my work at Simpson and Lowe, while Marie did most of hers at home. It contained little more than a drafting table, a large light, and a few metal filing cabinets.

I sat down at the table, pulled out the latest plans for my dream house, and began to go over the details again, searching for places where I could remove yet another enclosed area from what was already an impossibly airy and unreal space. But as I worked, I found myself increasingly unable to concentrate on the plans before me. It was as if the dream house had become, at last, pure dream, nothing more than idle whimsy, an idea for which I no longer felt any genuine conviction. It was Rebecca and her search that seemed real to me now, and I even allowed myself to hope that from time to time Rebecca might sense my presence beside her, silent, determined, armed as she was armed, with the same grisly instruments of night, the two of us equally committed to tracking down "these men," poking at the ashes they had left behind, closing in on their distant hiding places.

I remembered the photograph she'd shown me on Friday afternoon. I saw my father standing in the open, his army cap cocked to the side. The smile on his face had seemed absolutely genuine. It had given his face an immense happiness, a joy and sense of triumph that I'd never seen before. Not in life. Not in any other photograph. That day, April 1, 1942, I realized with complete certainty, had been his finest moment.

Rebecca had already noted that my mother had to have been pregnant with Jamie by then, but it wasn't the fact of my brother's technical illegitimacy which struck me suddenly. It was something else, a curious memory of something that had happened when I was eight years old, a year or more before the murders, but which I could now recall very clearly.

It was a spring day, and my father had been doing some kind of repair work in the basement. He'd asked Laura to bring him something from the garage. Laura had gone to find it, but after several minutes, she still hadn't come back into the house, and so my father had turned to me.

"Go get Laura," he told me.

I went up the stairs, out the kitchen door, and into the garage, expecting to find Laura still searching through the usual disarray to find whatever it was my father wanted. But she was sitting in a far corner instead, her body in a dusky, yellow light. A pile of blue papers was scattered at her feet, all of them spilling out of a small shoe box that had obviously fallen from the shelf overhead. She had one of the light blue pieces of paper in her hand, but she was no longer reading it. She was simply sitting motionlessly, deep in thought, her eyes lifted toward the dark, wooden ceiling.

I called to her, but very softly. "Laura?"

She looked at me directly, her body still motionless, except for the way her fingers slowly curled around the blue paper, as if to conceal it.

"What do you want, Stevie?" she asked stiffly.

"Dad wants you," I told her.

She drew her hands behind her, the blue note disappearing behind her back. "Tell him I'll be there in a minute," she said. "I have to clean up this mess."

I did as she told me, and for a while my father seemed satisfied that Laura was on her way. But later, with his typical impatience, he finally headed up the stairs and out to the garage. I followed behind him, a dog at his heels.

Laura was still in the same corner as we entered the garage, the same blue paper in her hand. She tried to hide it again, which surprised me, since I'd never before seen her try to conceal anything from my father.

His eyes fixed on the paper. "What is that?" he asked.

Laura didn't answer.

My father walked through the dusky light and drew the paper from Laura's fingers.

From my place at the front of the garage, I watched as he read it. When he'd finished, he turned to me.

"Go play, Stevie," he said.

I was in the backyard a few minutes later when the two of them came out of the garage. Laura was nestled beneath my father's arm, and they were walking slowly toward the house.

My mother came home a short time later. She'd been grocery shopping, I remember, and as she headed up the stairs, her arms around an enormous brown bag, my father stepped out of the house, took the bag from her, and returned it to the car. Then he motioned for her to follow him and the two of them walked past me and over to the very edge of the yard. I was too far away from them to make out any of what they said, but I remember having the distinct feeling that they were talking about the blue papers Laura had found in the garage.

After a while they walked back toward the house. They were still talking, and as they passed, I heard my mother say, "You told her not to . . ." She didn't finish, because Jamie suddenly came rushing around the corner of the house. At the sight of him, both my father and my mother froze, each of them staring at him with such frightened, startled looks that I had sensed even then that the blue papers, and everything that had happened since I'd seen Laura reading them, had had something to do with Jamie.

During the next few days, however, the entire incident slipped from my mind. Everything returned to its normal pattern, except that my mother seemed even more subdued. There were times, forever after that, when she seemed to flee from any notion of command. Steadily over the next few years, she became more vaporous, slowly giving up the prerogatives of wife and mother so that in the end she seemed more like some distant relative we'd saved from poverty or shame, one who lived with us but had no standing among us, no office or authority, incontestably by then the "poor Dottie" of my aunt's unforgiving judgment.

But for the rest of us, nothing seemed to change, and as I sat at my desk that morning, remembering the blue papers, it struck me that I wouldn't have remembered it at all if something else hadn't happened, something which I always believed was connected in some way to what had been written in them.

It was about three months later. My father had recently put a redwood picnic table under the large maple tree that stood beside the rear fence, and Laura and I had begun meeting there to play Monopoly or checkers or some other game. That particular day, Laura had begun to teach me chess. Slowly, with infinite patience, she introduced me to each piece. I had only played checkers before, and it was not easy for me to get a grip on this much more complicated game.

We'd been at it for nearly an hour before Jamie strode across the backyard and sat himself down on the bench beside me.

Laura hardly registered his presence. Instead, she continued to concentrate on teaching me the game. Jamie watched sullenly while she did it, as if evaluating each word my sister spoke, each gesture she made, second-guessing and inwardly ridiculing her, at times even smiling snidely when she got something slightly wrong or out of order and had to correct herself.

As the minutes passed, I could feel the air heating up and turning sour around us. It was as if the peaceful little island that Laura and I created when we were together had been invaded by a poisonous wind.

Finally, the storm broke.

"You're doing it all wrong, Laura," Jamie snapped. "It's stupid the way you're teaching him."

Laura didn't so much as look at him. She picked up the knight, and began to explain its move.

"You're going to screw it up, as usual," Jamie barked.

Laura's eyes shot over to him. "You're not supposed to talk like that in front of Stevie."

"I'm trying to keep him from being a loser, Laura," Jamie fired back. "The way you're teaching him this game, he'll play it like a sissy."

Laura's eyes narrowed lethally. "Nobody asked you, anyway, Jamie," she hissed angrily. "Nobody asked you to come over here and bother us."

Jamie leaned toward her threateningly. "I don't have to be asked," he said. "It's my yard, too, you know."

For a flaming instant, Laura glared at him with a terrible ferocity. Then she turned her attention back to the game, but not before muttering a single, indecipherable phrase. "Sort of," she said.

It had been said under her breath, but loud enough for us to hear it.

"What did you say?" Jamie demanded.

Laura didn't answer. She picked up one of the knights and pressed it toward me. I could see that it was trembling in her hand.

"What did you say, Laura?" Jamie repeated, only this time in a tone that was more than teenage anger. Cold. Severe. A prelude to explosive rage.

Laura locked her eyes on mine. "This is the knight," she said evenly, "it moves like this." She lowered the knight to the board and demonstrated the move.

Jamie continued to stare at her with a terrible, quivering hatred. I remember bracing myself, my own mind racing to decide what I would do if he lunged forward and hit her.

But he did no such thing. After a few more impossibly tense seconds, he simply rose silently and left us, a lean, disjointed figure striding awkwardly across the green summer lawn.

Laura had resumed teaching me about the knight by the time Jamie had finally disappeared into the house. She went directly to its moves, to various ways of using it. She didn't try to explain what she'd meant with that angry, nearly whispered "Sort of," and I never heard her say anything so cryptic to Jamie after that.

So what had my sister meant that day beneath the maple tree?

For well over thirty years, it was a question I'd never asked. Then, that Sunday morning, as Peter and Marie slept upstairs and I sat at my desk, with both Rebecca and her mission steadily gaining force in my own mind, I tried to find out. I went to the box I'd brought up from the basement the day before, hoping that the answer might be there.

Within a matter of only a few minutes, I discovered that it was.

EIGHT

Three days later, Rebecca had hardly taken her seat across from me at the restaurant before I handed her the document I'd found in the box. She took it from my hand and began to read it. What I gave her that evening was something she'd already asked for, my father's army records. After the war, he'd taken a few college classes under the GI Bill of Rights. A short application process had been required, and he'd submitted several forms to prove that he'd been in the army. One of them was a listing of his whereabouts during all that time. It began with Newark, New Jersey, where he'd been inducted in June of 1940, and ended with New York City, where he'd been mustered out on a medical discharge, an injured knee, in May of 1942. All the places my father had lived during those two years of military service were listed in the document, along with all of his official leaves. What it showed unmistakably was that he had lived at Fort Bragg, North Carolina, from July of 1941 until April of 1942, when he'd been given leave to return to New Jersey, and where, on April 1, he'd married my mother in a civil ceremony in Somerset.

When Rebecca finished reading, she looked up, her face very still. She had instantly put it together.

"Jamie was not your father's son," she said.

"No, he couldn't have been. My father was in North Carolina when my brother was conceived."

"And so he must have known that he wasn't the father of the child your mother was carrying. Even on the day he married her," Rebecca added wonderingly.

"Yes, he had to have known that."

She thought a moment, then asked, "So who was Jamie's father?"

"I don't know," I answered. "How could I know? It all happened a long time before I was born." Then something occurred to me. "Do you have the pictures you showed me last time?"

"Yes." Rebecca took them out and spread them across the table.

I lifted the one that showed my mother posed alluringly against the stone wall and handed it to Rebecca. "I think maybe the man who took this was Jamie's father," I said. "I mean, look at my mother, at the way her face is shining."

Rebecca let her eyes dwell on the picture as I continued.

"I think my mother was in love that day," I said. "She was satisfied in every way. I don't think my father ever made her feel like that."

Rebecca returned the photograph to the table. She remained silent.

"Reading all those romance novels, that was the way my mother went back to that time in her life," I told her. "She never forgot him. She never forgot the way he made her feel." I glanced over at the picture of my father. "Maybe that's what my father couldn't bear, that he was going to live the rest of his life in the shadow of my mother's first love."

"Which might explain your mother's murder, and perhaps even Jamie's," Rebecca said. "But what about Laura?"

I had no answer, and after a moment, Rebecca's eyes returned to the picture of my father on his wedding day. "Even though he must have known about the child, he looks very happy in this picture," she said.

"He was happy, I think," I admitted. "It's the only picture he ever looked that happy in."

She thought a while longer, then returned her attention to the military document that had revealed everything. "Where did you find this?"

"In some papers my aunt left me," I said, "but there was something else I couldn't find."

I told her about the blue papers, the ones Laura had found in the garage that day, the ones, I felt sure now, that had told her everything about Jamie, that he was only "sort of" a member of our family.

"So Laura knew," I said when I'd finished, "and she used that knowledge against Jamie at least once."

I went through the story of the argument beneath the maple tree.

"Do you think Jamie knew what Laura meant?" Rebecca asked.

"I don't know."

Rebecca considered everything I'd told her for a few seconds. "What were the blue papers?" she asked finally. "They weren't documents, were they?"

"No . . . I think they could have been love letters," I answered slowly, "from Jamie's real father. Letters she couldn't part with."

"Even at the risk of their being found."

"Yes."

And so all my old surmises about my mother had been wrong. "Poor Dottie" had swooned to someone's touch, had caught her breath, taken a stunning risk, and in doing that had lived for just a moment the life she only read about from then on, in novels piled beside her bed.

Rebecca leaned back in her seat and remained very quiet for a long time. She was still thinking about my mother, I believe, but my mind had shifted over to my father, to the smiling figure in the photograph, triumphant on his wedding day.

"He must have loved my mother a great deal to marry her knowing that she was already carrying another man's child," I said.

Rebecca didn't look so sure.

I remembered the look on my father's face the night I'd gone down into the basement, stopped on the third step, and watched him work silently on his latest Rodger and Windsor until his eyes had finally lifted toward me. I heard his words again: *This is all I want.*

"Or maybe all he ever wanted was just a wife and kids," I said.

Rebecca looked at me. "Except that he killed his wife, and two of his children," she said sharply, "slaughtered them one by one, in cold blood."

It was at that moment that the full ruin of my family struck me in all its horror. In a weird, nightmarish vision, I felt myself pass effortlessly through the walls of 417 McDonald Drive as if they were nothing more than stage scrims, solid at one moment, dreamily transparent at the next, so that I could see through the whole house at a single glance, see one day's death unroll before me in far more grisly and exact detail than I had ever been able to imagine it before.

My father's old brown van glides into the rain-swept driveway, its slick black tires throwing arcs of water into the air behind them. From its gloomy interior, my father's face stares at me from behind the van's black, serrated wheel, his eyes glowing from its gray interior like unblinking small blue lights. He does not linger inside the van, but emerges quickly and determinedly, then walks at a measured, unhurried pace toward the side door of the house. Once inside, he slaps his old gray hat softly against the side of his leg, sending a shower of shimmering droplets across the gleaming, checked tile of the kitchen floor. For a single, suspended moment, he stares about the room, taking in its empty, lifeless space, his face a rigid, wooden mask, with nothing moving in it but his eyes. They settle finally on the basement door.

He walks down the stairs to the tall metal cabinet he has always used to store his tools. He opens it in a single smooth, untroubled movement, all indecision long behind him, and withdraws a long object which years ago he had stored away, wrapping it in brown paper and binding it haphazardly with a length of frazzled twine. At the small workbench he had once used to assemble his Rodger and Windsor bicycles, he unwraps the shotgun and lays it out across the wooden worktable. For a few seconds he strokes its wooden stock deliciously, as if it were a woman's smooth, brown thigh.

Upstairs, each in their separate rooms, those who are about to die continue through the iron motions of their quickly dwindling lives.

Alone in his room, Jamie hunches over his desk, working mightily to keep his attention on the biology textbook the police photographs would later show still open on his desk.

A few feet down the corridor, Laura emerges from the bathroom, her body wrapped up in her long white robe. She enters her own room, walks to the small dressing table by the window, and begins to run a brush through her long dark hair.

Across the hallway, my mother rises from her bed. She stares about wearily, still in the fog of her late afternoon nap. She plucks one of her romance novels from the table by the bed and heads softly down the corridor to the stairs, moving down them slowly just as my father, still in the basement several feet below, presses two red, cylindrical 12-gauge shells into the twin chambers of the shotgun.

Upstairs, Jamie grimaces, shakes his head, closes the text, thinks better of it, and wearily opens it again.

Laura makes a final sweep through her hair, then opens the center drawer of her dressing table. She withdraws a tube of lipstick, pulls off its shiny cap, and leans in closer to the mirror as she brings its dark red tip to her mouth.

Below them, in the basement's faded light, my father turns and begins his ascent up the plain wooden stairs that lead to the kitchen.

Now on the first floor, clutching at the collar of her red housedress, my mother turns to the right and advances into the living room just as my father reaches the top of the basement stairs. She is in the solarium, easing herself down into one of its white wicker chairs by the time he steps out into the kitchen, the long black barrel of the shotgun weaving as he glances, very briefly, out the window toward the rain.

For a single, breathless instant, I see all motion stop, as if at that final, precipitous moment, my family had been given one more chance. I feel like screaming at them from my great distance: "Stop, please stop! We can find some other way!"

They do not hear me.

They begin to move again.

My father mounts the stairs toward the second floor, his eyes staring toward the upper reaches of the house until he passes the threshold and confronts a dimly lighted hallway and three closed doors.

Behind the first door to the right, Jamie fidgets at his desk. He leans back, peers out the window, finds no relief, and slowly returns to the open book.

Behind the second, Laura remains at her dressing table. She reaches into the dresser again and takes out a light green plastic compact. She looks at it, clearly displeased by its babyish appearance. She opens it anyway, takes the small beige pad from inside, and begins to rub it softly across her cheek.

Downstairs, my mother remains slumped in one of the little solarium's white wicker chairs. She lets her eyes drift up from the book for a moment, then stares out at the rain as she absently fingers a small green leaf on a hanging fern.

I see my father as he begins to move down the upstairs hallway, his eyes on the first door to his right. He shifts the shotgun into position as he nears Jamie's door.

Inside the room, Jamie turns as that same door opens seconds later. He stands up as my father enters, moving his desk chair against the back wall as he steps away.

Below, in the solarium, my mother's body bolts forward with the roar of the first blast. Her lips part as she draws in a startled, unbelieving breath. The book slips from her lap and flutters to the floor.

Above her, Jamie's body wheels to the left. His face disintegrates as his body lifts from the floor with such force that one of his tennis shoes flies off and slams against the side of my lower bunk, leaving a small, rubbery mark against its light, pine finish.

In the adjoining room, Laura freezes for an instant, as if locked in place by the horrific tumult she can hear next door. She stands up, stares about wonderingly, and lets the light green plastic compact drop from her fingers, its small round mirror cracking softly as it hits the floor.

Below her, my mother rises, stricken, from her chair. Her shoulder brushes against the curtain of long green vines. Her right hand rises, trembling, to her throat.

Upstairs, my father is on the move again. He strides toward the second door, a cloud of smoke trailing behind him as he closes in upon it.

Another blast shakes the house, and my sister's body plummets backward, the palm and two fingers of her right hand flying away as her chest explodes in a fine pink spray.

Through the translucent walls of the house on McDonald Drive, I see all that had been denied, diminished, or somehow brushed aside accumulate in the grim mortification of my mother's face.

Above her, my father breaks open the breech of the shotgun and draws out its two spent shells. In slow motion, I see their slender red cylinders slip from his long fingers and tumble through the thick, powdery air.

The reins which had held my mother in place for so long snap as if cut away by a flying dagger, and she bolts from the solarium and rushes toward the kitchen. Once there, she spins around wildly, unable to focus, too driven by terror to initiate a logical scheme to save her life.

Above her, my father moves from room to room, looking for her in their bedroom, their bathroom, everywhere. Time is passing while he hunts for her, the several minutes that Mrs. Hamilton noticed between the second shot and the last.

Time is passing, while my mother spins like a human top in the kitchen, spins and spins, until her eyes catch on the basement door. She darts toward it frantically, instinctively, an animal's flight to the underground safety of its earthen burrow.

My father is already coming down the stairs before she opens it. He is already in the solarium by the time she reaches the basement's cement floor. She is spinning again by the time he closes in upon the kitchen. She has already padded through the basement's puddled water and taken her place behind the cardboard box by the time he descends toward her from the dark at the top of the stairs. He stops on the third step from the bottom.

There is a third horrendous blast.

Queen for a Day comes to an end.

The vision ended abruptly, and I felt as if I'd been hurled against a bare wall. Reflexively, I jerked backward, my breath coming in quick, wrenching gasps. I could feel long lines of sweat move down my chest and back. A wave of tingling sharpness swept across my body.

In a kind of blur, I saw Rebecca lean toward me, her hand reaching across the table.

"Steve? Is something wrong?"

I shook my head, but fiercely, in a kind of manic up-and-down motion.

Rebecca stood up immediately. "Let's go outside," she said, then tugged me to my feet and led me out into the night.

For a moment, I leaned against a wall, still breathing heavily, unable to talk.

"Do you want to stop?" Rebecca asked. "You don't have to go on with this."

I shook my head.

"Are you sure?"

I nodded.

"Then let's go to my place," Rebecca said. "It's more private. We can just talk, if you want. About something else."

She walked me to my car, then pointed to hers. "Just follow me," she said.

I fell behind her, keeping a close distance, first through the town, then out toward the lake, the yellow beams of my headlights rising and falling as we moved along the wavy, unpaved road. I felt self-conscious and embarrassed, as if I'd cracked under too little pressure. There were moments when I wanted to turn around, to disappear into the darkness. But at the same time I was driven to continue, to follow Rebecca all the way, as if my father were in the car beside her, riding along, his blue eyes staring out into the nightbound trees.

I'd calmed myself down considerably by the time I reached Rebecca's cottage. It rested deep in a grove of trees, the lake only a matter of yards away, so that as I got out of my car, I could hear its waves lapping softly against the shore, which calmed me even more.

Rebecca didn't wait for me to join her, but walked quickly to her door. As I approached, moving across the moist grass, I could hear the keys tinkling softly as she drew them from the pocket of her skirt. She faced the door, her back to me, the long dark hair falling to her shoulders as she searched for the right key.

She found it quickly, opened the door, and turned on the small lamp that rested on a table beside it. I followed her inside, then stood silently, watching her as she moved about the room, depositing her things in various places, the briefcase on the table by the window, her small black handbag in a chair by the door. A few feet away, I could see her bed, cluttered and disheveled, through a partially open door.

"Would you like something to drink?" Rebecca asked.

"No, thanks."

She nodded toward a chair to my right. "Sit down."

I did, then watched as she took a seat opposite me, drawing her legs up under her in a gesture that seemed casual and unstudied, as if she'd become somewhat more at ease in my presence.

"I'm sorry about what happened in the restaurant," I told her.

"What did happen, exactly?"

"I saw it all. The murders, I mean. The way he killed them one by one."

"How much do you actually know about the murders?" Rebecca asked. "How they were done, that sort of thing."

"Not much, really," I admitted. "I know he used a shotgun."

"So what you 'saw'—I mean at the restaurant a few minutes ago—that wasn't based on anything you knew?"

"No."

"You never actually saw any of the bodies, right?"

"No," I answered. "I never went inside that house again." I shrugged. "I used to say that I never saw any of my family alive again, but actually, I never saw any of them at all."

I could remember a few things about that morning, however, and I told Rebecca what they were. I remembered my mother standing at the kitchen counter as I raced by her on my way to school. And Jamie walking far ahead of me, his cap pulled down against the morning rain. And I remembered Laura, the feel of her fingers wrapped around mine as we walked toward school together. "Bye, Stevie," she'd said, as she'd dropped me off at my school, then moved down the sidewalk, a slender girl with long dark hair, a body disappearing into a net of rain.

"Laura was the last one I saw," I told Rebecca.

"And she was walking alone? Not with Jamie?"

"They never walked together."

"But they went to the same school, didn't they, the one a few blocks from the grammar school where you went?"

"Yes, but they never walked together," I said. "I always walked with Laura."

"Who did Jamie walk with?"

"Nobody," I said. "He didn't have any . . ." I stopped, remembering something. I waited until it was clear in my head, then I told Rebecca.

"Someone put flowers on his grave," I said. "Not my mother's or Laura's. Just Jamie's."

"When?"

"Just before I left for Maine with Uncle Quentin," I answered. "Aunt Edna took me over to the cemetery so that I could say good-bye. They'd all been buried side by side, with Laura on one side of my mother and Jamie on the other."

It had been a cold, snowy day, the wind snarling around us as we'd climbed the low hill that led up to the graves. It had played havoc with Aunt Edna's long black coat, whipping at it madly while she struggled forward, tugging me along with her, sometimes harshly, so that I'd tripped occasionally and gone facedown into the snow. "Get up, Stevie," my aunt had kept saying. "Get up! Get up!"

It had taken us almost five minutes to reach the graves, and by that time Aunt Edna was exhausted. She clutched irritably at her coat and glared down at the three snow-covered mounds, each with its own gray stone. My eyes were drawn to the one on the right, to Laura's grave. A layer of snow nearly covered her name. I could make out only the large, ornate "L" and the faint outline of the final two letters. The date of her birth was completely covered, but I could see the word "November" carved below it, though the date and year were covered with snow.

Aunt Edna jerked my hands. "Say good-bye, Stevie," she snapped.

Obediently, I whispered, "Good-bye, Laura," then repeated the process with my mother and, at last, with Jamie.

"That's when I noticed the flowers," I told Rebecca. "They were small, blue flowers, and the wind had nearly stripped them, but I could see a few buds, nonetheless. There were no flowers on the other graves, just on Jamie's."

"Where did you think they'd come from?" Rebecca asked.

To my surprise, I recalled exactly where I

thought they'd come from. "Well, I remember looking at them and thinking to myself, 'He's still here.' " I stopped and looked at her somberly. Even to me, it seemed too bizarre to be true. "I was only nine," I admitted, "so who else could I have possibly thought might put them there? Who else would have cared enough to do it—and who was still alive—except my father?"

"Did your father care for Jamie?" Rebecca asked directly.

"I think he tried to, yes," I said.

"You never noticed him showing any particular resentment toward him?"

"No," I said. "Even now, knowing what we've learned, I still don't remember seeing any great resentment toward Jamie on my father's part."

"But they didn't get along, did they?"

"No, they didn't." I thought a moment, then added, "But Jamie was not a lovable person, and he was always after Laura, always belittling her. And since my father loved Laura so much, I'm sure that Jamie's behavior made it hard for my father to reach out to him." I glanced toward the window, fixed my eyes on the dark lake beyond it, the wild currents I imagined to be swirling just beneath its black, unmoving surface. "It was getting all tangled up," I said quietly.

"What was?"

"Us. All of us. We were getting all tangled up in things."

For a moment, I saw my father as I'd often seen him, standing alone by the fence, smoking. There were times when I'd awakened near dawn, gone to the bathroom down the hall, then returned to bed. As I'd crawled back beneath the covers, I'd sometimes glimpsed him there, a solitary figure, standing in the smoky gray of early morning light, very still and deep in thought, as if he were trying to find a way out.

"Maybe that's what he couldn't bear," I said.

"What were you getting tangled up in?" Rebecca asked.

The answer came to me without hesitation. "In each other," I said. "All knotted up in each other." I considered my answer longer, then added, "And in love, or faking it, anyway."

"Faking love?"

"Yes. Pretending to love, when we really didn't. That's the hardest thing in life. Imagine doing it for years." I saw my father by the fence again, caught in his arctic solitude. "The way my father did."

Rebecca said nothing, but I could see a growing intensity in her eyes, as if I had alerted her to something.

"The men you're studying, they were all doing that, weren't they?" I asked. "They were all faking love."

Rebecca responded with a question of her own. "If that was true, that your father was faking love, when did that begin?"

"I don't know for sure," I admitted. "But I knew who he loved the least."

So did Rebecca, and to demonstrate it, she drew another picture from her stack. It showed Jamie's body sprawled across the floor, his head like an exploded melon, scattered in bits and pieces across the floor and wall.

"Poor Jamie," I said softly. "He had no idea what was coming toward him."

I remembered all the times my father had gone out and shot baskets with my brother, how often even that had ended in some kind of brawl, ended with Jamie stomping up to his room, slamming the door behind him. At those times, my father had often lingered beneath the net, the ball bouncing up and down on the cement drive, rhythmic as a heartbeat, while he stared vacantly toward the backyard. I could see the look on his face, an expression of helplessness and bafflement, as if he were lost in a terrible bramble, pricked and bleeding, with no way out.

"My father was confused," I told Rebecca. "Maybe, in the end, he just wanted to get out of that confusion." I looked up at her emphatically. "Things were heating up in our house," I told her. "Tension. Hatred. Maybe he couldn't find any other way to clear the air." I considered it a moment. "So he just blasted his way out."

"A sudden explosion, is that what you're saying?" Rebecca asked. "That your father just blew up one afternoon?"

I nodded.

Rebecca said nothing.

"Maybe Jamie was the focal point of that confusion," I added after a time, "the center of the storm, you might say, but not the whole thing."

"Did you ever see them talking?" Rebecca asked. "Jamie and your father?"

I shook my head. "No."

"So they weren't faking love anymore?"

"No, they'd gone beyond that point, I think," I said.

It struck me that perhaps this was the line that my father, and all these men, had finally crossed, the one that divided genuine from counterfeit devotion. Somewhere, they had decided that they would no longer live behind their own paternal mask, that the long masquerade was over.

My eyes drew over to the picture of my father on his wedding day, the luminous smile that adorned his face. "Maybe that's where the fakery began," I said as I tapped the photograph softly, "from right here, from the very first day."

Rebecca watched me silently.

"So that his whole family life was a lie," I added quietly, in a voice that was even, controlled.

In a rush of images, I saw all the postcard moments of our family life, the holidays spent together, the bloated turkey on Thanksgiving, the lighted tree at Christmastime. I saw all our little celebrations, saw my father as he'd stood beside the blazing candles of countless birthday cakes. Each in turn, I watched him lift us into the uncluttered air, Jamie when he turned five, Laura the day she won the fourth-grade spelling bee, me on the day I first rode my bike without training wheels.

"All a lie," I repeated softly, my lips hardly parting with the words. "Can that be possible?"

Rebecca's eyes fell toward the picture of my brother in his ruin, a gesture that gave me the only answer I required at the time.

NINE

A week passed before we met again. As always, it began with a phone call to my office, and it ended with the two of us seated in the front room of her cottage by the lake.

From the beginning, it was clear that during the intervening days, Rebecca had thought a great deal about our last conversation. She began with a reference to it.

"We were talking about faking love," she said, as she took a seat opposite me. "You were saying that your father might have faked it from the beginning."

I nodded.

"What about his love for Laura?" Rebecca asked. "Was he faking that, too?"

I shook my head determinedly. "No. Absolutely not."

Rebecca took a picture from her briefcase and handed it to me. It showed Laura as she lay on her back, her chest blown open, her soiled feet pressed toward the camera. I gave the picture back to her.

"I don't care what that shows," I told her. "I saw his face when he was with her. She relieved him.

She gave him the only happiness he may have had in our family."

I could tell Rebecca remained doubtful.

"I know that my father loved Laura," I repeated, almost wistfully. "Because I loved her too. Especially toward the end. Especially that last year when it became . . ." I hesitated to say it, but found that I couldn't keep it back. ". . . romantic." I shrugged. "Or at least that's the way it felt."

Laura was sixteen that year, and so beautiful that there were times when I'd catch her in my eye, and simply stop, dead still, and watch until she passed from view. So beautiful that I'd begun to dream about her. They weren't the sweaty, lustful fantasies of teenage boys, but the atmosphere was always luscious nonetheless, a sensual world of glades and humid leaves, warm mists and jungle fragrances.

In dreams, Laura came to me in such places. Of course, it was never really Laura, but only a presence I recognized as her, a smell, a taste, but never the person that she really was, the teenage girl who ate dinner across the table from me, and slept in the room next door. Still, it was a powerful presence, and after each dream, I was left with the odd sensation of her actually having passed through me, like a wind through a cloud, leaving me in a strangely suspended state of excitement and delight. The following morning, while she ate her eggs obliviously across the table, I would smile inwardly, remembering my dream, and with the strange sense that I'd cunningly stolen something from her during the night, then triumphantly slinked away.

"I was in love with my sister," I said. "If we'd been allowed to grow up together, I'm sure I would have found another romantic object." I shook my head. "But she died at the height of her power over me, and so, I had all this love left over, like money I couldn't spend."

"You couldn't spend it with your wife?"

"It's not the same."

I half expected Rebecca to lean toward me and begin a wholly different inquiry, but she didn't. Instead, she looked at me very shrewdly, as if taking some part of me in for the first time. Then she said, "I know."

For a moment, we stared at each other softly. During that brief time, I felt an undeniable connection to her, a sense of having shared the same dark space. But it lasted only an instant, for almost immediately, Rebecca shifted in her seat, as if to break free of some invisible net.

"How about Laura?" she said. "Did she have a 'romantic object' in her life?"

I suppose it was not until that moment that I fully realized just how much I'd buried since the murders, how much I'd repressed.

"Yes, she did," I said. "A boy named Teddy Lawford."

Rebecca drew a small pad from the table beside her chair. "Was he from Somerset?"

"No. They met on Cape Cod. My father had rented a cottage there for the last week in August 1959." The nearness of that day in November struck me. "It was just three months before the murders."

Rebecca's eyes tensed slightly, but she said nothing. Instead, she merely allowed me to continue, her pen still poised above the white paper which bore nothing but Teddy Lawford's name.

"Teddy was seventeen," I began.

As I spoke, I could see him quite clearly in my mind, tall and lanky, with light brown hair. He had grayish eyes that seemed to change depending on the light, something Laura had later commented on. His amiable, divorced father was a large, beer-barrel of a man who'd spent his life selling auto parts in Boston. He'd rented the cottage next to ours for the summer, and Teddy had watched a series of families move in and out of it over the preceding weeks, some staying no longer than a few days before they were replaced by another. But we had been the first, I later heard Mr. Lawford say, who'd shown up with a lovely girl nearly his son's age.

"I think Teddy's father was anxious for him to meet someone," I said.

Rebecca looked at me. "You mean a girl his son could have a sexual experience with?"

"Yes, probably," I answered. "He must have seen Laura at some point, although I don't know exactly when that might have been."

Perhaps from behind the tattered paper shades of his own cottage, perhaps from the screened porch that looked out over the sea. In any event, Mr. Lawford had no doubt glimpsed her, had let his eyes settle upon her body as she moved along the side of the house, or strolled through the tall green sea grass to the beach below, all the time brokenly aware, as he must have been, that she was well beyond him, that he was too old and bald and fat to inspire anything but repulsion in such a beautiful young girl, but that she might make a suitable offering for his son.

"Mr. Lawford invited us over to his cottage the second night we were on the Cape," I said. "My mother hadn't really wanted to go. Jamie, either. But both of them had finally come along with the rest of us."

It was early evening, and a gorgeous red sun was lowering on the horizon. I'd never seen a sunset on the sea, or even the kind of deep blue light that descended upon us that evening. It was warm, and Laura was dressed in a pair of white shorts and a dark green blouse, its ends knotted at the front. I remember that Teddy came to attention as she walked into the backyard, his dark eyes clinging to her like talons.

"Teddy fell for my sister at first sight," I told Rebecca. "They hadn't even spoken, but he was crazy about her."

"So it wasn't exactly love," Rebecca said.

I shook my head. "Love? No, it didn't have time to be love."

But it was very powerful nonetheless, and it grew unabatedly during the entire evening, as Laura and Teddy inched their way into a different universe. The contrast between them and the rest of us must have been amazing. Jamie sat morosely by himself, dully watching the sea. My father and Mr. Lawford talked idly and passionlessly of business matters, my mother listening to them silently, her hands folded in her lap. As for me, I scuffled with Mr. Lawford's cocker spaniel, both of us rolling mindlessly across the sandy lawn.

And yet, even as I rolled around that evening, I could sense the emergence of a new state of being, a world that had suddenly sprung into existence, and which floated in the air between Teddy Lawford and my sister. I didn't know what it was, but only that it was something that had been mysteriously created, and that its movements were infinitely fast.

"It wasn't love," I told Rebecca once again. "But once you'd felt it, you wouldn't want to live without it."

Rebecca lifted her face slightly. "It was romance," she said firmly.

"Well, whatever it was, Teddy was in the full grip of it. He came over to our house the very next morning."

He was dressed in a pair of cutoff blue jeans and a white T-shirt, the sleeves rolled up above his shoulders. I saw him lope across the yard, pause a moment at the little stone walkway that led to our house, then bolt forward, as if, in those few hesitant moments, he'd thought it all over and decided the issue once and for all.

Though it was still early, Laura had been awake for a long time. I'd glimpsed her sitting alone on the screen porch, then later strolling absently in the backyard, making odd, aimless turns, her long hair blowing in the early morning breeze. Despite the chill, she'd gone into the yard wearing nothing but the bottom of her bathing suit beneath a loose-fitting blouse, purposely leaving behind her thin blue windbreaker, the one she'd tightly wrapped around herself while she'd remained on the porch.

"Laura had gone out to attract Teddy," I told Rebecca. "You might say, to display herself. She was very beautiful that summer, and I'm sure Teddy was completely overwhelmed by that."

And so, that morning I watched as Teddy bounded down the walkway toward our cottage, not even able to control his stride. I was at the window, and it was only a few feet from there to the door, but Laura was at the door even before I could get to it, answering his knock instantly. A wave of white light swept over her when she opened it, and for a moment, as I watched, she seemed encased in its radiance. She stood quite still, talking to him, her hands toying nervously with the loose ends of her blouse. I can still remember the words that passed between them, so ordinary they seemed to burst in the heated air:

"Oh, hi, Teddy."

"Hi, Laura. Have you already eaten?"

"No, not yet."

"There's a little diner down the road. It's not so great, but I go there for breakfast. You want to come with me?"

"Well, my father's still asleep, you know?"

I had come up quite close to them by then, walking very slowly from the window to the door, listening intently as I moved toward them.

Laura looked at me, and I noticed that, despite the chill, small beads of sweat had formed a moist line across her upper lip.

In an instant, she was gone, the two of them disappearing behind a curve in the road. She hadn't asked my father's permission. She hadn't said so much as a "see you later, Stevie" to me. It was as if a mighty wind had picked her up and blown her out the door.

"She was completely swept away," I told Rebecca. "I couldn't imagine what was going on in her. I couldn't believe that she'd just left without saying anything to my father."

He woke up an hour later, fully alert, the way he always did, as if, each morning, he returned to himself in a sudden, startling realization. He was dressed in a pair of blue trousers and a checked shirt, and he barely offered a passing wave as he headed for the kitchen. I heard him making a pot of coffee, then, after it was made, I saw him walk out onto the back porch and stare out across the field of high, green sea grass that stretched almost to the beach. The morning light was even brighter by then, and it framed him eerily as he stood, his back to me, peering out toward the bay, the black mug of coffee rising and falling rhythmically before he finally spun around, as if alerted by some sound, and looked at me:

"Where's Laura?" he asked.

"Laura?" I repeated hesitantly, stalling for time, but remembering the look she'd given to me as she'd left with Teddy, a look that had unmistakably commanded me to lie. "I don't know, Dad," I answered. "I haven't seen her."

He nodded slowly and lowered himself into one of the rusty metal chairs on the back porch. It was only then that the oddity of his initial question struck me. How had he known that Laura was not in the house, not sleeping in her bed like his wife was? I know that the question rose in my mind that morning, but only in a child's mind, quick, glancing, devoid of further investigation. It was not until I'd related the whole story of that morning to Rebecca that the answer actually occurred to me.

"He had expected to find her waiting for him on the porch," I told her. "And when he walked out onto the back porch and saw she wasn't there, he knew something was wrong."

"What did he do?"

"He had another cup of coffee."

And another and another, while the sun rose steadily and my mother slept mindlessly, and I wandered in the backyard, glancing apprehensively toward him from time to time. Something had gone wrong, and I knew it; some mysterious and confusing element had entered into our lives. I could see it in my father's face. For even though his features remained very still, I could sense that wheels were spinning wildly behind them.

My mother got up at around ten that morning, but she didn't join my father on the back porch. Instead, she mechanically made breakfast for herself, the usual boiled egg and toast, then walked out into the living room and ate it absently, as if it were merely tasteless fodder, fit for nothing but the maintenance of life.

I went out to play in the backyard. Mr. Lawford's spaniel spotted me and ran over for another round of tussling in the grass, and this occupied me fully for quite some time. The strange dread I'd felt vanished in the frolic, and so it was not until I saw my father come to his feet that I even noticed that he still remained on the back porch.

He stood very tall, a lean man with wavy black hair, the checked shirt billowing slightly as he came out into the yard. He didn't notice me at all, but walked directly to the edge of the yard, the place where it began its sharp decline toward the beach.

I walked over to him and stood at his side, looking down, as he did, toward Laura.

"Laura came back about an hour later," I told Rebecca, "but not by way of the road. She came up the beach instead, and she was alone."

Alone, because she must have known that whatever lie I'd come up with to tell my father, it surely hadn't included Teddy.

Standing beside my father, I could see her moving slowly, her head bowed slightly, as if she were looking for shells. She was barefoot, her brown leather sandals dangling from one hand, as she waded through the weaving lines of white lacy foam.

"There she is."

That was all my father said, and it was no more than a whisper, three words carried on a single, expelled breath. Then he returned to the house, without waiting, as I did, for Laura to make the hard climb up the stairs along the sandy hill to our cottage.

She was out of breath by the time she reached me, her long hair slightly moist with sea spray. She wasted no time in getting to the subject:

"I saw Dad up here."

"He went back into the house."

"What did you tell him?"

"That I didn't know where you were."

"Good. Thanks, Stevie."

"Where were you, Laura?"

She didn't answer me, but only walked directly back to the house and joined my father on the small back porch. While I played in the backyard, I could see them sitting together, their faces gray behind the screen, smoke from my father's cigarette drifting out into the summer air.

A few hours later we all went down to the beach, trudging cautiously through the deep sea grass, my father lugging a huge picnic basket, Jamie dragging along behind, looking as morose as he had the preceding day.

Teddy came bounding down a few minutes later. My mother invited him to have one of the ham sandwiches she'd made, and he accepted without hesitation. For a time, he chatted amiably with us all, although his eyes often fell upon Laura with a deadly earnest. Neither of them gave the slightest impression of having met earlier that morning, but I remember having the distinct impression that my father knew that they had. Perhaps Laura had told him while the two of them sat behind the gray screen. Or perhaps he'd sensed it in the looks that sometimes passed between Teddy and Laura while we all sat together on the blanket my mother had spread over the sand.

It was very hot that day, and not long after lunch, Laura, Teddy, and I all went into the water for relief. My mother, who never swam, gathered everything up and wandered back to the house, leaving my father alone on the beach. He sat there for several hours, his long legs sticking out of a dark blue bathing suit, watching us distantly, with that strange attitude of concentration which I'd only seen in the basement before, and which I associated only with the assembling of fancy European bicycles. And yet it was there on his face, that look of intense study and attention.

It was not directed at me, of course, but at Laura and Teddy as they moved farther and farther out into the sea. Glancing toward them from time to time, I would see hardly more than two heads bobbing happily in the blue water, although I am sure now that my father saw a good deal more.

Rebecca looked at me quizzically. "What more did your father see?" she asked. "I mean besides what was obvious, two teenagers attracted to each other."

"I'm not sure, but I think it was something about life." I remembered Rebecca's earlier remark about what she was looking for in these men. "Maybe something unbearable," I added.

I could see my father's face as it had appeared that day. Although in his youth he'd been a pale, skinny boy, middle age had filled him out a bit. He was still slender, of course, but his face had aged into an unmistakable handsomeness, his sharper features less bird-like, the eyes more deeply set and piercing. His curly black hair framed his face well, and when the wind tossed it, as it did that afternoon, it gave him a wild, curiously appealing look. Because of that, I realized that I'd been completely mistaken in what I'd just told Rebecca. "No, he didn't look like a man about to break," I said. "He didn't look like that at all."

I watched her quietly for a moment, certain now that I was following behind her in some strange way, covering ground she'd already covered.

"My father wasn't some little gray man who crumbled under pressure," I said finally. "Why have I always wanted to think of him that way?"

I instantly thought of the other men Rebecca had chosen for her study. None of them had been inept or inconsequential; none had seemed to lack a certain undeniable dignity.

I saw my father again as he'd appeared that day on the beach, his legs stretched out before him, leaning back slightly, propped up on his elbows, his eyes focused on Laura and Teddy as they bounced up and down in the heaving waves.

In my imagination, his features took on a classical solidity and force, almost the military bearing of one who had chosen to defend the city, no matter what the cost.

I looked at Rebecca, amazed by my own reassessment. "My father had a certain courage, I think."

It was then that the utter loneliness of my father hit me with its full force, the darkness within him, his long silence, the terrible hunger he carried with him into the basement night after night, and which, I realized now, Laura had sensed as well, and perhaps even tried to relieve from time to time, like someone visiting a prisoner in his cell.

Rebecca looked at me questioningly. "Did something happen on the Cape, Steve?" she asked.

I nodded. "Yes."

Rebecca seemed almost reluctant to continue, as if she felt herself being drawn down in a world even she was not quite prepared to enter. "Do you want to stop now," she asked, "or do you want to go on?"

"I want to go on, Rebecca."

And so I did.

I told her how Teddy and Laura had spent almost all their time together after that first morning, how my mother had remained almost like an invalid, reading her romance novels, how, at last, my father had seized the gray back porch like a conquered province, sitting hour after hour in the little metal chair, his eyes trained on the sea.

Finally, I arrived at the place where I'd been heading all along, that last night on Cape Cod.

"Nothing really strange happened until the end of that week," I began, "the night before we headed back to Somerset."

Early that afternoon, it had begun to rain. By evening, it had developed into a full summer storm, with sheets of wind-blown rain slapping against the cottage's rattling windowpanes. While the rest of us retreated into the house, my father remained on the back porch, still in that same chair, his eyes fixed on the violently churning sea.

"Lost in thought, that's how I'd describe him," I told Rebecca. "Lost in thought."

"But you don't know what he was thinking about?"

A possibility occurred to me: "Killing us, perhaps."

"Why would you think that?"

"Because, over dinner that night, he did something cruel to my mother."

She'd called him in to a hastily prepared dinner of hot dogs and baked beans, and he'd taken his usual seat. He looked preoccupied, intensely engaged in something within him. He remained silent while the rest of us chatted, mostly about the things that still had to be done before we could leave the next morning. A couple of times during the meal, Laura had tried to engage him, but he'd only answered her in quick, terse phrases, little more than a yes or no, sometimes not even that, but only a brisk nod of the head.

My mother had watched all of this for some time, yet had said nothing. Finally, she got up and headed back to her chair in the living room, inadvertently leaving one of her novels on the table near my father. She was almost all the way out of the room when he called to her suddenly:

"Dottie."

She turned quickly, as if surprised by the sound of her name in his mouth, unsure of the context in which he'd used it, already gathering her red housedress around herself more tightly:

"Dottie."

My mother had already turned all the way around to face him before he spoke to her again. She didn't answer him, but only stood, very still, as if waiting for his next word.

My father added nothing else for a moment, and I remember he looked regretful that he'd called her name at all. Still, he had started something which he could not help but finish:

"You forgot to take your book, Dottie."

And with that, he picked it up and hurtled it toward her violently, its pages flapping hysterically in the air until it struck my mother in the chest and fluttered to the floor.

My mother stared at him, stricken, and my father seemed to collapse beneath her broken, helpless gaze. His face was ashen, as if mortified by what he'd done. He stood up, walked over to where the book lay lifelessly on the floor, retrieved it, and handed it to my mother:

"I'm sorry, Dottie."

She took it from him, retreated into the living room, and slumped down in her accustomed position. The book lay in her lap. She made no effort to read it that night. Instead, she remained in her chair, the yellow lamplight flooding over her, her eyes fixed on the small painting that hung on the opposite wall.

I gave Rebecca a penetrating look as the thought struck me.

"She knew it was coming," I said. "From that moment, I think, she knew he was going to kill us."

Rebecca didn't question this. She jotted a note in her black book and looked back up.

"What was Laura's reaction to what your father did?" she asked.

I remembered the look on her face in great detail. She had been sitting across from me, so that the book had flown between us as it hurtled toward my mother. Laura's eyes had followed it briefly, then shot over to my father. What I saw in them astonished me.

"It was admiration," I told Rebecca. "Laura

looked at my father as if he'd done something gallant, like he was some kind of knight in shining armor." I released a sharp, ironic chuckle. "All he'd done was throw a book at a helpless woman," I said. "That's not exactly Sir Lancelot, is it?"

"Then why did Laura look at him that way?"

"I don't know."

She didn't seem to believe me. "Are you sure you don't know?"

"What are you getting at, Rebecca?"

Before she could answer, I already knew. It had undoubtedly been admiration that I'd seen in my sister's eyes, but I hadn't guessed the nature of what it was she admired until that moment.

"Action," I said. "She admired him for actually doing something. It was hostile, and it was cruel, but at least it was *something*."

It was perhaps the same thing Quentin had admired not long before he died, muttering about how my father had "taken it by the balls." I thought about it a little while longer, remembering the softness in my sister's eyes, the love she had for my father, the small, almost undetectable smile that had quivered on her lips as she'd glanced over at him that night. It led me to the final moment of my narrative.

"That wasn't all my father did that night," I said.

Rebecca looked at me thoughtfully. I knew that she could hear the slight strain that had suddenly entered my voice as I began:

"It was much later that night, and . . ."

I'd already been in bed for several hours when I heard someone moving softly in the adjoining room. I crawled out of bed, walked to the door, and opened it. In the darkness, I could see Laura as she headed stealthily toward the back porch, through its creaking screen door and out into the yard. Her posture was different than I'd ever seen it, slightly crouched, as if she were trying to make herself smaller, less easily seen.

I followed her as far as the back porch, then stood, staring through the gray metal web of the screen. I could see my sister as she made her way across the wet grass, the white folds of her nightgown rippling softly in the wind that came toward her from the sea. In that same wind, her long hair lifted like a black wave, falling softly to her shoulders and down her back.

I remember that I pressed my face into the screen, as if trying to pass through it bodilessly, like a ghost, and float out toward the tall green reeds into which she had wholly disappeared.

I stood for a long time by the screen, half expecting Laura to reemerge from the sea grass, perhaps with a shell in her hand, or some article she'd forgotten to retrieve from the beach earlier in the day.

But she didn't come back, and so, after a moment, I drew away from the screen and turned back toward the house.

That was when I saw my father.

He was sitting motionlessly in the far corner of the porch, his long legs folded under the metal chair, his light blue eyes oddly luminous in the darkness. In the eerie stillness, he looked like a serpent sunning itself on a stone, but entirely inverted, drawing warmth and comfort from the darkness.

He didn't speak to me at first, but merely let his eyes drift over to me, hold for a moment, then leap back to their original position, peering out at the wall of gently waving reeds. Then he spoke:

"Go back to bed, Stevie."

"Where's Laura going?"

"Go back to bed."

His eyes returned to me, and I felt myself shrink back, moving away from him cautiously and fearfully, as if he were coming toward me with a knife.

Within seconds I was back in my room, but I couldn't sleep. My mind latched on to Laura, to her white gown billowing in the breeze, and I remember feeling frightened for her somehow. Normally, the fear would have come from the simple knowledge that she was out in the darkness alone. But that wasn't the origin of my dread. It was him. It was the feeling that he was going to go after her, stalk her in the reeds, do something unimaginable.

I looked at Rebecca, shaken suddenly by my own unexpected insight. "So I was really the one who knew all along that he was going to kill us," I told her. "I was the one who sensed it. Not my mother or Jamie or Laura."

Rebecca's face was very still. "Go on," she said.

And so I did, relating the story in as much detail as I could recall, reliving it.

After a time I walked back to the porch, although very stealthily, intending only to peer surreptitiously around the corner of the door to assure myself that my father was still there, that he hadn't followed my sister into the reeds.

But he was gone, the chair empty, a cigarette butt still smoldering in the little ashtray he kept beside it. I knew that he hadn't returned to the bedroom he shared with my mother. I don't know how I knew this, but it was as clear to me as if I'd seen him disappear into the tall grass or heard the creak of the screen door as it closed behind him. I knew, absolutely, that he'd decided to go after my sister.

I stood, frozen on the porch, poised between the warmth of my childhood bed and the darkness beyond the house. I don't know what I thought, if I thought anything at all. Perhaps I was already beyond thought, already operating at a more primitive level, sensing the storm that was building within my father the way an animal lifts its face to the air and senses danger in the bush.

"What did you do?" Rebecca asked.

"I went after my father."

A curious expression rose in Rebecca's face. "You weren't thinking of it as going after Laura?"

"No."

And it was true. Even as I opened the screen door and stepped out onto the wet lawn, I knew absolutely that I was pursuing my father rather than moving to protect my sister, that my intent, shadowy and vaguely understood, was to join him in the tall grass, commit myself to whatever it was he had committed to the moment he'd crushed the cigarette butt into the ashtray beside his chair and headed out into the night.

The grass was tall and still wet with rain, and the blades, as they pressed my arms and legs, felt very cool and damp. The ground was soft, and I could feel my feet sink into it slightly with each step. The reeds had parted as my father had moved through them, leaving a wide trail for me to follow, already crouching as I went forward, moving slowly and secretly, as if I already had much to hide.

The trail led down the hill toward the sea. I could hear the waves tumbling not far away, but I couldn't see them until the clouds parted suddenly and a broad expanse of light fell over the beach. It was then that I glimpsed my father's head, saw his tangled black hair and sharp, angular face just for an instant before he sank down, squatting over the wet earth. I could tell by the motionlessness of the grass that he'd stopped, and for a moment, I stopped as well and stood, sinking imperceptibly into the rain-soaked ground.

For a little while I listened intently, my head cocked like some primordial creature. I could hear only the waves as they tumbled toward shore a few yards away and the wind as it swept through the reeds that surrounded me.

I don't know exactly when I began to move forward again, or why, or what I was thinking as I did so. I remember only the sudden desire to penetrate more deeply into the green wall and the inability to draw back once I'd begun to move again.

I walked slowly, very silently, as if stalking a prey almost as cunning as myself. I remember shifting to the right somewhat, because I didn't want to come upon my father. I'd glimpsed his position in a wedge of light, and I carefully edged myself away from him as I continued to slink forward through the reeds.

I didn't stop until I heard a shifting in the grass, the slow, rhythmic friction of blades rubbing softly against other blades. As I continued forward, I could hear someone breathing, then two people breathing in short, quick spasms.

I stopped and peered out, gently drawing away the curtain of reeds that blocked my vision. That was when I saw her.

"Laura," Rebecca whispered.

"Yes."

At first my sister's body appeared to me in a blur of white and black, her long hair shifting back and forth over her naked shoulders. She seemed to be rising and falling on a completely separate cushion of pale flesh. I could only partially see the body beneath her, the one which shuddered violently each time my sister rose and fell above it. It came to me only as a headless ghost, white against the dark ground, moaning softly each time my sister lifted the lower part of her body then eased herself down upon him again.

I could see his slightly hairy thighs, the nest of dark hair into which they disappeared, and finally the long pale shaft that seemed to pierce and then withdraw itself from the body of my sister.

It was 1959, I was nine years old, and so I'm sure I didn't know what was happening there in front of me. Still, I knew that it was something powerful, occult, primitive, and at last profoundly private. I felt the need to withdraw, to sink back into the reeds and return to my bed, but something held me there, and for a moment, I continued to watch, shamed perhaps, but also mesmerized by the spectacle before me.

I don't know how long I watched, but I do remember that during that time the idea that my father could be anywhere near such a scene completely left me. I remained fixed on the two bodies, as if dazzled by the continually building intensity of their motions, the rising force and deep needfulness I could hear in their breathing.

Suddenly, my sister arched her back and released a long, luxurious sigh. She shook her head, and her dark hair brushed back and forth along the lower quarters of her naked back. Then she fell forward in a spent, exhausted motion, the wall of her flesh suddenly collapsing so that I could see the green reeds beyond her, and deep within those reeds, my father's pale blue eyes, motionless and vaguely hooded, with nothing at all in them of the voyeur's seamy lust, but only staring toward mine in an instant of unspeakable collusion.

For a few seconds, we continued to stare frozenly at each other while Laura and Teddy hurriedly dressed themselves, took a final, strangely passionless kiss, then rushed away, Laura moving up toward our cottage, Teddy toward his.

Once both of them were out of sight my father stood up and started walking back to the cottage. I trailed after him, just a few feet behind. He didn't look back at me. Perhaps he was too ashamed. I will never know.

Rebecca peered at me unbelievingly. "You mean that he never said anything to you about that night?" she asked.

"No."

"Did he seem different after that?"

"Yes, but not toward me," I answered. "Only toward Laura."

Rebecca's pen remained motionless above the still nearly blank pad. She'd taken very few notes, but I knew she'd absorbed every bit of my story, every nuance and detail.

"How did he change toward Laura?" she asked.

"He got even closer to her," I answered. I considered it a moment, trying to find precisely the right word. "He became . . . more tender."

For the first time Rebecca looked vaguely alarmed, as if the word had caught her by surprise.

Still, it was undoubtedly the right word to describe the change that came over the relationship between Laura and my father during the few weeks before he killed her.

"They were very tender with each other after that night on the beach," I said. "They'd always been very close, but they got even closer for a while." I did a quick calculation in my head. "My sister had seventy-nine days to live."

The starkness of the number, the brevity of my sister's life, shook me slightly, but only slightly, not with the disoriented unease I'd experienced in the restaurant days before.

Still, Rebecca noticed the reaction. "This is hard, I know," she said.

Her eyes were very soft when she said it, and I knew that I wanted to touch her, and that everything about such a grave desire seemed right to me at that moment, while everything that stood in the way of its completion, the whole vast structure of fidelity and restraint, seemed profoundly wrong.

"Rebecca, I . . ."

I stopped, quickly glanced away from her, and let my eyes settle once again on the lake beyond her window. The clouds had parted by then, and the moon was bright against its ebony surface. It gave the sense of a world turned upside down, of the past devouring the future, of all life's elements twisted and inverted, so that I seemed to be staring down into the waters of the sky.

TEN

It was nearly midnight by the time I got back home that evening. I'd expected to find Marie either working in her office or asleep. But she was waiting in the den instead, sitting beneath the reading lamp, her face very stern when she spoke to me.

"Where have you been, Steve?" she asked.

I looked at her innocently. "What do you mean? I've been at work."

"You mean at the office?"

"That's right."

"I called the office," Marie said. "I spoke to Wally. He said that . . ."

"I was doing a site inspection," I interrupted quickly. "At that office complex on the north side of town."

She looked at me a long moment, and I could see the wheels turning, the whole machinery of her suspicion fully exposed in her eyes.

"A site inspection at night?" she said doubtfully.

"We began it in the afternoon," I told her. "Then we had a long meeting in the general contractor's trailer."

For a moment she seemed vaguely embarrassed, as if by her own dark thoughts. "Oh," she said, her voice less accusatory, though a strained quality lingered in it. Then she smiled faintly. "Well, anyway, I'm glad you're home," she said.

"Me, too," I told her, though I knew it was a lie, that I wanted to be with Rebecca instead.

"Any more questions?" I asked half jokingly.

"I guess not."

I offered a quick smile, then headed upstairs. It was a gesture of flight, I recognized, a darting-away from the seaminess of the lie I'd just told Marie, perhaps even a flight from the uneasiness and foreboding I'd felt at the moment of telling it.

Once alone in the bedroom, I thought of my father, of the way he'd hurled the book at my mother's chest that night on Cape Cod. I wondered if he'd felt the same restriction I felt now. Had there been some place outside his home that had called to him with an irresistible urgency? Later on that balmy summer night on Cape Cod, as I remembered now, I'd glimpsed him in the yard, standing beside my mother in the moonlight, his arm draped loosely around her shoulder. They'd returned from a long walk, and for a moment, as they'd stood together in the darkness, they'd actually looked like a couple in love. For a moment, he'd drawn her in more closely and kissed her hair. I wondered now if that gesture had been nothing more than part of a vast deception. Had my father really wanted to be with her that night? Had he wanted to be with any of us? Or had he secretly yearned for another life, one in which every moment was filled with challenge and surprise, a life from which we blocked him simply by being alive?

I thought of each of us in turn. I saw Jamie in his sullen anger and isolation; Laura in her reeling moods, walking the house in the blue twilight; my mother forever locked within the folds of her red housedress; myself, a small, ordinary boy, indistinguishable from any other. Last I saw my father, still distant and mysterious, a figure walking behind us, the grip of the shotgun nestled, almost gently, in his hands.

I remembered Rebecca's purpose again, her search for whatever it was in life that these men had been unable to bear, and in my father's case it occurred to me that the unbearable thing for which Rebecca was still searching might have been nothing more mysterious than ourselves, that we were, each of us, in our own individual lives, unbearable to him, the living proof that his life had come to nothing.

I walked to the bedroom window, parted the curtains, and looked out. The lights from the suburban street seemed dull and lifeless. For years I'd been able to look out that same window without the slightest sense of disturbance. Now the very look of it made me cringe, for it seemed to me that my life, like all the other lives around me, possessed only the manageable level of risk, and no real jeopardy at all. Lived within its confines, we hunted the appropriate game, settled for the reachable star. We made the roads straight and flat. We turned on the light before we headed down the corridor, and grabbed the railing as we inched cautiously down the padded stairs. We grew old in a world of shallow breaths, feared both gasps and sighs.

And yet, for all that, the very next morning I went on with my routine as if nothing were changing in my life. I sat at the breakfast table and made small talk with Marie and Peter. Dutifully, I asked about Marie's latest bid, about Peter's work in school. But even as I listened to them, their voices sometimes faded, their faces drifted off into a blur, as if they were becoming mere white noise.

"Finish up, Peter," I heard Marie say as she got to her feet, "you're going to be late for school."

I remained at the table while Marie went upstairs to finish dressing and Peter darted to his room to get his jacket. Seconds later, I heard him dash by me. He gave me a quick "Bye, Dad," then bolted out the door.

"Are you still here?" Marie said later when she came into the kitchen.

I looked at her. "What time is it?"

I could see that the question struck her as odd. "You're wearing a watch, Steve," she said.

"Oh," I said, then glanced down at it, but didn't move.

"Shouldn't you be leaving?" Marie asked.

"Yeah, I guess."

I got up and went to my car. As I began to guide it out of the driveway, Marie came out of the kitchen and walked toward me. I stopped the car as she came near.

"You don't look well, Steve," she said worriedly. "Do you want to stay home today?"

I shook my head. "No, I'm fine," I said with a small, dismissive smile.

Marie didn't smile back. "You need to take care of yourself, Steve," she said in a voice as full of real concern as I'd ever heard, a voice that should have comforted and relieved me, but didn't.

I shrugged. "I'm fine," I repeated, then let the car begin to drift away again.

She said nothing more, but simply stepped away from the car and watched, without waving good-bye, as I glided down the driveway. Now, when I think of her, I often see her in that pose, standing in the grass, her arms folded over her chest, watching silently as I drifted from her sight.

Once at my office, I went directly to my desk and began working on the library I'd been designing. But even as I worked, adding lines and filling in details, I felt that I was continually returning to the house on McDonald Drive. Curiously, I no longer dreaded these returns. Instead, I seemed to move back toward that lost place with an increasing sense of rendezvous and complicity. My companion was always Rebecca, and I sometimes felt that I was walking hand in hand with her through the separate murder rooms. I could hear her voice, as if in whispers, pointing out details, the open textbook on Jamie's desk, my sister's bare feet. The bodies of my dead family seemed to lie sensually before us, as if we were joined in the rapture of my father's crime.

It was over a week before I saw her again, and it seemed an infinitely long time. Each time the phone rang on my desk, I hoped that it would be she, whispering to me with a grave intimacy, as if we were lovers, bursting with breathless communications.

She called on a Wednesday afternoon, and we met at her cottage the following evening. I expected to exchange a few pleasantries, but Rebecca got right down to business instead.

She'd gotten some additional information from Swenson, she told me, and even as we began where we'd left off the week before, I sensed that she was holding something back. Even so, I didn't press the point. By then I'd become quite willing to go at whatever pace Rebecca set. Perhaps I'd even sensed that to know everything Rebecca knew would dull the intensity of the journey we were making together—something I didn't want to happen. What I wanted was to feel that intensity and peril all the time, to tremble forever at the edge of some sudden, apocalyptic discovery.

And so I followed Rebecca's lead, anticipating nothing, merely letting her questions guide me back.

"You said that things became more tender between your father and Laura after that night on the beach," she said.

"Yes."

"But they'd always had a close relationship, hadn't they?"

"Yes," I said. "But he seemed to pay even more attention to her after that. It was almost as if he were studying her, trying to get an idea of what was going on inside."

"And you only noticed this change after you'd returned from the Cape?"

"Yes."

We'd gotten back on a Monday night, Labor Day 1959, all of us crammed into the dark brown station wagon. My father drove, of course, while my mother sat in the front seat, her right shoulder pressed tightly up against the door, her face pale and bloodless as she stared straight ahead. Her eyes seemed lifeless, drained of light, and the sallow skin of the face that surrounded them made her look like a department store mannequin.

Laura and I sat together in the back seat while Jamie lay crouched up and constantly complaining in the small square of trunk space that lay just behind us. He had absented himself as much as possible from the rest of us during the preceding week, but this last effort at self-imposed exile was certainly his most extreme, a punishing act of ostracism which Laura found ridiculous and contemptible, but which my father, lost in his own thoughts, seemed hardly to notice.

We'd planned to leave early that Monday morning, but things had gotten scattered and confused during the day, and we'd finally pulled away from the little cottage at nearly four in the afternoon. By that time, the off-Cape traffic had reached its dreadful end-of-season peak, and we'd staggered along toward the Sagamore Bridge at a snail's pace, inching down the highway one jerk at a time, Jamie groaning uncomfortably with each movement of the car.

It was nearly midnight by the time we got back to the house on McDonald Drive, but my father didn't seem particularly tired. He pulled himself briskly out of the old station wagon and immediately began to unload the week's supplies while my mother staggered wearily into the house, then up the stairs to the bedroom.

Laura regarded my mother's bedraggled retreat into the house as nothing more than a way of avoiding the work involved in unpacking the car, and she clearly resented it.

"Why doesn't Mom help unpack?" she demanded sharply as my father handed her a large cardboard box. "The rest of us have to work at it."

My father did not reply. He simply drew another box from the back of the car while he listened as Laura railed on about my mother.

"Why is she so special?" she asked hotly. "Why does she get to go up to bed?"

Once again, my father refused to answer her. Instead, he yelled for Jamie, tossed him a heavy box, and commanded him to take it into the basement. Then, when Jamie was safely out of sight, he turned toward Laura, his eyes staring pointedly into hers. There was a kind of fierceness in his gaze, and I remember being quite drawn by the strangeness of it, as if he were about to pronounce some vital truth that he'd kept to himself all these years, waiting for the right moment to reveal it. But when he spoke, no such great truth emerged. Instead, after he'd settled his eyes on Laura for a moment, he said to her, almost in a whisper, but very distinctly nonetheless, and with that air of unchallengeable authority he often had, "You should know."

Rebecca wrote the words in her notebook, then looked at me. "Where were you when your father said that?"

"I was standing next to Laura."

"What did Laura say?"

"She didn't say anything."

"What do you think your father meant by, 'You should know'?"

"I have no idea," I told her. "But Laura knew what he meant. I know she did, because of the way she reacted."

I was standing only a few inches from her. I saw her fire her final question, then heard my father's reply, his voice neither sharp, nor angry, nor resigned. Instead, it seemed to carry a sense of severe scolding which struck Laura like a slap in the face, so that she shrank back from him immediately and lowered her eyes. Then, almost in the same motion, she stepped toward my father again, placed her hand very briefly on his shoulder, then turned and made her way into the house. She did not come back out to help us unload the car, but remained inside with my mother.

"Actually *with* my mother," I told Rebecca emphatically. "In the same room with her, not just the same house."

It wasn't until we'd finished unloading the car that I finally returned to the house. My father and Jamie continued putting various things away in the garage outside, but that was heavy labor, unsuited for a nine-year-old boy, and so I'd left them and gone back inside. It was nearly one in the morning by then, and I was very tired and wanted to get in bed as soon as possible.

I'd passed the threshold of the stairs and was headed down the corridor toward the room I shared with Jamie when I saw Laura and my mother. It was enough to make me stop.

"They were together in my mother's room," I told Rebecca. "Sitting side by side on the bed. I'd never seen my sister sit that close to my mother. It seemed very strange."

They were facing away from me. My mother had changed into her red housedress, and she was bent forward slightly, as if she were about to pick something up from the floor. I could see that Laura had draped her arm over my mother's shoulder comfortingly, and though I didn't know it then, the soft shaking motion I noticed in my mother's body undoubtedly was caused by the fact that she was crying.

Rebecca looked up sharply from her notebook. "Crying?" she asked.

"It must have been that," I said. "I don't know what else it could have been."

"But what was she crying about?"

"I don't know. Maybe it was some sort of delayed reaction," I said. "You know, delayed from earlier, when my father had thrown that romance novel at her."

"And Laura was comforting her, you said?"

"Well, not exactly," I answered, remembering it with a fierce clarity.

Rebecca looked at me, puzzled.

"It wasn't real," I said, "the sympathy. None of what Laura was doing was real. Not the way she'd slung her arm over my mother's shoulder. Probably not even the words she must have said to her while they sat on the bed together."

Rebecca looked at me doubtfully. "How do you know that?" she asked.

"By the way my sister looked at me," I answered, glimpsing that look again, a chill moving over me, as if a ghost had suddenly drifted past, brushing my shoulder with its pale robe.

"It was a strange look," I added.

In all the years I'd known her, Laura had never glared at me in such a forbidding way as she did that night. I'd climbed the stairs wearily, innocently seeking only the shortest route to my bed. I hadn't meant to eavesdrop. And yet, as Laura's head swiveled slowly in my direction, I saw her face stiffen hideously, her eyes take on a dreadful anger.

"She looked like an animal," I told Rebecca, "trapped, like a creature driven into a corner."

Rebecca jotted a note into her notebook, but didn't speak.

Even then, as I told Rebecca about that one brief incident, the look in my sister's face chilled me, and I remembered that during the few seconds she'd stared at me, I'd felt as if I were under fire, bullets slamming toward me, chewing up the floor beneath my feet, riddling the plaster wall behind me, spewing dust into the air.

"I all but dove into my room," I said, "just to get out of her sight."

But I'd done more than that. Once in my room, I'd locked the door behind me, then pressed my back against it like some terrorized child in a grade-B horror movie.

I'd still been standing in the same position a few minutes later when I felt the doorknob turn.

"Stevie? You in there?"

It was Jamie.

"Stevie?" he called again. "Stevie, you in there?"

I opened the door, glancing around his lean body toward the empty corridor. The door to my mother's room was closed. To my right, only a few feet down the dark corridor, the door to Laura's room was closed too, though I could see a line of bright light just beneath it.

"What's the matter with you?" Jamie demanded irritably. "You hiding something? Why was the door locked?"

I shrugged, unable to come up with an explanation that would have made any sense to him. "I didn't know it was locked," I said finally.

To my surprise, Jamie didn't challenge the completely illogical nature of my answer, perhaps because the childhood sense of the magical and miraculous which lingers on in adolescence was still so much a part of the way he saw the world that he could casually accept the otherwise impossible notion that doors could sometimes lock themselves.

In any event, he merely walked to the bed, pulled himself up to his upper bunk, and lost himself in one of the sports magazines that were always piled in a jagged stack at the foot of his bed.

For a long time, I remained in the room, sitting in the lower bunk. The weariness I'd felt before as I'd trudged up the stairs had disappeared, and in its place I could feel nothing but a disquieting tension. After a time, it drove me from my bed to the window. By that time, Jamie had fallen asleep, the sports magazine still open on his chest.

It was a clear summer night, and I could see the whole shadowy stretch of the backyard as if it were illuminated by a pale blue light. It was very warm, as well, and the window was fully open, a light breeze rustling the curtains quietly.

I don't know how long I stood by the window, but after a time, I heard the door at the side of the house—the kitchen door, the one that Mrs. Fields would approach only a few weeks later, then shrink back from in sudden dread—I heard it open, then close, and after that, the muffled sound of footsteps as they moved down the short flight of stairs to the walkway which divided the house from the garage and which led in a gentle curve to the backyard.

My father appeared seconds later, walking alone over the dark green lawn. He was taking long, slow strides, as he moved from the western to the eastern corner of the yard, then back again, a cloud of white smoke trailing behind him like the pale exhaust of an old steam engine.

I don't know exactly how long he paced the yard alone that night, but only that after a few minutes, I heard the kitchen door open again.

This time it was Laura.

She came around the corner of the house, dressed in her white sleeping gown, her long dark hair hanging in a black wave down her back. She was barefoot, and I could see her white feet as they padded across the dark green grass toward where my father stood, now leaning slightly against the solid wooden fence he'd built along the rear edge of the yard.

He didn't turn toward her, although he must have heard the door open, just as I had heard it. He didn't turn because, unlike me, he already knew who'd opened the kitchen door.

"It was obviously a prearranged meeting," I told Rebecca, "something the two of them had already planned."

Rebecca didn't look surprised, and I could tell from her face that she'd fully accepted the conspiratorial nature of my father and my sister's relationship, its eerie sense of secret conclave.

"Laura walked over to him," I went on, "and the two of them stood by the fence and talked for a long time."

From just behind the plain white curtains, while my brother lay snoozing a few feet away, the sports magazine rising and falling to the rhythm of his breath, I watched as my father and sister talked quietly, but very intently, their eyes resting steadily upon each other.

It was probably exactly that feeling of intensity that kept me posted by the window during the next few minutes. It was in every element of their posture, in every glance that passed between them, even in the sharp whispers I could hear but not make out, as if their voices were distant instruments scraping at the air.

They were in plain sight, of course, both of them posed starkly against the moonlight, and yet I felt the inexplicable need to hide behind the white shroud of the bedroom curtains. I didn't know why, but only that despite their outward show of openness, the fully illuminated yard, even the nearly ostentatious brightness of my sister's gown, the predominant mood of their meeting was surreptitious and collusive. Perhaps even a little arrogant, as if they both presumed with perfect certainty that the rest of us were sleeping in the dark house, that no matter what they said or how loudly they said it, neither Jamie nor my mother nor I would hear or see anything.

"It was as if, as far as they were concerned, we were already dead," I said.

Rebecca glanced down at her notebook, as if trying to avoid my eyes. "Did you ever get any idea of what they talked about that night?" she asked, but in a voice that was deliberately flat.

"No."

But I suspected even then that it was something of the deepest significance to them both. My father had remained rigidly in place throughout the conversation, his eyes focused intently on my sister. For her part, Laura had remained almost as motionless as my father. From a distance, she appeared locked in a stony, reptilian stillness which went against the often frantic quality of her movements, the fidgety fingers and continually bouncing feet. It was as if this stillness had been imposed upon her by the gravity of what was transpiring between them, the sheer awesomeness of its content.

"So you never heard any part of what they said?" Rebecca asked, as if she were still in doubt about the truth of my first answer.

"Well, only a few words at the very end," I admitted, "but that was after they'd come back into the house."

I'm not sure how long they'd talked together before my father suddenly nodded sharply, as if in conclusion, then began walking back toward the house. Laura walked beside him, her hand holding to his arm. When they had made it almost halfway across the yard, my father stopped, looked down at my sister for a moment, then lifted his right hand and very gently stroked her hair. It was a gesture that seemed to melt her, so that she leaned toward him and buried her face in his shoulder. My father looked away from her, as if unable to bear what he'd seen in her eyes. Then, in a slow, surprisingly dramatic movement, he lifted his face toward the bright, overhanging moon. They stood in just this position for a long time, she in her pale gown, he in his stone-gray work clothes, the light washing over them, so that they looked vaguely like marble figures, motionless and cold.

Then they separated and walked, without touching, back toward the kitchen door. Seconds later, I heard them pad up the short flight of stairs toward their separate rooms.

I ran to the door of my room and opened it slightly. Through the small slit, I could see my father and Laura as they mounted the stairs, moving slowly, until they came to a stop at the top of the landing. For a brief, suspended instant, they stood, facing each other silently.

Then my father said, "Are you all right?"

And my sister said, "Yes, I'm fine."

With that, they headed up the corridor, moving directly toward my room. I shrank away from them, not wanting to be seen, and eased my door back so that it was almost closed when they passed. Because of that, I could see only the broad outlines of their two bodies as they swept by my door, featureless and without detail, little more than gliding shapes.

I heard my father say, "Tomorrow."

And my sister said, "So soon?"

My father did not answer her. Or, if he did, it was later, in some place beyond my hearing. For after that, I heard nothing but the sound of his feet as they moved on down the carpeted hallway, then the sound of his bedroom door as it opened and closed.

Minutes later, I heard Laura open the door to her own room, so I know that for a short time she stood alone in the unlighted corridor. I don't know why she waited for those few extra minutes, or what thoughts played through her mind as she stood in the darkness outside her room, as if afraid to go in alone.

"And that's all you heard them say?" Rebecca asked.

"Yes."

She glanced down at her notes, quietly, thoughtfully, as if she were processing and rearranging information that she alone possessed. Watching her, I felt as if she'd rowed out onto a dark lake, leaving me on shore.

"The 'tomorrow' your father talked about," she said finally, "that would have been the first Tuesday in September?"

"I suppose."

"The first day of school," she added, almost to herself. Then she came back to me suddenly, her dark eyes darting over to mine. "Did anything unusual happen that next day?" she asked. "Did you notice any change in anything?"

"No," I said.

Again, Rebecca appeared to draw into herself,

her mind deep in thought, as if she were unable to accept what appeared to be the routine notion that "tomorrow" had been nothing more than my father's idle reference to the beginning of school, and Laura's whispered reply just a schoolchild's regret.

I leaned forward slightly. "Should I have seen something different that day?" I asked. "Was something going on?"

She didn't answer, but only flipped back a few pages in her notebook, scanning the lines she'd written until she found the right one.

"You said before that when Laura and your father were down by the fence, that they hadn't been concerned that anyone in the house might be watching them," she said.

"That's right."

"You said that it was as if they thought the people in the house were already dead."

I knew then what she was getting at. "How long had he been planning it, Rebecca?"

"Maybe longer than you think, Steve." She waited, trying to gauge how the latest information might affect me. "At least three or four months," she said finally.

"How do you know that?"

"Because of something Swenson found," she told me. "Travel brochures. A lot of them."

Occasionally, I'd seen my father reading an adventure novel, always slowly, taking weeks to slog through each one. I'd also seen him idly turning the pages of the local newspaper. But I'd never seen him browsing through anything that resembled a travel brochure.

"He found quite a few of them in that little office your father had at the rear of the store," Rebecca added, without emphasis.

It was little more than a stockroom, as I recalled then, small and cramped, but more secure, with many locks. It was the place he'd kept the unassembled Rodger and Windsor bicycles before bringing them home. Once or twice I'd seen him there with Nellie Grimes, the bookkeeper he'd hired some years before, but on all other occasions, he'd been in the room alone. Because of that, it was easy for me to think of it as the place of his solitude, the cluttered little room which he'd set aside for his plotting, the careful working out both of his crime and his escape.

"These brochures," I said. "Where did they come from?"

"He got them through the mail," Rebecca answered. "There was no indication that he ever went to a travel agency."

I shrugged. "I don't ever remember seeing any travel brochures around the house."

"That's because they weren't mailed to McDonald Drive," Rebecca said. "They were all mailed to the hardware store downtown." She paused a moment, then added, "Some had been mailed as long as three months before the murders."

I leaned back, as if unable to absorb this latest bit of information, the full-blown proof, as if any had still been necessary, of my father's plot.

"The brochures were from all over," Rebecca said. "Mexico, Europe, Asia, South America. That's why they weren't much help to the police."

"So they never had any idea where he went?"

"Not until they found the car," Rebecca said.

"That was in Texas, wasn't it?" I said tentatively, only vaguely recalling something Quentin had told me. "Near the Mexican border?"

"Right on the border, actually," Rebecca said. "In Laredo."

I nodded. "That's right," I said. "I remember that Quentin told me about them finding the car."

"Swenson brought it back," Rebecca said, "but no one ever claimed it."

So that it still sat in the shadowy corner of the police garage in Somerset, as Rebecca went on to inform me, a dark, eerie symbol of my father's flight. I could see it there, rusting, abandoned, the odor of my father's cigarettes still lingering in the ragged brown upholstery, dust gathering on the black, serrated wheel where he had laid his hands.

"You could claim it if you wanted," Rebecca added softly.

I shook my head wearily. "No, I don't want it," I whispered.

But I remembered it, nonetheless, as I told her.

Then I related a time when my father had driven all of us far out into the woods, to where an old cabin, not much more than a log shack, sat in a primeval forest.

It was probably four years or so before the murders, and we'd all gone out in that same old car in which he'd later made his escape—Laura and Jamie and I scrunched up together in the back seat; my mother, looking vaguely content on the passenger side; my father, his big hands on the wheel, smiling with a kind of gleeful adventurousness as we bumped along the barely passable road.

He'd stumbled upon the cabin while hunting as a boy, and I suppose there was something about it which had suddenly called him back. "I want to show you all something," he'd said at the breakfast table that morning.

We hit the road about an hour later, drove for a long time, paved roads eventually giving way to unpaved ones, then at last on to what were little more than ancient logging trails. It was already early in the afternoon by the time we finally reached the cabin.

It was set in a deep wood, near a winding brook, and I could tell by the way my father looked at it that it represented something to him, perhaps his ideal of a forest paradise, remote, primitive, and uncomplicated. When he looked at it, his face took on the kind of expression I would later see in paintings of the saints when they saw God, that here before them was the true, abiding majesty. That day, he even seemed like them, saintly, a father out of the great book of fatherhood, a man of mythic kindness and commitment, capable of making an epic sacrifice.

He played with us in the forest, a long game of hide-and-seek, in which we skirted behind bushes and fallen trees, while my mother watched us from her place on the cabin's small, dilapidated porch. We played tag, and he ran after us, lifting Laura into the air each time he caught up with her, their faces nearly touching as he lowered her to the ground again.

Toward evening, it began to snow, and while the rest of us gathered up our things and prepared to leave, my father walked out into the woods again and stood alone among the trees, his arms lifted slightly, hands open, catching snowflakes in his palms.

As I finished relating this episode, I realized that my eyes had grown moist.

"I'm all right," I assured Rebecca quickly, gathering myself in again. "I just got a little nostalgic, I guess."

It was more than that, though. I'd entered a new realm of feeling in regard to my family's slaughter. I realized that it was no longer the explosive instant which horrified me, as it had in the restaurant days before, but the long decay of love, the slow stages of its dissolution.

I could see that Rebecca understood that, but what she could not have known was that only part of my anguish was connected to the dark reliving of my family's death. The rest had to do with me, the volcanic discontent I had come to feel in the presence of everything that had grounded and sustained me in the past. It was as if that airy, unreal dream house I'd been working on for so long was now the only one in which I wanted to live. It was without walls. It had no foundation. It was pure fantasy. And yet it seemed right in a way that made everything else seem wrong.

After a moment, my eyes settled upon Rebecca. "They actually saw the monster, didn't they?" I asked. "My father and the rest of them? Whatever it was that was eating them alive, they actually looked it in the eye."

Rebecca didn't answer me directly, but grew distant, perhaps even apprehensive. "Maybe we should end the interview for tonight, Steve."

"Why?"

"I just think it would be best," Rebecca said firmly, leaving no doubt that the interview was over.

She walked to the door, opened it, then followed me out into the darkness, slowly walking me to my car as a swirl of leaves played at our feet.

"I'm sorry this is so hard for you," she said.

"It's a lot of things, Rebecca," I admitted. "It's not just my past."

At the car, I stopped and stood very near to her. I could almost feel her breath.

"When do you want to meet again?" I asked.

She watched me hesitantly, but said nothing.

I smiled. "Don't worry, Rebecca. I'll go all the way through it with you."

She nodded. "In all the other cases, there were no survivors," she said. "I guess I should have known how hard it would be for you, but I just hadn't had the experience before."

"It's okay," I assured her.

I opened the door and started to get in, but she touched my arm and drew me back around to face her.

"You should only go as far as you want to, Steve," she said. "No farther."

"I know," I told her.

I could feel her hand at my arm, and I wanted to reach up and hold it tightly for a long time. But I knew that close as it seemed to me, her hand might as well have been in another universe.

"Well, good night, then," she said as she let it drop from my shoulder.

"Good night," I said, then got into my car.

It was still early, so I stopped off at a small restaurant and had a sandwich and a cup of coffee before going home.

Marie was at the sink when I walked into the kitchen. Peter was at the table, chopping celery.

"You're home early," Marie said. "We're making a tuna dish."

"I've already eaten," I said idly.

Marie's eyes shot over to me. "You've already eaten?"

I nodded obliviously.

"You got off early and didn't come home to have dinner with Peter and me?" she asked, in a voice that struck me even then as deeply troubled, as if in this small twist of behavior she'd already begun to detect the approach of her destruction.

"I guess I did," I said, then added defensively, "Sorry. I just wasn't thinking."

Marie looked at me brokenly, but I did nothing to ease her distress.

"I'm going to lie down for a while," I said, then headed up the stairs.

Once upstairs, I lay down on the bed, my eyes staring at the blank ceiling. Below me, I could hear Peter and Marie as they continued to make their dinner together. Below me, as I realize now, they were shrinking. I should have seen it, like a murderous vision, as I lay alone on my bed that evening. I should have seen Peter fleeing down a dark corridor, Marie cringing behind a cardboard box. I should have seen the circle tightening, felt the first bite of the noose.

But that evening I felt nothing but my own distress. I remembered Rebecca as she'd stood beside me only a short time before, and I knew that I'd wanted to draw her into my arms. Perhaps, at the time, I'd even imagined that she was all I really needed to solve the riddle of my life. But I realize now that Rebecca was only the symbol of those other things I had wanted even more.

"In the deepest and most inchoate longings of these men," Rebecca would later write, "there was a central yearning to be embattled, a fierce need for a fierce engagement, so that they saw themselves in that single, searing instant not as killers slaughtering women and children, but as soldiers in the midst of battle, men heroically and perilously engaged in the act of returning fire."

It was months later, and I was alone, when I read that passage. By then, I was wifeless, childless, homeless. Everything was gone, except my one need to "return fire" as my father had, in an act of sudden and avenging violence.

ELEVEN

During the last days of October, as fall retreated and the first wintry rains began, I felt as if some sort of countdown had begun. It wasn't a radical change, only a shift in direction, a sense of moving into the final phase of something. There was a helplessness about it, a feeling that I no longer controlled my life, that perhaps, a creature of disastrous circumstances, I had never actually controlled it. It seemed my father had destroyed that web of connections which might have given me context, a place to stand in the world. After that, I'd drifted here and there, but always in reaction to something outside myself. I was an accidental architect, an accidental husband, an accidental father—an accidental man.

"They felt their lives were dissolving, didn't they?" I said to Rebecca at one of our meetings toward the end of October.

Her reply went to the center of how I'd come to feel. "No," she said. "They felt that in some way they had never lived."

But rather than thinking of myself at that moment, my mind focused once again on my father, and

I remembered how, in the days preceding the murders, he'd seemed to sink into a profound nothingness. For many hours he would sit alone in the solarium, silent, nebulous, hardly there at all. At other times, he would stand by the old wooden fence, his hands deep in his pockets, staring emptily across the lawn. At the very end, he had even stopped answering the phone when it rang at the house on McDonald Drive. It was as if he could no longer imagine that the call might be for him.

"He'd become a worthless shell," I told Rebecca at one point. "He'd been stripped of everything by then."

It was the word "stripped" that seemed to catch in Rebecca's mind. She repeated it slowly, as if it had conjured up something even darker than my father's crime.

"Stripped to the bone," I said assuredly. "There was nothing left of him."

I recalled the dreadful baiting which Jamie had continued to inflict on Laura, and how, in the last weeks, my father had sat by and let it go on day after day. The force that had once moved him to defend my sister had dissipated.

Rebecca didn't challenge my description of my father's disintegration, but I could see that it disturbed her. For a time, she even seemed curiously disoriented, as if she'd lost her way somehow. At the next meeting, her questions skirted away from the final days of my family's life. Instead, she concentrated on other issues, our routines and schedules, the division of chores, all the minutiae of my family's existence.

Then suddenly, during the second week of November, she regained her direction. It was as if after standing poised at the edge of something for a long time, she'd now decided to plunge over the side.

I arrived at her cottage late on a Thursday afternoon. She'd already started a small fire in the hearth, and it was blazing warmly when I arrived.

"It's cold out," she said as I came through the door.

I nodded and began to take off my coat.

"I like November," she added. "I think it's my favorite month."

It struck me as an odd choice. "Why?"

She thought a moment. "I guess because it's cold enough to make it clear that winter really is coming," she said, "and that we need shelter."

I shook my head. "Too rainy," I said. "Too confining." I shook my shoulders uncomfortably. "It gets into your bones."

I sat down in my usual seat, then waited for Rebecca to ease herself into the chair across from me.

But she didn't do that. She took a seat at the table by the window instead, her briefcase already open before her. For a few seconds, she hesitated, her eyes glancing first out the window, then back to her briefcase, then at last to me.

"Do you remember saying that these men had actually seen the monster?" she asked. "That they'd looked it in the eye?"

"Yes."

"We have to do that, too," she said. She picked up a single photograph and handed it to me. "We have to look it in the eye."

It was a picture of my father standing in front of the hardware store on Sycamore Street. It had been taken the day he'd opened the store, and all of us were with him. I, an infant, slept obliviously in my mother's arms, while Jamie and Laura seemed to hang like small sacks from my father's hands.

It was the first photograph she'd shown me in which we were all together, and something in it frightened me so much that I actually drew back from it unconsciously, as if it might strike out at me.

I handed the picture back to her. "Okay," I said. "Now what?"

She looked at me evenly. "As a picture, a family tableau, it's practically idyllic," she said.

"Yes, it is. So what?"

"We've been through each of the relationships in your family," Rebecca said. "Now we have to look at the possibility of something outside the family that might have had some bearing on the murders."

It was then I knew that we were racing toward the end of it. She'd gotten as much information about my family as she expected to get from me. Her final task was simply to assure herself that in getting the story of my family as it related to its destruction, she'd gotten the only story there was, that there were no loose ends, that my father fully and completely conformed to her archetype of "these men."

"You mean another person?" I asked. "Someone connected to my father? A lover, something like that?"

"Yes," Rebecca said.

The very idea seemed preposterous to me. It was as if I could accept the fact that my father had slaughtered his family more easily than the notion that he might have loved someone outside the circle of that destruction.

"I don't think he was the type to have another woman," I said offhandedly. "Of course, a love affair is not something he would have talked about with a nine-year-old boy."

Rebecca looked at me. "Would he have talked about it with Laura?"

The question brought back a quick play of memory.

"Maybe," I said. I remembered how, during the weeks before her death, my sister had appeared to stiffen and grow cold toward my father, to give him unmistakably hostile glances. I'd noticed the change at the time, but been unable to understand it.

"I can say that things did change between Laura and my father," I added. "At first, after we came back from Cape Cod, they seemed closer than ever. But not long after that Laura withdrew from him."

Suddenly I saw this change as the key to everything. The last link my father had had with us, his love for my sister, had abruptly broken. His one and only tie to us had snapped, setting him free to kill us all.

I remembered the look on my sister's face when she'd glanced at my father from time to time during the last month of her life. The sense of admiration that I'd always seen in her eyes was entirely gone. It had been replaced by something deeper and far grimmer.

"She seemed very disappointed in him," I said. "It was as if she'd come to despise him."

Rebecca said nothing.

"Maybe that was what my father couldn't bear," I added after a time, "the fact that he'd lost Laura."

"Or that she'd simply come to love someone else," Rebecca added cautiously, "the way teenage girls inevitably do."

I saw my sister again in the long green reeds, the arch of her white back in the moonlight.

"You mean Teddy Lawford?"

"He wrote quite a few letters to Laura," Rebecca told me. "Swenson found them in one of the drawers of her dressing table." She reached into the briefcase and withdrew a single sheet of paper. "Laura wrote him back, too," she said, as she handed me the paper. "This is a copy of the last letter she wrote to him."

"Where did you get it?" I asked as I took it from her hand.

"Swenson got it from Teddy when he went up to Boston to interview him about the murders."

"Swenson interviewed Teddy? Why?"

"He considered him a suspect for a while," Rebecca said. "But Teddy had been at the University of Michigan on the day of the murders." She nodded toward the letter. "It's dated November 15."

While Rebecca looked on, I read what was probably the last letter my sister ever wrote:

> Dear Teddy:
>
> Hi, I hope you are okay, and that everything is still going well at college. I wish I could say things are better here, but they're not. They're worse than ever. Jamie's a bastard, like always, and Stevie's just a kid. My father stays in the basement, but I don't go down there anymore. If I ever see you, I'll tell you what he did. I don't want to say it in a letter. Someone might see it, and I don't know what he would do if that happened. He's such a fake, Teddy, such a cheat.
>
> Teddy, sometimes I get really scared. I

feel like something's going to happen, but I don't know what.

Damn, this is a depressing letter. I'm sorry, but it's just the way I feel. Maybe something will brighten me up in the next few days. If it does, I promise to write and let you know.

Love,
Laura

Once I'd finished reading, I handed the letter back to Rebecca. She kept it in her hand, waiting for me to speak. When I didn't, she repeated the line that had struck her as the most important: " 'If I ever see you, I'll tell you what he did.' " Her eyes bore down upon me. "What do you think Laura meant by that?"

"I have no idea."

" 'Fake.' 'Cheat.' Why would she use those words?"

I realized that Rebecca had gone full circle, returning to her original point. "Another woman, you mean," I said. "You think it's possible that he was cheating on my mother, and that Laura found out, and somewhere in all that, he decided to kill us?"

Rebecca didn't answer, but I could tell that her earlier questions had been generated by more than speculation.

"If your father had a lover," she said, "then he can't be included in my study."

"Yes, I know, Rebecca," I said. "But is there some reason why you think he might have had another woman other than Laura's letter?"

She hesitated a moment, looking at me with an

expression which always signaled the fact that she was about to reveal something she had previously kept hidden. "Well, there's a detail that always bothered Swenson," she said. "He was never able to track it down exactly, and I think you're the only person who might know what it means."

"What detail?"

"The fact that almost five months before the murders your father bought two tickets on a flight to Mexico City," Rebecca answered, the revelation completed. She glanced down at her notebook. "He made the reservation on June 15, 1959. The flight was scheduled to leave from Idlewild Airport in New York City."

"On what day?"

She looked up at me. "November 19."

I felt a sharp pang. "The day of the murders," I said.

"But he canceled those same tickets over a month before the murders," Rebecca added. "On October 10. So, on November 19, as far as we know, he had no travel plans."

I repeated the most relevant aspect of what she'd told me. "But the main thing is that before that, he'd reserved two tickets, not just one."

"He made the reservation in his own name," Rebecca said pointedly, "one for him and one . . ." She stopped for a beat, ". . . for someone else."

"And this 'someone else,' " I said, "there was no name?"

Rebecca shook her head. "He made the reservation by phone, and he never gave a name for the second person."

"For his lover, you mean."

"If he had one," Rebecca said doubtfully.

"You don't think he did?"

"If I'd thought that, I wouldn't have gotten this far in studying him," Rebecca said. "Even Swenson was never able to trace him to any other person." She shrugged. "Everything about your father points to a family man."

"Everything except that ticket."

"Yes."

I let it all pass through my mind slowly, trying to think if I'd ever seen the slightest sign that my father had had his own version of Yolanda Dawes, some pale, slender female with thin, spidery arms, the mythical destroyer of homes. I thought of various possibilities. There was Mrs. Hamilton, the minister's wife who lived across the street, but she was far older than my father, matronly and overweight, hardly a candidate for romance. Next door, Mrs. Bishop, even older, lay bedridden with rheumatoid arthritis. There were other women in the neighborhood, younger, sleeker, their legs tightly bound in the pedalpusher pants so common at the time, but it didn't seem possible that they would have cast a longing glance at the middle-aged man in gray work clothes who sometimes cruised by in his old brown van.

Then, quite suddenly, I thought of someone.

"Well," I said hesitantly, not wanting to emphasize the point, "there was this one woman who worked for my father."

Rebecca's eyes bored into me. "Who?"

"Her name was Nellie Grimes," I said. "I didn't know her very well."

"Was she a neighbor?"

"No. She just worked for my father."

A divorcée, with a three-year-old daughter, Nellie had begun to work in the hardware store in the fall of 1956. My father had needed someone to straighten out the store's tangled bookkeeping system, but after doing that, Nellie had stayed on to handle the part of the business my father despised, the dismal mountain of paperwork involved in keeping the store stocked, billing credit customers, even paying the store's own bills. He'd never liked any of the minutiae of running his own small business, and after Nellie came on, he'd turned all of it over to her. Thorough and highly organized, Nellie had quickly become indispensable to my father, a woman, as I'd once heard him describe her, "of many talents."

" 'Of many talents,' " Rebecca repeated as she wrote the phrase in her book. "Who did he say that to?"

My own answer surprised me. "My mother."

"So your mother knew about Nellie Grimes?"

I labored to dismiss the disquieting notion that there might have been an edge of cruelty in my father's description of Nellie, as if he were bent upon making the contrast between "poor Dottie" and a woman of "many talents" as painful as he could.

"Well, she knew who Nellie was," I answered casually. "All of us knew who she was, that she was this woman who worked for my father." I shrugged. "But I don't think it occurred to any of us that there might have been something going on between them."

I thought of all the times I'd seen my father and Nellie together, simply standing in one of the store's cluttered aisles, or hunched over Nellie's desk in the back, the two of them trying to straighten out some incongruity in the books. Everything had always looked perfectly normal between them. Neither had ever exhibited the slightest sense of a clandestine relationship, of secret hideaways or kisses stolen behind a potted palm.

"It always seemed like an ordinary, professional relationship," I said.

Rebecca gave me a penetrating look. "Then why did you bring her up?"

"Just as a possibility," I answered, dismissing it at the same time. "Nothing more than that."

But it was more than that.

I knew that it was more because of the force with which Nellie had suddenly returned to me. I hadn't thought of her in years, and yet I saw her exactly as she'd appeared during the time she'd worked for my father.

She was a short, compact woman with curly light brown hair, always neatly dressed, her lips painted a bright, glossy red. She had called me Skipper for some reason, and at the little birthday party my mother threw for me three months before her murder, Nellie gave me a blue captain's cap with a large golden anchor stitched across the front. Her daughter was named May, and at the party she'd stood, looking a bit confused, in a lacy white dress, a small, willowy child with long, blond hair and a vacant look in her light green eyes.

"Why did this woman in particular come to mind, Steve?"

"Opportunity, I suppose," I said. "I mean, they were alone in the store a good deal. It would have been easy for him."

"Would that have been enough for your father to have an affair?" Rebecca asked. "Just that it would have been convenient?"

The word "affair" struck me as an inappropriate one to use in terms of any relationship my father might have had with Nellie. It seemed too worldly and sophisticated a word for either one of them. Had the "affair" existed at all, it would have been carried out in cheap motel rooms off noisy, commercial roads. Or, perhaps, even worse, just a quick, sweaty tumble in the back of the hardware store. As such, it didn't strike me as the sort of thing my father would have done.

"No, I don't think so," I told Rebecca. "Besides, he never struck me as being driven in that way. Toward sex, I mean, just for itself." I thought a moment longer, my father's face returning to me, clothed in the curling smoke that had always seemed to surround him. "Love might have attracted him, though."

"Could your father have gotten that from Nellie Grimes?" Rebecca asked.

I considered Nellie carefully once again, recalling the round face and hazel eyes, the somewhat large and rolling hips, but more important, the buoyancy of her manner, the uncomplicated happiness and jollity that seemed to pour from her, and which was so different from the general gloominess and withdrawal which characterized my mother.

I nodded. "Maybe," I admitted.

My father kept a small army-surplus cot in the back of the store, and for an instant I saw him lying upon it, wrapped in Nellie's somewhat flabby arms, his old gray work clothes stripped away and bundled sloppily in a pile beneath the creaking springs of the old metal cot. It was not a vision I could sustain, however.

I shook my head. "I can't give you any particular reason, Rebecca, but I just don't think my father would have been attracted to Nellie Grimes."

"Do you know what happened to her?" Rebecca asked. "There's no indication in the investigation that she was thought of in connection with the murders."

"Well, she wasn't working at the store when it all happened," I explained. "She'd stopped working for my father by then."

"When did she stop?"

I tried to recall the time exactly, but found that I could come up with only a general approximation. "Toward the end of the summer," I said. "Sometime in the middle of August, I think."

"Do you know why she left?"

"No."

"Do you know where she went?"

"I don't know that either," I said. "But I do remember the last time I saw her."

It had been in the railway station downtown. My father had driven her and May, who was six years old by then, to the train late one summer afternoon, and I had come along with them, May and I bouncing about in the back of the van, along with a varied array of battered old suitcases, while my father and Nellie sat up front, talking quietly.

My father had been dressed in his usual work clothes that day, but Nellie had dolled herself a bit in a black polka-dot dress to which she'd added a round, pillbox hat with a short black net that hung from her forehead to just beneath her upper lip, and which, though long out of style, had given her an unmistakable air of mystery.

Once at the station, my father had lugged the suitcases to the appropriate ramp, then we had all waited for Nellie's train. It had not been long in coming, and during that short interval, my father and

Nellie had smoked cigarettes and talked quietly while May and I darted here and there among the other passengers. I caught none of the conversation that passed between them except, at the very end, as the train was already pulling into the station, its cloud of billowing steam pouring over them, I saw my father take a plain white envelope and press it into Nellie's hand. He said nothing at all, but the look which passed between them at that instant was very beautiful and grave, deeper than a casual farewell.

For a moment, I labored to bring back those two lost faces. I saw my father peering down at Nellie, his large, sad eyes settling delicately upon her as he placed the envelope in her hand, then gently folded her fingers around it. She was staring up at him, pressing her face closer to him as if reaching for his lips. She seemed to strain toward him unconsciously for a moment, then to pull back, instantly aware that he would not bend toward her, not so much as a single, tender inch.

Then she stepped away, bent down to me, lifted the black net from her face, and kissed me softly on the cheek. "Bye, Skipper," she said. She looked at me a moment, then smiled brokenly, and added, "Maybe someday." After that, she quickly grabbed May's hand, and the two of them disappeared into the train. My father and I hoisted the bags on after her, but she was not there to take them from us, and I had the strangest sense that she was just inside the first car, standing with her back pressed against its cold metal wall, crying.

"There might have been something between them," I told Rebecca, "but only on her side, not his."

"So you don't think that second ticket to Mexico could have been for Nellie?"

Because there seemed no other, more likely, candidate, I let myself consider the thought once again, probing at it almost academically, using little bits of logic and deduction to piece together my father's phantom love affair.

Then a chilling thought occurred to me.

If it was true that the two tickets to Mexico had been for my father and Nellie, then what had they planned to do with May?

For an instant, I saw her exactly as I'd seen her that day in the train station, a little girl in a burgundy dress, disappearing into the gloomy, rattling depths of the railway car. A few months later had she died as my mother, Laura, and Jamie had died? In some distant city, perhaps even at the same time, had Nellie Grimes done to her daughter what my father had done to Laura?

From the grim notion of such a murder, it was easy for me to imagine it in all its awesome detail.

I could see May in her room, playing with her doll, a record on the little dark red plastic music box she had carried with her onto the train that day. She was humming along with its scratchy tune while she dressed a pink, rubbery doll whose heavy lids closed each time the head was tilted back. Alone, sitting Indian-style on the checkered quilt that covered her bed, humming to herself while her fingers tugged softly at the doll's little wool dress, she barely looked up as the door to her room crept open and Nellie Grimes stepped into it as if from a cloud of thick gray smoke.

I sat back in my seat, startled by the vividness of

my own imagination, by the way it had driven me toward a firm and uncompromising denial.

"No, that second ticket couldn't have been for Nellie," I said with absolute certainty, "because two tickets would mean that they'd have had to kill May, and I don't believe my father would have had anything to do with such a murder."

Rebecca looked at me cautiously. "You don't think he would have had anything to do with the murder of May Grimes even though he had been willing to kill . . ."

"The rest of us, yes," I said. I shook my head at the absurdity of my own reasoning, but I couldn't rid myself of the notion that, for all he'd done to my mother, Laura, and Jamie, my father would not have brought May Grimes within that murderous circle.

"He wouldn't have killed May," I said again. "He killed us because we'd done something to him. We weren't like May. We weren't . . . innocent."

I stopped, stunned by the hard and unforgiving judgment I had just rendered upon my murdered family. I tried to draw my scattered thoughts into a coherent whole. "It's just that we were unhappy," I said finally, giving up. "Desperately unhappy."

I stopped again, waiting for the next question, but Rebecca knew I'd supply the story anyway.

"I think my mother tried to kill herself once," I said softly, "but I can't be sure." I drew in a long, weary breath, then continued. "It was toward the end of October," I said. "I know because it was the night of the fireworks. It was sort of a village Indian summer celebration. The town had this big festival in October, and we always went together, the whole family."

It had been a clear, unseasonably warm night,

and I was dressed in just a pair of jeans and a T-shirt. The town fireworks display went off at nine, and for a few blazing minutes we'd all watched as the dark sky exploded with brilliant shards of multicolored light. It had lasted for only a short time, certainly no more than ten minutes, and yet, during that interval we'd actually seemed like a family that might endure, taking the days in ordinary stride, weathering the usual storms.

After the fireworks, we went to a local diner, and my father ate quite heartily, which was unusual for him. So unusual, in fact, that it seemed curiously faked, as if he were acting a part, forcing himself to appear less troubled than he was. My mother sat beside him, and from time to time, while Laura and Jamie and I dined on our usual hamburgers and french fries, my mother and father talked quietly to each other.

"We got home around eleven that night, I suppose," I went on. "My mother looked very tired. We all noticed it. Jamie actually took my mother's arm as she got out of the car. Laura saw it, too. After my mother had sat down in the living room, she went into the kitchen and made her a glass of warm milk."

"And your father?"

"He didn't do anything," I said. "He just sat across from my mother until we all went upstairs to bed."

As always, Jamie fell asleep almost instantly. I could hear him snoozing contentedly in the upper bunk. Laura was more high-strung, and that night, like many other nights, I heard her walking about in the room next door long after everyone else had fallen asleep.

But that night, I heard something more than the

familiar sounds of Jamie's breathing and Laura's rustling about in her own room. I heard the door of my mother's bedroom open softly, a tiny squeak I had long ago recognized, but had rarely heard at such a late hour. I got up at once, walked to the door of my room, and opened it. In the corridor, I could see my mother as she came out of her bedroom, then, without turning on the light in the hallway, made her way slowly down the stairs. She was all the way down the stairs before I ventured out of my room. I walked down the same corridor, but stopped at the top of the stairs. From there I could see the light in the downstairs bathroom go on, and hear my mother as she opened the white wooden medicine cabinet that hung above the sink.

"What did you do?" Rebecca asked.

"I waited until she started back up the stairs," I told her. "Then I just went back to my room."

But I didn't fall asleep, and about two hours later, I heard the same squeaking hinge that told me my parents' bedroom door had opened once again. Just like before, I walked to the door of my room, opened it slightly, and looked out. From that position, I could see my mother as she staggered toward the staircase once again. But this time she was weaving unsteadily and moaning softly, her arms wrapped around her stomach.

I started to move toward her, perhaps to help her down the stairs or to wherever it was she was trying to get to that night, but then I saw my father come out of the bedroom. For a moment, he stood very still in the doorway, watching her silently, his light blue eyes glowing, cat-like, in the moonlit hallway. Then, as if in response to a sudden signal, he rushed toward her, gathered her into his arms, and walked her back into their bedroom.

I remained at my door for a long time, but I didn't see either my mother or my father again that night. I could hear my mother coughing and gagging, and I knew that she was in the bathroom that adjoined her room, probably bent over the sink or the toilet. After a while, I returned to my own room and lay down on the lower bunk.

"At the time," I said, "I thought it was just a bad stomach."

Rebecca looked up from her notes. "Why did you ever come to think it might be something else?" she asked.

"Because of what happened the next morning."

I had gotten up early, just at dawn, a little boy needing to go to the bathroom. The light was pouring through the high window to the right of Jamie's desk, and some of it spread out into the hallway when I opened the door and headed for the downstairs bathroom.

It was located to the left of the stairs, just off the kitchen, and when I reached the bottom of the stairs I saw my father working furiously inside its cramped space. He was going through all the drawers of the small cabinet that we used to store such things as toothpaste and extra rolls of toilet paper. The door of the mirrored medicine chest that hung above the small white porcelain sink, and which my mother used to store the family's various medicines, was open. My father had assembled a large number of bottles and plastic pill containers along the rim of the sink, and he was intently reading the labels of each of them in turn, his eyes squinting fiercely as he read. After reading a label, he would either return the container to the medicine chest or drop it into the plain gray shoe box he'd placed on top of the toilet.

"So from all this, you've come to believe that your mother had tried to kill herself that night?" Rebecca asked.

"Yes."

"And that the next morning your father had tried to find out what she'd used so that he could get rid of it?"

I nodded. "Because later that morning, I saw him put the shoe box in his van."

Rebecca scribbled a few notes into her notebook, then glanced up at me. "When did you see your mother again?"

"Later that day," I answered. "She looked very weak. Like an old woman, frail."

But she looked more than weak, more than frail. She looked devastated.

I had arrived home from school just a few minutes earlier and was busily making myself a peanut butter sandwich when I saw her make her way shakily down the stairs. The house was empty save for the two of us. Neither Laura nor Jamie had gotten back home yet, and my father was still at work in the hardware store downtown.

"She must have heard me fiddling around in the kitchen," I told Rebecca. "That's probably why she came down." In my mind, I saw her drag herself down that long flight of stairs, still exhausted and probably in some kind of pain, so that she could say the three barely audible words as she drew herself into the kitchen.

" 'Welcome home, Stevie,' that's what she said to me. That's all she said. Just 'Welcome home, Stevie.' " I shook my head. "Poor Dottie," I said.

"She died in that same old red housedress she wore when she came down to the kitchen that afternoon."

Rebecca's pen stopped dead. "No, she didn't," she said. "She was killed in a regular skirt and blouse."

"She was?"

"Yes," Rebecca said. "Why did you think she'd been wearing the red housedress?"

I shook my head, astonished and a little unnerved by my own weird conjectures. "I don't know why I thought that," I said.

Rebecca watched me with a kind of eerie wariness, as if, perhaps, she already did.

TWELVE

Peter was at the small desk in the den, intently tracing a map, when I got home from my evening with Rebecca. It was part of that night's schoolwork, and he was working at it diligently, as he always did. He barely looked up as I passed, and when he did, a fringe of blond hair fell over his right eye.

"Hi, Dad," he said, then returned to the map.

I nodded toward him as I headed on down the corridor. I could see the light shining in Marie's office, and some part of me wanted to avoid it, to slink up the stairs, away from her increasingly uneasy gaze. But the stairs themselves rested at the end of the corridor. Only a ghost could have made it past her door unseen.

She was behind her desk, as usual, a classical piece playing softly in the background, something I didn't recognize.

"How's it going?" I asked casually as I stopped at her door.

She glanced up and smiled somewhat tiredly. "Fine," she said. She was wearing her reading glasses, but she took them off to look at me thoughtfully for a moment, her face very quiet, one part of it in shadow, the other brightly illuminated by the lamp at her right.

"Everything okay?" I asked.

"I suppose so," Marie answered in a strange, uncertain reply.

"All your projects moving along?"

It clearly struck her as a spiritless question, with an answer neither wanted nor expected, but she did not make an issue of it. Instead, her mind appeared to shift to a more casual concern. "I thought we might call out for a pizza for dinner," she said.

I nodded. "Fine with me."

The thoughtful look returned, studious, concentrated, as if she were trying to read something written on my forehead. "You've been getting home at such odd hours for the past few weeks, it's hard to know exactly when to cook," she said.

I nodded. "We're finishing up a few big drafting jobs at the office," I told her, though she had not asked for any further explanation of my unusual absences.

"Finishing up?" she asked. "So things should be back to normal soon?"

"Yeah, pretty soon."

She smiled, though a little stiffly. "That's good," she said.

"Anything else?" I asked.

The question seemed to strike her as more serious than I had meant it. She looked at me solemnly. "Should there be?"

I shook my head. "Not that I know of."

"Okay," Marie said, but with an unmistakable tone of resignation, as if a chance had been offered, but not taken. Then she reached for the phone, though her eyes never left me. "With anchovies?" she asked, in a voice that sounded unexpectedly sad.

"Yeah, that's fine," I told her, drawing away from the door. "I just need to go wash up."

I walked up the stairs to our bathroom and washed my hands. As I did so, the phrase Marie had used, "back to normal," lingered uncomfortably in my mind. For Marie, it meant the return to a precious predictability and routine. To me, however, it meant the end of something exciting and full of unexpected discovery. As I dried my hands that evening, I felt like a man who'd lived for many years on a deserted island, only to spot, for a single, shining hour, the approach of a long white ship, the dream of rescue growing wildly with each passing moment, until, after an excruciating interval of anticipation, the great ship had drifted once again toward the far horizon, and, at last, disappeared beneath the flat gray of the sea.

"Steve?"

It was Marie calling from downstairs, but I couldn't answer. I stood, as if transfixed by the misty glass of the bathroom mirror.

"Steve, the pizza's here."

The pizza had arrived, and moving as if on automatic pilot, I went downstairs, paid the delivery boy, and brought the large square box into the kitchen.

Peter and Marie gathered around, and I methodically gave each of them a slice, then got one of my own, eating it silently with them at the kitchen table.

Across from me, I could see Peter's blond head lowered over his plate, but I didn't think of him, or of Marie. Instead, I returned to my father.

I saw him in his long silences, in the lair he'd made for himself in the gray basement. I saw him as he watched each of us go through our daily, unexalted lives, and I wondered at the process by which we had been reduced to nothing in his eyes. Nothing, at least, beyond profound intrusions. Had he spent night after night in the house on McDonald Drive, listening mutely to our squabbling, and thought only of how he might be released from us, set free, at last, to go to . . . what?

Was it to his own, still undiscovered version of Rebecca?

Was it the pain of not being with her that he had, at last, found impossible to bear?

It was hard to imagine, and yet I had no choice. I wondered if during the long, drab dinners at our kitchen table, my father had dreamed of a "someone else" while he'd listened absently to our quarreling or our dull school day gossip. Had he dreamed of spiriting her away to his own dream house, a cottage in the hills, perhaps? And each time, had that rapturous vision foundered on the banks of our daily bickering and mundane pettiness?

I remembered that as a child, I'd noticed moments when my father had stared vacantly out the window or sat in isolation in the little, vine-draped solarium. Perhaps, on those occasions, he'd let himself be carried away by the intensity of his need.

I also saw him in his van, staring at my mother as she crouched over her flower bed, and I marveled at how easily I could put Marie in the place of "poor Dottie," how easily I could shrink her down to a small, dry pebble.

Later that same night, as I walked out into the backyard, my feet trudging through the dry, steadily accumulating leaves, I thought again of how lost my father had looked as he'd sat alone in the brown van.

I saw his face, deep-lined and webbed in misery, but with a terrible edge of purpose within it, his eyes shining through the smoke, cold and without pupils, mere round, ice-blue orbs.

After a time, I returned to the house. I watched television with Peter, then chatted with Marie for a few minutes after he had gone to bed, a dull conversation which appeared to annoy her after a while, so that she finally marched up the stairs and went to bed.

I went to my office, sat down at my desk, and began to add a few passionate but unreal lines to my "dream house." The house had become even more vague and insubstantial during the last few weeks, with turrets and towers and unsupported balconies, a house that could exist only in a world that had forsaken gravity, along with all the other laws that govern earthbound things.

It was the phone that finally interrupted me. I picked it up, and to my immense surprise, it was Rebecca.

There was something urgent in her voice, and for a moment I allowed myself the fantasy that she had been seized by the same deep yearning for me that I had so long felt for her.

"It's me," she said.

"Yes, I know."

"I won't be able to meet with you on Wednesday afternoon. I have to check on a few things."

I could clearly hear her reluctance to say more. I could also hear the sound of engines in the background, the rustle of passing voices.

"You're at the railway station," I said.

"No, the bus station," she said. "I'm going to Somerset. To see Swenson."

"When will you be back?"

"By Saturday."

"So we can meet at the usual time that day?"

"Maybe a little later, if that's all right," she said. "I'll let you know." I heard a pneumatic door as it opened. The strain returned to Rebecca's voice. "I've got to go," she said. "My bus is leaving."

Then she hung up.

The phone was still in my hand when Marie came to the door. She was dressed in a sleek, white sleeping gown, her hair in disarray.

"Who was that?" she asked drowsily.

I said the first name that occurred to me. "Wally," I told her.

She seemed to awaken suddenly, the veil of sleep dissolved. She looked at me, puzzled. "So late?" She glanced at the clock which hung on the wall to her left. "It's past midnight."

I shrugged. "He just wanted to talk about a problem we'd run into earlier today."

She smiled, but distantly. "I didn't think Wally ever cared that much about anything at work."

She knew him well, and she was right. Wally had never been the type to give his work a second thought once he'd left the office. He'd been a bad choice, but I was stuck with him.

"He's been a little more concerned with things lately," I said. "Maybe he's a little worried, too."

"About what?"

"I don't know," I said with a shrug. "Mr. Lowe's opinion of him, I guess."

Marie smiled at the mention of Mr. Lowe's name, a quiet, respectful smile.

"Anyway, we straightened it all out," I added quickly.

"Good," Marie said. She looked at me softly. "So, are you coming to bed soon?"

"It won't be long," I assured her.

She nodded and drew herself back out into the corridor. "Good night, then," she said as she disappeared into its darkness.

I sat back in my chair and let my eyes settle on the telephone. Marie had already vanished from my mind, but merely by staring at the phone I could all but feel Rebecca's breath still surging toward me through its stiff black lines.

I got up early the next morning. While still in bed, I reached up and touched my face. I could feel the scratchy texture of my morning beard, and it reminded me of the dream I'd had a few weeks before, a dream of waking up in a place I didn't recognize, a small room with an old sink and a battered armoire. I remembered the short white curtains and the warm, tropical breeze that had lifted them languidly, revealing a rust-colored landscape of tiled roofs and dark spires.

A few minutes later, I walked downstairs. Everything in my house, I realized, looked old and encrusted, and had lost its power of attraction. It was a feeling which Rebecca had already begun to explore. "For these men, perhaps, for all men," as she finally wrote, "the sense of permanence in human relations rarely issues a truly romantic call, rarely speaks in thrilling whispers or attains the electrifying jolt of a lover's voice." The capacity to imbue long and enduring relations with just that kind of highly charged romanticism, she added, "was the single greatest achievement of the female imagination."

Whether true or not of all men, Rebecca's insight was true enough of me. For it was undoubtedly the "thrilling whisper" rather than the "sense of permanence" that I wanted as I stood among all the things and people who'd gathered around my life.

"You tossed a lot in bed last night," Marie said as she came down the stairs.

I gave her a weak smile. "I've got a lot on my mind," I told her. I didn't add anything else, but merely allowed her to assume that my recent agitation was related only to my work, that there was nothing growing in me that she should fear.

Peter came bounding down the stairs a few minutes later. He wolfed down the cereal Marie had poured into the bowl, then headed out to the driveway for a couple of hoop shots before he left for school. I could see him playing happily in the sun as he leaped about the cement driveway, ducking and swooping, pretending that the opposite team was closing in upon him.

"You know, he's a pretty good basketball player," I said as Marie rose and headed for the stairs.

She turned toward me and smiled weakly. "Like his dad was," she said, almost wistfully, as if remembering the former life of a loved one who had already died.

She was still upstairs when I left the house a few minutes later. I passed Peter on the way to my car, stopped to make a couple of shots, then drove away. In the rearview mirror I could see his hair shining in the early morning sun.

I arrived at my office a few minutes later. I had barely gotten to my desk when Wally stepped up to it.

He smiled brightly and slapped me on the shoulders. "You got lucky, old chap," he said.

"What do you mean?"

"I have to go into New York today, and Mr. Lowe told me to take you along."

"To do what?"

"I'm delivering the latest drawings on the Global Apartments project," Wally told me. "Old Man Lowe thinks you should be there in case there are any questions."

Normally I would have dreaded such a trip. My love was drawing in my private cubicle, the seclusion of creating isolated forms. I hated meetings of all kinds, especially client meetings. But that day such a ride into the city struck me as a respite, a way of regaining the strength which had been drained from me during the night.

We took the old U.S. 1 rather than the highway, moving through shady Connecticut villages until we reached the crowded suburbs of New York. Wally drove in his usual style, casually, with his arm slung out the open window. He was about twenty pounds overweight, and his reddish hair had thinned considerably since the days he and Marty Harmon and I had first worked together at Simpson and Lowe, but there was still a raw and vulgar boyishness about him, a quality that appeared to attract some people as much as it repelled others. The young secretaries often flirted with him openly, while the older ones, married or looking toward marriage, thought him a pathetic clown.

That day, as we drove through the bright, still summery, air, Wally lit one cigarette after another, often bobbing the lighted tips wildly as he spoke. He related tales of his various jobs, his youth, finally his travels, either alone on business trips, or with his wife and family.

"You don't get out much, do you, Steve?" he asked at one point. "Out of Old Salsbury, I mean."

"Not much."

"When was the last time you were in New York?"

"Years ago. I can hardly remember."

Wally shrugged, letting the subject drop.

I thought of the night before, the excuse I'd made to Marie about Rebecca's call.

"Listen, Wally," I said as we headed through the last stretch of road that led into the city, "if Marie ever mentions anything about my getting a call from you late last night, I . . ."

Wally's eyes shot over to me. "You need an alibi, Steve? Someone to cover for you?"

"Well, it's just that last night . . ."

"She called, right?" Wally said with a slow smile. "She always does, in the end."

"Who does?"

"The other woman," Wally said flatly. "She always says she'll never call you at home, but she always does."

"This was a little different," I said quickly.

Wally looked at me pointedly. "It couldn't have been too different," he said, "or you wouldn't have had to lie about it, would you, old buddy?"

He was right, of course. But only partly right. For though Rebecca was not my lover in any technical sense, she had come to represent one: the flight from life's heaviness, the possibility of escape.

"So is it love?" Wally asked lightly.

I didn't answer.

Wally's smile broadened. He didn't press the question, but settled instead for a different one. "It's the woman who came to see you in the office that day, am I right?"

I nodded faintly, reluctantly.

"Whew!" Wally said, pretending to wipe a line of sweat from his forehead. "Hot, hot, hot."

I watched the road, adding nothing, feeling neither shame nor the absence of shame, but only the disquieting sense that I had cheapened the nature of my own feeling for Rebecca by being unable to explain it.

"Does she live in Old Salsbury?" Wally asked.

"A little ways outside it."

"Do you see her a lot?"

"Not too often."

Wally shrugged. "Well, just tell her to ease up on the old home phone, you know?" he said. Then he grinned impishly, one worldly man to another. "Either that, or keep me well-informed in case . . ." He stopped. "What's your wife's name?"

"Marie," I said.

Wally nodded briskly, then finished his sentence. "In case Marie calls me up sometime to find out where the hell you are."

"She'd never do that," I assured him. "She'd never try to track me down."

"Don't kid yourself, buddy," Wally said. "If she starts really chewing at it, she'll track you down all right."

I shook my head. "No, she wouldn't," I told him. "She'd rather die first."

Suddenly I felt my eyes grow cool and vacant, and there must have been something in my voice, because I felt the car veer to the right, then come to a noisy halt along the bank of the road. I turned toward Wally. He was staring at me worriedly.

"Whoa, now, buddy," he said.

I glanced at him quickly, defensively, as if some part of a secret plot had been uncovered.

"You look a little weird, Steve," Wally added. He reached over and squeezed my shoulder. "You don't want to let things get out of hand, you know?"

"What do you mean?"

"With this woman," Wally said, "the one who's fucking your mind." He looked at me pointedly, giving me his best advice. "You don't want to burn the house down, you know?"

"Burn the house down?"

He smiled indulgently. "The first time a woman comes flying into things, it really jerks your tail into a knot, I know," he said. "But then, when that one's gone, another one comes along, and after two or three times like that, you realize that it's all just fun and games, that there's no need to get all knotted up about it."

I shook my head. "It's not like that with me," I told him. "It's not just fun and games."

He laughed at my boyish innocence. "So, I guess you're one of these men that has to take it seriously, right?" he asked.

I didn't answer. I had no answer.

Wally watched me soberly. "Listen, Steve, you can play around with this woman, have your fun and all that, but when it's all over, you need to go home and warm your feet at the same old fire." He waited for me to answer. "I'm talking about your wife, Steve."

"Marie," I said, but my voice was little above a whisper.

Wally gave me a penetrating look. "You have to be careful and not get things mixed up, that's what

I'm saying." He paused a moment, his eyes watching me closely. "When they get mixed up, bad things can happen," he added darkly. "Remember Marty Harmon?"

I nodded silently.

"He was one of these men that couldn't keep things straight," Wally told me firmly, "and look what happened to him."

Suicide, of course, had "happened" to Marty, but it had never occurred to me that I was in the least like him, or that I might ever reach such a state of physical and spiritual exhaustion. It wasn't death I wanted, it was a different life.

The realization that swept over me at that instant was as close as I had ever come to a full understanding of how far I had been swept out to sea, of how deep my discontent actually was.

"I can't go back," I muttered weakly.

"To wherever you were before this woman, you mean?" Wally asked. "Of course you can."

I shook my head slowly.

Wally leaned toward me, his eyes intent, troubled. "Listen, I'm trying to give you some advice, Steve," he said sharply. "I gave Marty the same advice, and he didn't take it either." He stopped, looked at me very severely for a moment, then added, "I mean, you don't want to end up like . . ." He stopped again. "I mean, when your father . . ."

I stared at Wally, stunned not so much that he would make a connection between me and my father, as that he would actually say it to my face.

"I don't even remember who told me about it," Wally said, his voice softer now, conciliatory, "and, believe me, I don't mean . . ."

"That I could murder my family?" I asked harshly.

"No, no, no, no. I would never have said that, Steve," Wally answered. "It's just that when you see a man hurting, well, you see a man who might lose control." He shrugged. "I just keep remembering Marty, you know? He wasn't a bad guy. He was just a guy that got it all screwed up."

"I'm not Marty Harmon," I said firmly. "And I'm not my father either."

Wally looked at me quietly, resigned that there would be no point in continuing the conversation. "Okay, Steve," he said at last, "we'll just drop it, okay?"

"Yeah, let's do."

With that, Wally edged the car back onto the road and drove on silently. We never spoke seriously again, nor did he ever mention my father, my family, or even the unknown woman he has no doubt come to blame for their destruction.

Now, when I remember that afternoon, I think of it as the last chance I had to save us all. I knew that Rebecca was leaving, that her study was very nearly done, that very, very soon my life would go "back to normal," with nights at home with Peter and Marie, days at work, summer visits to that very lake along whose bank Rebecca's cottage still rested in a grove of trees.

So what would have been missing in a life lived like that? Certainly not love, as Marie was soon to tell me. Certainly not comfort. There would have been no ignominy in my return to normal.

What would have been missing? The mythical dream house without walls or firm foundation. The thrill of awakening in an unknown country, the exhilaration of an endless setting forth. Surprise. The allure of the unexplored. And finally, love, at its sharpest instant, the moment when it fuses with desire.

Much would have been missing.

But not everything.

THIRTEEN

Rebecca returned to Old Salsbury the following day just as she'd said she would. It was a Saturday, but I wasn't at home when she called. Neither was Marie. It was Peter who answered, then later gave me the message.

"A woman called," he said. "She asked for you. She left her name and number."

He'd written it down on a small square of white paper, which he handed to me dutifully.

I glanced at the paper, pretending that I didn't recognize the name he'd written in large block letters beside the number: REBECCA.

"Did she say what she wanted?" I asked casually.

Peter shook his head. "She just wanted you to call her back, I guess." He shrugged and darted away.

A few seconds later, as I sat at my desk, dialing Rebecca's number, I saw his lean body as it darted across the backyard and disappeared around a tall, nearly leafless tree.

She answered immediately.

"It's me," I said.

"Yes, hi," Rebecca said. "I just wanted to let you know that I'd gotten back to town."

"Was it a worthwhile trip?"

"Yes." Her voice seemed to tighten somewhat. "There were some new developments."

"I'm surprised to hear that. I thought you already knew everything."

"Sometimes it's just a question of one thing leading to another."

"Well, what did you . . ."

"Not now," Rebecca interrupted quickly. "We'd planned to meet today. Can you make it in the evening? Say, around seven?"

"All right."

"Okay, see you then," Rebecca said as she hung up.

I held the receiver for a moment, almost as if it were her hand. I felt it cool, then let it go, and walked out into the backyard and stood beside the covered pool.

Peter was poised on the other side. He smiled a moment, then lifted his arms until his fingers touched. He held himself suspended in that position for a moment, pretending he was about to dive onto the broad black tarpaulin that stretched across the now empty pool.

"Good form," I said. "You look like a real pro."

He seemed pleased by my attention. "They're teaching us at school," he said. Then he ran over to me, his blond head bobbing left and right.

"What if there were water in the pool," he said, "and one time I started to drown?"

"I'd come in after you."

"What if there were sharks in the water?"

"I'd come in after you," I repeated.

He smiled broadly, then dashed away again, this time around the far corner of the house.

Marie returned an hour later. She looked tired as she got out of the car and headed toward the house. From my place in the den, I could see her move wearily up the stairs that led to the kitchen and disappear inside the house. I expected her to join me, but she never did, and so, after a time, I went to look for her. She was not in her office, so I went upstairs.

I found her in our bedroom, lying faceup on her side of the bed, her arms folded neatly over her chest. She'd kicked off her shoes, but otherwise she remained in the same formal business clothes she'd worn to New Haven earlier in the day. A bright shaft of light fell over her from the parted curtains, and I could see small bits of dust floating weightlessly in the flooding light.

"How'd it go?" I asked.

She did not open her eyes. "Not great. They didn't like some of the designs."

"They never like them in the beginning," I told her. "They have to be critical at the first presentation; otherwise they feel like they're being led by the nose."

Marie took a deep breath, then let it out slowly. "I'm tired," she said.

"It was a long day," I said, "the drive alone, you know?"

She opened her eyes and gazed at me softly. "Let's go out to dinner tonight, Steve," she said, almost plaintively, as if asking a favor, "just you and me." She smiled. "We could use a night out, don't you think?"

It was a simple request, not much asked nor expected, and yet I couldn't grant it. Rebecca would be waiting for me at her cottage. It was to her that I had to go.

I shook my head. "I can't, Marie," I said. "I have to go into the office."

Her eyes narrowed. "On a Saturday night?"

"It's the final meeting on that library," I said. "I have to finish the designs."

She looked at me doubtfully. "On a Saturday night?" she said again.

"I'm supposed to be at the office by seven," I told her. "Wally's coming in, along with a few guys from the drafting department. We're going to work through the night if we have to."

Her eyes lingered on me a moment, then she turned away and closed them again. "You'd better start getting ready then," she said. "It's almost six."

I walked over to the bed and sat down beside her. "I have a little time," I said.

She didn't answer, but only continued to lie stiffly beside me.

I touched her cheek with the side of my hand.

She drew her face away instantly. "No, no," she said, a little brusquely, "I want to rest."

I stood up and walked into the adjoining bathroom. Once there, I showered and dressed myself. Marie was still lying on the bed when I came back into the bedroom. She didn't stir as I left her, didn't so much as open her eyes.

Peter was in the family room when I got downstairs.

"Why are you all dressed up?" he asked, as I stepped in to say good-bye.

"I have to go into the office," I said.

"When will you be back?"

"Not until late. There's a lot to do."

He smiled jokingly. "So I guess I shouldn't wait up for you, huh?"

I shook my head. "No, I don't think so." I waved good-bye, then headed outside.

I'd already backed the car nearly halfway toward the street when I glanced back toward the house. I could see the gray eye of the television as it glowed dimly toward me from the shaded window of the family room. It gave me the eerie sense of being watched, and so I let my eyes retreat from it, drifting upward, along a wall of brick and mortar, until our bedroom came into view and I saw Marie standing at the window, watching me from afar. For a single, delicate moment, we stared mutely at each other, two faces peering outward, it seemed to me, from two different worlds. Then, her eyes still gazing at me with the same penetrating force, she lifted her arms very gracefully, like the wingspread of a great bird, grasped the separate edges of the bedroom curtains, and slowly drew them together. They were still weaving slightly as I let the car drift on down the driveway and out into the street.

"Hi, Steve," Rebecca said as she opened the door. She stepped aside to let me pass.

I took a chair not far from the window. Outside, I could see the still gray surface of the lake. It looked like a sheet of slate.

Rebecca took the chair opposite me, so that we faced each other directly, as if we were about to begin some kind of intensely demanding game.

"We're close to the end, I think."

Something in my face must have puzzled her, because for a moment she stopped and regarded me closely. "We've gone through each member of your family," she explained, "and their relationships."

I nodded but said nothing.

"There are things I'll never know, of course," she added. "Your father still seems very mysterious to me."

"My father," I repeated softly. Curiously, I suddenly thought of him almost as a rival for her attention, a dark, majestic figure whose profound experience of life and death utterly dwarfed the humdrum banality of my own.

I felt the need to bring him down. "Are you sure he's worth knowing any more than you already do?"

"Yes, I am."

"But you're sure he fits your criteria, aren't you?" I asked. "You're sure that Nellie Grimes, for example, had nothing to do with the murders."

She nodded. "Yes, I'm sure of that," she answered.

"You found her, didn't you?" I said. "You found Nellie."

She shook her head. "Not exactly. Nellie Grimes died eight years ago. But I found her daughter, May. She lives not far from Somerset."

"How did you find her?"

"Through Swenson."

"I thought he hadn't known anything about Nellie."

"He's never mentioned her to me, that's true," Rebecca told me, "but only because he'd never thought of her as actually connected to the case." She paused a moment, then went on. "After the murders, Swenson talked to a lot of people who'd known your father. He was trying to get some idea of where he might have gone after the murders. One of the people he talked to was Grimes." She reached into her briefcase and handed me a picture of a woman standing on a small wooden porch. "She was living in Hoboken," she went on. "Swenson remembered seeing May playing in the backyard despite the drizzle. He said her dress was muddy, and that her hair was wet and stringy, but that Nellie didn't seem to care."

It was hard to imagine May in such a state, or her mother's indifference to it. In all my other memories of them, they'd been dressed as well as they could afford to be, always neat and clean, as if waiting to be put upon display.

"Nellie Grimes was not doing very well at that point," Rebecca added.

"What did she say about my father?"

"She said that he'd always been very kind to her," Rebecca answered, "and that he'd given her some money when she'd left Somerset."

In my mind I saw the envelope pass from my father's hand to Nellie's.

"She also told Swenson that she didn't believe your father had killed his family," Rebecca added.

"Then who did?"

Rebecca shrugged. "She only said that she was sure it was someone else," she said. "Then Swenson asked her directly if your father might have been involved with another woman, and she said absolutely not. She told him that she knew for a fact that your father was not that kind of man."

I remembered the way Nellie's face had lifted toward my father that day in the train station, and I suspected that it had lifted toward him in just that same tempting way many times before. In isolated places, no doubt, where no one could have seen him answer to the intensity of such a call, but he'd drawn back on those occasions, too, resolutely, with his own unfathomable pride.

Rebecca looked at me as if she expected me to contradict her, then added, "May also had a very high opinion of your father."

"But she was just a child," I said. "What could she have known about him?"

"Actually, she remembered him quite well," Rebecca said. "Very clearly, even down to the gray work clothes he always wore."

For a moment it struck me as intimate knowledge, and I felt a strange resentment toward May Grimes, as if she'd usurped my place as the sole surviving witness.

"How would she have known anything about my father?" I asked.

"May evidently spent a lot of time in the hardware store," Rebecca continued. "There was no place for her to go after school, so she played in the back room. Sometimes your father would come back there and try to entertain her a little." She smiled. "May remembered that he bought her a Chinese checkers set and that they used to sit on the floor and play together."

I could not bring the image to mind very easily, my father sitting on the bare cement floor with a little girl, playing Chinese checkers, trying to help her pass the long boring hours of a winter afternoon.

"She remembered something else," Rebecca said, the tone of her voice changing. "They were playing together one afternoon. May thinks it was just a few weeks before the day your father took her and her mother to the train station." She paused a moment, as if hesitant to go on. "They were alone in the back room," she continued finally. "May had been staring at the board, making her next move. When she finished it, she looked up and noticed your father staring at her. She said he looked different, very sad. She asked him if there was anything wrong. He didn't answer exactly. He only said, 'This is all I want.' "

I felt my skin tighten, but said nothing.

Rebecca watched me cautiously, gauging my mood. "I remembered you telling me that he'd said the same thing to you."

"In exactly the same words." I shook my head helplessly, my father's mystery still as dense as it had ever been. "What was going on in him?" I asked, though very softly, a question directed toward myself as much as toward Rebecca.

Rebecca, however, actually offered an answer. "At that point, when he said that to you in the basement," she said, "he was probably very depressed."

I could see that she was leading into something.

"Depressed about what?"

"Well, he'd finalized his plan by then, of course," she said. "He'd canceled the two plane tickets, for example." She looked at me significantly. "He did that on October 10."

I knew then that the "new developments" she'd mentioned on the phone earlier had to do with those two mysterious plane tickets. She'd tracked down their enigmatic meaning and was about to lay her findings before me like a parting gift.

"Why did he cancel those tickets?" I asked. "You know, don't you?"

Rebecca leaned forward, settling her eyes on me with a deep, probing gaze. "You remember the night before you came home from the Cape? You saw your father and mother talking together, and he had his arm around her."

"That's right."

"And the next night, the night the family got back to Somerset, you saw your father and Laura beside the fence in the backyard."

I nodded.

"You said that they looked as if they were engaged in a very serious conversation," Rebecca went on. "Then later, you saw them come up the stairs, and it was at that point that you heard a few words pass between them."

"That's right."

Rebecca drew her black notebook from the briefcase. "I want to be sure I have this exactly right." She flipped through the notebook until she found the page she wanted. "This is what you heard," she said. Then she quoted it: "Your father: 'Tomorrow.' Laura: 'So soon?' Your father: 'Yes.' " She looked up. "The 'tomorrow' that your father mentioned would have been September 3."

"Yes."

"Let me ask you again: do you remember anything about that morning?" Rebecca asked.

I tried to recall it, but it remained a blur of activity. My mother had prepared the usual breakfast of cereal and toast, and after eating, Laura, Jamie, and I had all gone back upstairs to finish getting ready for school. The only thing that seemed different was the fact that my father had still been at home when we'd all left the house about a half hour later.

"My father stayed home that morning," I said to Rebecca. "He usually left before we did, but that morning, he didn't." I drifted back to that day again, but only far enough to regain one last, minuscule detail. "He was sitting at the kitchen table as I passed," I added. "I was racing for the door, you know, excited to be going back to school, but he shot his hand out, grabbed my arm, and stopped me. 'Kiss your mother good-bye, Stevie,' he said. And so I did."

Rebecca looked as if I'd just confirmed something that had only been a conjecture before.

"He'd never asked me to do that before."

"And then you went to school just like always?" Rebecca asked.

I nodded. "Yes, we all went together. Well, at least Laura and I did. Jamie always went ahead of us."

"Did you and Laura talk about anything in particular that morning?"

"No," I said. "We just walked to school like always. She left me at my school, then walked on to hers, about three blocks down the road."

"When did you see Laura again?"

"She was waiting at the corner for me right after school," I said. "She always did that."

For a moment, as I remembered her standing on the corner waiting for me that afternoon, her books in her arms, her long dark hair falling over her shoulders, I felt her loss again, but this time with a piercing depth, as if all the conversations I might have had with her in life, all the good and comforting times we might have had together, had suddenly swept over me in a great wave of imagined days. I saw us share all that we had not been allowed to share, the keenest experiences of adulthood, marriage, parenthood, the approach of middle age, all that my father had abruptly and mysteriously canceled as surely as he'd canceled those two plane tickets to Mexico.

"I loved my sister," I said, though barely above a whisper. "And I think she loved me."

Rebecca's next question came at me like a slap in the face. "And Jamie," she asked, "did you love him?"

I answered without hesitation. "No."

"Did anyone in the family love him?"

"I don't think so," I answered. "He always seemed alone."

Alone in his bunk, alone at his desk, alone beneath the tree in the backyard, always alone.

"So Jamie never waited for you after school?" Rebecca asked.

"No, only Laura did that," I answered. "She was always there, waiting on the corner, just like she was that first day of school."

Despite the warmth of the weather, as I recalled then, the first leaves of autumn had already begun to drift down upon us. I saw them fall slowly, but thickly, as Laura and I made our way down Ontario Street, and I felt a great sadness settle upon me, like the leaves.

"The leaves were falling," I said to Rebecca. "They were very red."

But they could not have been red, I realized. I was not thinking of leaves. I was thinking of my sister's death, and Jamie's and my mother's. I was thinking of their thickly falling blood.

"Did you and your sister talk much on the way home that afternoon?" Rebecca asked.

"Not that I recall."

"You walked silently, all the way home?"

Something came back vaguely, a tiny detail. "No, I don't think we walked all the way home together that day," I said slowly, unsure. "I think she went into Oscar's, that little convenience store on the corner."

Rebecca looked at me doubtfully. "Why would you remember that?" she asked.

"Because it was so unusual," I answered. "But I do remember it now."

I saw Laura turn to me, felt her hand release mine. "Go on home, Stevie," she said. "I'll be there in a minute." Then she walked away, moving slowly toward the convenience store, and finally disappearing inside of it. As I headed home, I saw her standing by the window, her eyes fixed on me, as if she were waiting for me to leave.

"So you walked the rest of the way home by yourself?" Rebecca asked.

I nodded. "Laura told me to go on home without her, and so I did."

"Was Jamie home when you got there?" Rebecca asked.

"No," I said. I could feel it returning to me slowly, a picture of that afternoon. "No one was home," I added, "not even my mother."

It had never occurred to me before, but for the first and only time I could remember, my mother had not been at home when I arrived from school. I had returned to an empty house.

"I was alone in the house for a while," I said, "then Laura arrived, and Jamie a few minutes after that."

Jamie had gone directly to our room, but Laura had walked into the solarium instead. Later, when I'd approached her, skipping jauntily across the living room carpet, she'd looked up at me fiercely, and snapped, "Stop it, Stevie." Then she'd turned away, letting her eyes drift out toward the empty street.

"Laura was not in a very good mood that afternoon," I told Rebecca. "I could tell that something was bothering her."

Rebecca glanced down at her notebook. "When did your mother get home?"

"Soon after the rest of us, I guess," I told her. Then I remembered something else. "My father brought her. They came home in his van."

Once again an odd certainty swept into Rebecca's face. She leaned forward and began to dig through the briefcase, finally withdrawing several sheets of paper. It looked like a report of some kind, very official, with all the pages stapled together in the left-hand corner.

"This is the autopsy report on your mother," she said. "I had never read it because the cause of her death was so obvious." She flipped back the first two pages. "But while I was with Swenson yesterday, he made an aside about your mother being 'doomed anyway.' " She lifted the report toward me. "When I asked him what he meant, he gave me this."

She'd already turned to the page that mattered. She'd even underlined the relevant passage. I read it, then handed the report back to her, dazed.

"She had a brain tumor," I said, astonished. "Is that why she tried to kill herself?"

Rebecca nodded. "Probably."

I saw my mother as I'd seen her that night, trudging wearily down the stairs, shoulders bowed, head down, a single shaky hand gripping the wooden banister. How alone she must have felt at that moment, how sealed within a black solitude.

"Your mother's doctor told Swenson that your mother had come in for an X-ray examination on

September 3, and that your father had come with her," Rebecca said.

"September 3," I said, laboring to make those connections I was certain Rebecca had already made. "So when my father and Laura had that conversation by the fence the night we got back from the Cape, he was telling her that my mother was sick, and that she was going for an examination the next day?"

"Probably," Rebecca said. She looked back down at her notebook, read a few pages to herself, then glanced back up at me. "The doctor said that your mother arrived on schedule for her appointment. He remembered that your father brought her in, and that later, when the examination was over, he came to pick her up."

"Yes, he brought her home that afternoon," I told her.

Rebecca seemed hardly to hear me. "Over the next few weeks the doctor had several conversations with your father," she went on. "The kind of conversations male doctors had with men in those days."

"What do you mean?"

Rebecca seemed surprised by the question, as if any further explanation should have been unnecessary. "Well, in certain cases a doctor and the husband of a female patient would get together to decide just how much a wife should know."

"And so this doctor, he talked to my father about my mother's illness, but not to her?"

"Yes," Rebecca said. "According to Swenson's case notes, the doctor told your father that your mother's tumor was inoperable, and after that, they discussed quite a few alternatives. The doctor called several specialists in the field. He got back answers that weren't very encouraging."

"I see."

"And finally, on October 10, the doctor told your father that there was nothing that could be done," Rebecca said, "that your mother was going to die." Her eyes drifted down to her notebook, then back up to me. "The two tickets to Mexico City were canceled that same afternoon."

The realization swept over me like a lifting breeze. "So the second ticket was for my mother," I said. "He'd planned to take her away at some point, a surprise vacation, something like that."

Rebecca nodded. "There was no other woman, Steve."

For a brief interval, I thought it all over again, everything Rebecca had just revealed. There was still something that didn't fit, and after a moment, I realized what it was.

"But when we were unloading the car the night we got back from Cape Cod, and Laura started complaining about my mother, my father snapped at her, remember? He said, 'You should know.' "

Rebecca looked at me without expression.

"And Laura went up to my mother's room and sat down on the bed beside her and put her arm around her."

Rebecca nodded.

"Well, my father couldn't have meant that Laura should know about my mother's illness," I said, "because Laura couldn't have known about it that night. She hadn't been told yet."

"Probably not," Rebecca admitted.

"But she went up to my mother's room anyway," I added. "So she must have known something."

Rebecca glanced down at her notes, as if expecting to find an answer there.

"And if my mother was already dying, why did my father bother to kill her?" I asked.

Rebecca sighed. "There's still something missing, isn't there? Swenson thought so, too. He never thought it all added up. He never found a motive."

"A reason for my father to have done it, you mean?"

"Yes."

"Well, that's what you're still looking for, isn't it?"

Rebecca stared at me in earnest. "I know what it was in all these other men," she said, "but I'm still not sure about your father."

I said nothing, but only looked past her, out toward the lake. Night had nearly fallen by then, but beyond the water, I could still make out a dark line of thunderclouds as they rumbled in from the west.

"Motive is everything," Rebecca said, though only to herself. "There's no question that your father did it. His fingerprints were all over the shotgun. There were no other fingerprints." She thought a moment longer, then glanced toward me. "The only question is why?"

I continued to watch the wall of dark gray clouds as it closed in upon us. My father's face swam into my mind, then dissolved almost instantly, a figment, an enigma.

"It may rain tonight," I said softly, as if to avoid any further inquiry into the foggy labyrinth of his mind.

Rebecca nodded. "It was raining that day in November," she said thoughtfully. Her mind seemed to latch on to an unexpected possibility. "Maybe something happened that day in particular. Maybe something happened that brought it all together."

"And sent my father over the edge, you mean?"

"Yes."

I remembered the changing faces of my father, those features that slowly descended from the joy of his wedding day to the bleakness with which he'd stared toward my mother from the smoke-filled cab of the old brown van.

"I don't think so," I told Rebecca. "I don't think something just happened that day, something out of the blue, that caused my father to pick up that shotgun."

Rebecca nodded. "No, probably not," she said. Then she pulled a single sheet of yellow paper from her briefcase. "All right," she said, "let's start again. Let's start from October 10, the day your father learned that your mother was dying. We'll go from there to the end."

I said nothing, but merely waited for her to guide me back toward that day, as I knew she'd always planned to do.

"Your mother was dying," Rebecca began. "How did things change in the family because of that?"

"I never knew she was dying," I told her. "No one ever told me. And I don't think Jamie knew, either."

"Why do you think that?"

"Because he was the same old Jamie up until the moment my father murdered him," I said. "He was always up in his room, always alone. Nothing changed with Jamie."

"So you don't think he ever found out about your mother?"

"I don't think so," I said. "He certainly never changed in his attitude toward her."

"What was his attitude?"

"That she was a maid," I said, "someone who washed clothes, cooked meals, vacuumed up that gray grime that my father was always tracking up from the basement."

"That's the only way Jamie saw your mother?"

"More or less. I don't think he gave her much thought."

Rebecca wrote my observations down in her notebook, then glanced up again. "Do you think Laura ever knew just how serious your mother's illness was?"

"Oh, yes, of course she did," I said.

I saw my sister in the solarium once again, sitting sullenly in the wicker chair as she had that September afternoon, snapping at me to "stop it," without adding what must have been the final, unsaid portion of that sentence: "Don't you know your mother's sick, don't you know she may be dying!"

"Laura looked quite upset the afternoon before my mother came home," I told Rebecca. "And after that, for the next few days, she looked very strange." I shrugged. "At the time, I couldn't have known what was bothering her, but I did notice that she seemed . . ." I stopped, searching for the right word. "She seemed dazed," I said finally, "like she couldn't quite figure out what to do, how to handle it."

"Did she treat your mother differently after that?"

"Yes," I said. "For a time, she treated her much more gently."

Rebecca's eyes narrowed questioningly. "What do you mean, 'for a time'?"

Even though it had been my own phrase, it struck me as being almost purposely vague, just as it had clearly struck Rebecca as being so.

"Well, for the first few weeks, Laura was very gentle and helpful," I explained.

It was easy for me to recall all the little gestures of kindness my sister had made toward my mother during that brief time. She'd helped her in the kitchen, gone shopping with her on Saturday afternoons, and had been generally more tender toward her than she'd ever been.

"But that kindness didn't continue?" Rebecca asked.

"No, it didn't," I said. "It lasted for a few weeks, more or less until my mother tried to kill herself."

"How did it change after that?"

"Laura seemed to withdraw from her," I said. "From my father, too. At about the same time."

"That would have been around the middle of October, then?"

I nodded.

"Jamie was the only one who stayed the same during all those weeks," I added, then thought a bit more of it, remembering how often he'd begun to bait my mother, too, as if one target were no longer enough for his steadily building spitefulness and anger. "Actually, I think he got a little worse," I said. "He was sharp with my mother during those last weeks, but he also began to pull away entirely. From all of us, I mean. It was as if he couldn't stand being in the same house with us anymore."

Growing more sullen with each day, bitter in

what must have been a terrible, homebound loneliness, I remembered that Jamie had begun to absent himself almost entirely from the family during the last weeks of our time on McDonald Drive. He'd never joined us in the little den anymore, or even gone on those rare family outings to the drive-in movies. Instead, he'd sealed himself in his room, remaining there for hours at a time, coming down only to eat quickly, and after that, trudging up the stairs again.

"Toward the end," I told Rebecca, "Jamie was just a face in the hallway or on the other side of the dinner table. My mother didn't like to be around him. Neither did I. And, of course, Laura hated him."

"You left out your father," Rebecca reminded me. "What did he think of Jamie during this time?"

Once again I recalled the moment years before when all three of us, Laura and Jamie and myself, had erupted into noisy battle in the backyard. My father had stepped out onto the second-floor patio and stared down silently, bringing the conflict to an immediate end. Even from that distance, I could tell that his eyes had swept smoothly from my upturned face to Laura's, then back to mine, leaving out the third point in what should have been the triangle of his assembled children. Even in that moment of disciplinary concern, his eyes had not once moved toward Jamie. The following years, it struck me now, had only widened the abyss which separated them.

"I think that toward the end, my father just gave up on Jamie."

"In what way?"

"Gave up trying to love him, to be a father to him."

"Do you think Jamie felt that 'giving up'?" Rebecca asked.

"Yes," I said.

And for the first time, I saw Jamie captured in the deep well of his isolation. Not really his father's son, yet unaware of that dreadful fact, he had been kept outside the circle of our kinship, a prodigal and an outcast. To have killed him in so lonely and bereft a state, the only one among us who had never loved nor been loved by another, struck me as the single, saddest aspect of my father's crime.

A wave of empty, helpless grief must have passed over me at that moment, because when I looked back toward Rebecca, she appeared almost frightened by what she saw in my face.

"We don't have to finish everything tonight," she said.

Finish everything. Those were the words she used. And so I knew that within hours, perhaps minutes, I would be returned to that dreadful state of "back to normal" to which Marie had seemed to look forward with such anxious anticipation. I felt a pall descend, the atmosphere thickening and congealing around me. My destiny was being sealed. I was being buried alive. It was almost more than I could bear.

"Do you want to stop for the night, Steve?" Rebecca asked.

I lifted my head. "No, let's finish it tonight," I told her, now anxious to finish everything, to leave Rebecca behind, to go on to whatever it was that awaited me, and to do it quickly, cleanly, without ever looking back.

She nodded, glanced down at her notes, let Jamie slip back into his long oblivion, and renewed her focus upon Laura.

"You said that Laura treated your mother very gently for a time," she began.

"It was just a brief change," I said quickly, already pushing toward the next question, driving forward relentlessly, almost a man in flight.

"And after that how did Laura treat her?"

"She went back to the same attitude she'd always had toward her," I answered. "She seemed resentful of her. She avoided her most of the time, but once in a while, she would say something rather harsh."

"Harsh? Like what?"

"I can't remember any specific word," I told her crisply, almost curtly, urging her on at a steadily accelerating pace.

"You don't remember any particular episode of harsh treatment?" Rebecca asked.

"No."

"Did Laura act this way in your father's presence?"

"No. Never."

"And you said that this change occurred about a month or so after you got back from Cape Cod?"

"Yes."

"In early October then?"

I nodded.

Rebecca wrote the date down in her notebook. "But your father didn't change, is that right?"

"No, he didn't."

"Do you recall any particular incident between them? Some special act of kindness?"

"No."

Rebecca continued to pursue the point. "Did

anything at all strike you as different in your family during this time?"

"No."

"So as far as you know, nothing at all changed in the family during the month before the murders?"

I shook my head. "Nothing."

And yet, as I sat there, responding to Rebecca's questions with clipped, one-word answers, I could nonetheless feel the slowly building sense of doom that had begun to invade those final days. A heaviness had descended upon us, as if the house at 417 McDonald Drive had been filled with a thick, transparent gelatin through which Laura, Jamie, my mother, and even my father moved slowly and trudgingly, like weary, exhausted creatures, struggling to draw what were their final breaths. One by one, each of them isolated from the other, I saw them all a final time: Jamie, embittered by successive waves of rejection, entombed behind the closed door of his room; Laura slouched sullenly in the wicker chair of the solarium; my mother in her bed behind the tightly drawn floral curtains, a bomb already lit inside her brain; and finally my father, alone now in the basement, bereft, solitary and morose, slowly turning forward the thin black wheel. They had all been dying during those last weeks, I realized, like flowers past their season.

It began to rain, and Rebecca rose and closed the window. "And so everything remained the same up until the last day?" she asked as she returned to her seat.

"The last day," I repeated, remembering it now as fully as I thought I ever would.

"It was raining," I said.

It was raining, and had been raining for days.

The lawns along McDonald Drive were brown and soggy. Rain battered against the windowpanes of our rooms and thumped down loudly against the mock Tudor gables. The white cords of the basketball net hung limply in a gray, sodden web. The day before, my mother had hung our laundry beneath a bright mid-morning sun, but now, drenched and rain-beaten, it drooped heavily toward the saturated ground. Alone among all our clothes, only my sister's bra had been set free by a sudden burst of wind. It lay in a mangled, mud-spattered pile beneath a line of bathroom towels.

"Did everything seem normal that morning?" Rebecca asked.

"Yes, everything seemed 'normal,' " I said evenly, almost choking on the word. "We were all back to *normal* on that last day," I said bitterly, my voice coming through nearly clenched teeth. "Maybe that's what my father couldn't bear."

I saw Rebecca's face stiffen. "What do you mean?"

"Maybe that's why he killed them," I said coldly. "Because the kind of life they represented made him sick."

Rebecca's eyes narrowed. "What kind of life are you talking about, Steve?" she asked, but warily, as if she were closing in on a dangerous animal she'd studied and knew well.

"A pinched, little life," I said, brutally, the raw edge of my own vast discontent piercing through the mask behind which I'd hidden so long. "A dull, stupid life, with nothing in it that lifted him, that gave him hope, that had some possibility of escape."

Rebecca's face filled with recognition. "Escape from what?" she asked.

"From *them,*" I blurted. "From the way they were killing him before he decided to take it by the *balls* . . . and kill *them* instead."

The words seemed to hit her like bullets. She drew away from me, her eyes glaring fiercely. Her lips parted, but she didn't speak. Instead, she closed her notebook with an abrupt finality.

"I think we can end it here," she said, in a steely voice, her tone beyond any feeble gesture I might make at either apology or explanation.

I started to speak, but she rose instantly, walked to the door, and jerked it open. "I'll send you all the materials I've collected on the case," she said tensely.

I remained in my chair, my own last words washing over me like a hot wave.

"Rebecca, I . . ."

She remained at the door, her body rigid. "I'll also send you a copy of the book," she added.

I knew that all she might have felt for me before that moment—respect, esteem, perhaps even some affection—had been reduced to this single, brutal and explosive kernel. She'd seen the face of "these men" in my face, and there was no way for me to creep back into my former self.

And so I nodded to her as I passed, saw her eyes dart away, then stepped out into the rain.

FOURTEEN

I walked out into the rain, moving resolutely toward my waiting car. I didn't glance back toward Rebecca's cottage to see if she lingered by the door or watched me leave from behind the short white curtains of her tiny living room.

I could feel an immense emptiness within me, a sense of having been filled for a time, then gutted absolutely. As I drove down the curving road which led from Rebecca's cottage, I felt that some part of me had been blasted away by the same fire that had taken my mother, my brother, and my sister to their isolated graves.

It was still raining heavily when I pulled onto the main road, the leaden drops coming toward me like a hail of silver bullets, splattering onto the hood and windshield of the car, sending small bursts of water back into the dense, nocturnal air.

For a while, I drove on determinedly, biting down on my aching emptiness, trying to remove all the preceding days from my mind. I wanted to forget that I'd ever met Rebecca Soltero, heard her voice, or entertained a single one of her darkly probing questions. I wanted to forget all that she'd unearthed in me, the hunger and dissatisfaction along with the gnawing, nearly frenzied, urge to burst out of the life my own choices had created, as if in one, explosive act I could erase and then reconstitute an existence which, without explosion, offered no way out.

The lights of Old Salsbury glimmered hazily through the weaving veils of rain. I swept through its slick, deserted streets, past shop windows crowded with blank-faced mannequins and on toward its prim outer wall of white Colonial houses. I felt my head drift backward almost groggily, my mind reeling drunkenly in a fog of pain. I had never known so deep an anguish, or experienced so complete a sense of irredeemable collapse.

The house was dark when I pulled into the driveway. For a time I didn't go in, but remained in the car, instead, poised motionlessly behind the wheel, staring hollow-eyed at the black, unblinking windows. For a moment I closed my eyes, as if in an effort to make it all disappear, the whole intransigent structure of my life. When I opened them again, I realized that they were moist, glistening, that I had, against the force of my will, begun to cry.

I waited for a long time after that, waited to regain a stony composure. Then I got out of the car and walked toward the short flight of cement steps that led to the side entrance of the house. I could feel the rain slapping ruthlessly against me, but I walked slowly anyway, so that by the time I entered the house, my hair hung in a wet tangle over my forehead.

Down the corridor I could see a light burning softly, and for an instant, I thought that Marie must still be working in her office. Then I realized that the light was coming from farther down the hallway, from my office, rather than Marie's.

She was sitting very erectly in the black leather chair behind my desk, the surreal outlines of my mythical dream house spread out before her. When she spoke to me, only her mouth seemed to move; the rest of her body, her arms, her hair, the clean, classically drawn lines of her face, everything else appeared to hold itself firmly within a marble stillness.

"Where have you been, Steve?" she asked.

"At the office, you know that."

She shook her head firmly. "You weren't at the office."

"What are you talking about, Marie?"

She looked at me as if this last, despicable lie was hardly worthy of attention. "I went to the office," she said.

I started to speak, but found that I had no words. I felt my lips part, but no sound came. I knew that I was helpless, literally naked, before her. She was armored in the truth, and I was a worm wriggling beneath its dark, approaching shadow.

"Peter fell out by the pool," she said. "He hit his head."

"Is he all right?" I asked quickly.

"He's fine," Marie answered stiffly. "That's not the point now."

I knew what the point was. I could sense it hurling toward me like the head of a spear.

"I had to take him to the hospital," Marie went on. "The doctor wanted him to stay there a little while, and I thought you'd want to come and be with him."

"Well, of course I'd want to . . ."

She lifted her hand to stop me. "I drove to the

office to get you, Steve, but you weren't there. No one was there except the night watchman. He told me that no one had been in the office all night." Her eyes narrowed slightly. "Not Wally or any of those other men you said were going to meet you there."

I struggled to save what I could see sinking in the murky gray water, my wife, my son, sinking away from me forever.

"Marie, I was . . ."

"I know where you were," Marie said coolly, though without rancor, and entirely without fear, calm and self-possessed, ready to amputate the diseased and frightful limb.

"You were with her," she said, lifting a small square of white paper toward me.

From my place in the doorway, I could see the large block letters Peter had printed so neatly across the page: REBECCA.

I shook my head. "Marie, it's different, it's . . ."

She rose gracefully, like an ancient woman warrior, beleaguered, betrayed, her forces wounded all around, but still in full command. "I guess I always expected that you'd have some little fling somewhere along the way," she said, then added, "most men do."

"Marie, I . . ."

Again her hand rose, palm out, silencing me.

"But I never expected you to forget us, Steve," she said, "I never expected you to forget Peter and me."

I said nothing.

"And you did that," Marie said. "You forgot us. Maybe only for a little while, but an hour would have been enough."

She stepped out from behind the desk and headed for the door. The force of her character pressed me out into the corridor as she swept by me, marched down the hallway, then ascended the stairs. As she disappeared up them, I would have died to hold her, died to kiss her, died to have been the man she had always expected me to be.

I was still standing, stunned and speechless, when she came down the stairs again, this time with Peter sleeping in her arms. I could see the white bandage with its single spot of blood wrapped around his delicate blond head. I knew that she was going to her parents' home in the mountains. She would stay with them awhile, but only long enough to get her bearings. Then she would make her life over again, in some other place, perhaps even with some other man. Certainly, she would never come back to Old Salsbury or to me.

"Marie," I said softly, calling to her.

She turned as she reached the door, glancing back toward me, her face framed by the dark window, the space between us completely silent except for the hollow patter of the rain.

"Marie," I said again.

She looked at me almost mercifully, no longer as a husband, but only as another man who had lost his way. "Things weren't perfect," she said. "They never are." She watched me for a moment longer, as if in grave regret that what had been so obvious to her could have been so lost to me. "Things were missing, I know that," she added. "Things always are." She paused, her two dark eyes upon me like the twin barrels of a shotgun. "But it was never love, Steve," she said in her final words to me, "it was never love that was missing."

She turned then, and headed out into the rain. I walked down the corridor, parted the curtains, and watched as she laid Peter down in the back seat, then drew herself in behind the wheel. As she let the car drift down the driveway, I saw her eyes lift toward our bedroom window, close slowly as the car continued backward, then open again as it swung to the left and out into the slick, rainswept street.

Within an instant, she was gone.

For the next few hours, I wandered the house like a man who had awakened in a foreign city. Nothing looked familiar anymore. I heard ghostly, floating voices that seemed to speak to me in a language I had once understood, but which my long neglect had made incomprehensible, a language of connection, of duty, of belonging, a language which spoke of things present, rather than things missing, and as I listened to that language, I yearned for the oldest and most familiar objects in a house that was suddenly brand-new.

I don't remember into exactly what part of that house I had wandered when, hours later, I heard the knock at the door.

Two men were standing on the small porch when I opened it, one younger, bareheaded, one older, with glasses and a large gray hat.

"Steven Farris?" the older one said.

I nodded.

He reached into the pocket of his rain-soaked jacket and brought out a small, yellow badge. "Could you come with us, please?"

I rode in the back of a dark, unmarked car. I don't remember anything being said between the time I got in and the moment when the car finally pulled in behind a large brick building that I didn't recognize. I'm sure they spoke to me, but I can't remember what they said.

It was still raining when the car stopped and the older one turned to me.

"Are you ready, Mr. Farris?" he asked.

I must have nodded, because he got out immediately and opened the rear door of the car.

I followed him up a cement ramp, through a pair of double doors, then down a long corridor which ended at a flight of stairs.

"Just down here," the older one said.

We went down the stairs together, then into a small, green room where two metal stretchers rested side by side against the far wall.

By the time we reached them, the younger one had joined us. Still, it was the older one who drew back the white sheet that covered what was left of Peter's face.

I nodded. "My son," I said.

He covered him again, then stepped over to the other stretcher and repeated the same slow movement, drawing back the stiff white cloth.

She lay on her back, stiffly, her arms pressed neatly against her sides.

"My wife."

The sheet drifted back over her unmoving face.

The older one turned, and I followed him out of the room and back to the car. I took my place in the back seat and rode silently through the darkness, past the winding, unexpected curve that had brought my family to its death.

It was nearly dawn by the time the car pulled into the driveway again, returning me to my empty house. For a moment I continued to sit in the back seat, motionless, unable to move, as if paralyzed.

During that interval, I don't remember seeing or hearing anything. Then, as if in response to a signal I couldn't see, the older one turned toward me, his eyes gazing at me softly. "It's terrible right now, I know," he said, "but in the end, you will find your way."

You will find your way.

In my mind, I heard those words many times in the days that followed. I heard them as I paced the empty, voiceless rooms of my house or sat beside the covered pool, watching the late fall leaves gather on the dull black tarp. I heard them as Mr. Lowe, by then aware of exactly why my wife and son had been on the road that rainswept night, watched me disappointedly from the small square window of his office.

You will find your way..

I heard the words again and again, but still I couldn't find my way.

Things began to fall apart. I couldn't sleep, and barely ate at all. I burned my "dream house" plans, and sat for long, dull hours in the family room, the dim green eye of the television watching me from its place across the room. All my former occupations fell away. I couldn't read, couldn't draw, couldn't engage in conversation. At work, I sat at my desk, a silent, eerie specter, warily watched by the others as if at any moment I might pull a pistol from beneath my jacket and do to them what they all knew my father had done to my mother, brother, sister. At times, I would see the same, distant apprehension in their eyes that I'd sometimes glimpsed in the eyes of Aunt Edna so many years before, a suspicion that my father's poisoned blood had been passed on to me.

But although my fellow workers at Simpson and

Lowe couldn't have known it, they had nothing at all to fear from me. The revenge that was steadily building in my mind was not in the least directed toward them. I'd found another figure upon whom I'd begun to concentrate all my grief and rage.

William Patrick Farris.

During the weeks immediately following what everyone continually referred to as "the tragedy," I came to hate my father more than I'd ever hated him. I hated him for more than the ancient crime of my family's murder, hated him for more than what he'd done to my mother, Laura, and Jamie. I hated him for what he'd done to me.

Done to me, yes.

For it seemed to me at that time that my father had brought everything to pass, that almost everything could be laid ultimately at his door. Had he not killed my family, Rebecca would never have come to me, and Peter and Marie would still be alive. Even more, however, I blamed him for the poison in my own blood, for what I'd inherited from him, the dark impulsiveness and cataclysmic discontent that had led him to kill my mother, Laura, and Jamie, and which he had bequeathed to me. I thought of Peter and Marie, and went through the steps by which I'd murdered them as surely as my father had killed his own wife and children. It was a legacy of blood, passed down from father to son, and because of it, as I reasoned at last, it was necessary for both of us to die.

Night after night, I went through the packet of papers and photographs Rebecca had sent me by then. I no longer felt them as a link to her, but only as a way to keep alive my hatred, both of my father and myself. One by one, I stared at the photographs or read over the police reports. I savored each blood-soaked image, drank in every word, my eyes heavy in the early morning light, but glaring still at each macabre reminder of the hideously destructive nature I had inherited from him.

I grew bloated on our evil. I could think of nothing else. I lost my job, sold my house, and moved into a cheap hotel, but I didn't drink or sink into madness. That would have dulled the fierce edge I wanted more than anything to retain in what was left of my life. I didn't want to forget what the two of us had done. I wanted to remember every harrowing detail until the time of our executions.

Slowly, the plan emerged. I would track him down by moving through the places he'd moved, looking steadily for some clue both as to how he had been formed and where he might have gone.

As the weeks passed, I journeyed back to the little house in which he'd lived out his solitary youth, then to the hard-scrabble warehouse on Great Jones Street, and finally along the dreary line of small New Jersey towns through which he'd wandered, looking for work, finding none, moving on, in a trail that struck me, even then, as terribly forlorn.

I went through all the papers my Aunt Edna had left me, searching for addresses where he'd lived, references to places he'd been. I went to rooming houses that were now libraries, cafés that were now clothing stores, rural meadows that were now bald, grassless tracks of suburban housing. I traced names: cousins, co-workers, people he'd lent money. I found them living in back rooms, asylums, basements, old hotels. I found them dead, as well, wild boys and dancing girls reduced to names carved in gray stone.

I lost track of time. Hours glided into days,

weeks into months. My father's trail, never warm, and mostly fanciful, grew cold, and in the end I was left with a list of names and dates and places that were no more able to guide me to him than the random scribbling I might read from a bathroom wall.

In the end, you will find your way.

It was the older detective who'd said that to me as I'd sat, dazed and unmoving, in the rainy driveway that night. But now, when the words returned to me, I realized that they were carried on a different voice, the one which had guided Rebecca before me, and which, after so many years, so much brutal evidence, still dared to suggest that something didn't fit.

It was easy to find him. Swenson, after all, was not hiding from anyone.

A woman met me at the door. She wore a green dress dotted with small white flowers, and her hair was pulled back into a frazzled reddish bun.

"My name is Steve Farris," I told her.

It was a name she clearly recognized. She stepped back and eyed me with a keen vigilance from behind a pair of large, tortoiseshell glasses.

"I guess you want to see Dave," she said.

I nodded. "Is he here?"

"Sure he is," the woman said. "He can't get out anymore." She stepped away from the door. "Come on in," she said. "He's in the back."

I followed her down a short corridor, then into the shadowy bedroom where he lay. His condition seemed worse than Rebecca had described. Propped up by three large white pillows, he sat in a small metal bed, his lower body covered by a worn, patchwork quilt, the air around him little more than a cloud of medicinal fumes. There was a cylindrical orange oxygen tank at his right, and as I entered, he drew its yellow plastic mask from his mouth and watched me curiously.

"This is Steve Farris," the woman said.

Swenson nodded to me, then swung his head to the right, as if trying to get a somewhat better look at me.

"You need anything, Dave?" the woman asked.

Swenson shook his head slowly, his eyes still leveled upon me.

The woman walked over to his bed, drew the blanket a little more snugly over his stomach, and disappeared out the door.

During all that time, Swenson's eyes never left me.

"The son," he said finally in a breathless, ragged voice.

"Yes."

He motioned for me to take a seat near the bed, then returned the mask to his mouth and took in a quick, anxious breath. The face behind the mask was pale and ravaged, though his green eyes still shone brightly from their deep sockets.

"Rebecca thought you might come by here," he said, after he'd withdrawn the mask again.

"She did?"

He inhaled a long, rattling breath, lifted the mask again, then let it drop. "She said there were things you might want to know." His pale skin seemed strangely luminous in the gray light, as if a small candle still burned behind his eyes. But it was the eyes themselves that I could still recognize from that moment he'd turned to face me so many years before, those same eyes settling quietly upon me as I'd sat stunned and silent in the back seat of his unmarked car.

"Smart woman, Rebecca," Swenson said shakily, his head drifting slightly to the left. "Very smart."

"Yes, she is."

The green eyes bored into me, a young detective's eyes, swift and penetrating, but now embedded in a slack, doughy face. "What do you want to know about your father?" he asked.

It was a question which, as I realized at that moment, had never actually been asked of me, and which I'd never actually asked myself. What *did* I want to know? Why *had* I come so far in order to know it?

"I want to know what really happened," I told him. "I want to know exactly what my father did."

"That day, you mean?" Swenson asked. The mask rose again, the great chest expanded beneath the patchwork quilt, then collapsed. "November 19, 1959," he added, as the mask drifted down and finally came to rest in his lap.

He'd said the date not to impress me with his memory, but to suggest how it had remained with him through all the passing years, how he'd never been able to rid himself of his own, gnawing doubt, the persistent and irreducible presence of something in that house that didn't fit. And yet, at the same time, he seemed reluctant to begin, as if still unsure of where it might finally lead.

"My father had planned it for a long time, hadn't he?" I said.

Even as I said it, I saw our lives dangling helplessly over the fiery pit of my father's dreadful calculations. One by one, it seemed, he'd weighed the separate elements of our lives and deaths. Like a Grand Inquisitor, he'd heard the evidence while staring at my red-robed mother from the smoky fortress of his old brown van, or tinkering with his latest bicycle in the chill dungeon of the cement basement. One by one, we'd come before him like prisoners naked in a dock. Day by day the long trials had stretched on through the months, until, in a red wave of judgment, he'd finally condemned us all.

After that final condemnation, as I supposed at that moment, it had been only a matter of working out the technical details. Perhaps he'd considered various weapons for a time, carefully weighing the advantages of knives, guns, poisons, before finally deciding on the shotgun for no better reason than that he'd bought it years before, that it rested quietly in the green metal cabinet in the basement, that it was ready-to-hand.

"How long had he been planning it, do you think?" I asked Swenson, coaxing him forward, as one might nudge a man, ever so subtly, toward the edge of a cliff.

Swenson shrugged. He started to speak, but stopped abruptly, and returned the mask to his mouth. He took in a long breath, then let it out in a sudden, hollow gush. "If he planned it early, then he must have changed his plans," he said.

I said nothing, but only waited, as it seemed to me I had in one way or another been waiting all my life.

"Did Rebecca think he had a plan?" Swenson asked.

It was odd how far she seemed from me now. I saw her poised over her black briefcase, withdrawing papers in her usual methodical manner, showing me only what was relevant at that particular moment, concealing all the rest. I could recall the tension of my lost desire, but only as something remembered by another man, a story told by someone else, so that now when she came forward in my mind, it was as little more than a messenger sent to me by my father.

"I think so," I told him.

He looked vaguely surprised to hear it. He stared at me quietly, his breath coming in long hard pulls and quick exhalations. "Well, maybe he did," he said. The mask lifted, lingered for a moment at his mouth, then fell again. "But maybe he didn't." He tried to go on, but his breath could not carry the weight of another sentence. He took a quick inhalation, then added, "He got away, that's for sure."

"All the way to Mexico," I said.

Swenson nodded. "Using nothing but back roads," he said, "or we'd have picked him up for sure." He coughed suddenly, a hard, brutal cough, his face reddening with the strain. "Sorry," he said quickly, then returned to his story. "He left all his money in the bank." He looked at me pointedly as he drew in another aching breath. "Does that sound like a well-thought-out plan?"

I looked at him, puzzled, my eyes urging him to go on.

Swenson shifted uncomfortably, the large head sinking and rising heavily, its little wisps of reddish hair floating eerily in the veiled light. "He left the house at around six o'clock."

In my mind I could see him go almost as clearly as Mrs. Hamilton had seen him, a figure in a gray hat, carrying nothing with him, not so much as the smallest bag.

"He went downtown to the hardware store after that," Swenson said. A short cough broke from him, but he suppressed the larger one behind it. "Several people saw him go in, but since he owned the place, nobody made anything of it."

"What did he do in there?" I asked.

"He cleaned out the cash register," Swenson answered. "Took every dime." The mask rose again, then fell. "Then he went to that little store near your house."

"Oscar's?"

Swenson nodded. "He bought a lot of food and stuff for the trip." He stopped. The mask climbed up to his mouth, settled over it for a long, raspy breath, then crawled back down into Swenson's lap. "And he made a phone call."

"A phone call?"

"From that little phone they had out front," Swenson said, without emphasis. "We don't know who he called," he added, "but the kid that was standing behind him, waiting to use the same phone, was sure that he never got an answer."

"Someone else," I said in a cold whisper, "he was calling someone else." The face of Nellie Grimes came toward me, lifting slowly, gently, as if offering a kiss.

Swenson's great head drifted to the left. "Someone else, that's right."

"Rebecca told me that you spoke to Nellie Grimes," I said.

Swenson returned the mask to his lips, sucked in a long breath, then let it drop unceremoniously from his mouth. "It wasn't her."

"Then who was it?"

Swenson wagged his head wearily. "I don't know." He brought the oxygen mask to his mouth again, took in a long, noisy breath, and let it fall back into his lap.

I could feel a tidal fury sweep over me as I imagined him at that phone, still working feverishly to carry out his escape. It was a rage which Swenson could see in its full, thrusting hatred, and it seemed to press me back roughly, like a violent burst of wind.

"You're looking for him, aren't you?" he asked.

I stared at him icily, but did not speak.

"You want to kill him for what he did that day," Swenson said. He seemed neither shocked nor outraged by the truth he'd come upon. By then, no doubt, he'd slogged through a world of death. His only word was one of caution.

"There'll be more to do after that," he said.

"What do you mean?"

He lifted the mask to his face, leaned into it, and took in a long, rattling breath. "Someone else," he said when the mask lowered again, "like you've already said."

"Someone else, yes," I asked. "Someone waiting for him at an airport or a bus station, or just on a corner, waiting for him to pull up in the car."

Swenson shook his head slowly, ponderously, as if there were heavy weights inside his head. "No," he said. "Someone who was already with him. Someone in the house." He looked at me intently. "Someone helping him."

I stared at him, astonished. "Helping him?" I whispered. "Helping him kill us?"

Swenson nodded. "We followed your father's tracks down into the basement," he said. "They were very bloody, and they went all the way down to the third step."

"Yes, I know."

"But that was as far as they ever went," Swenson added laboriously, wheezing loudly now. "The only tracks on the basement floor were the little ones your mother made through those pools of water that had seeped in from the rain."

I nodded, waiting, as I knew I must, for the thing that didn't fit.

"But if your father had fired at your mother from the third step," Swenson added, "then he would have riddled the box she'd hid behind." His head shifted back and forth, as if with the weight of what he knew. "But that box wasn't hit at all," he added. He brought the mask to his face and sucked in a long, mighty breath. "It hadn't been moved, either," he added as he lowered it slightly, "because if someone had moved it, it would have left a smear of blood." He looked at me pointedly as he returned the mask to his mouth, took a long, heavy breath, then lowered it again. "Someone walked around that box and shot your mother," he began again, his voice high and tremulous now, breaking with the effort these last words had cost him. "Maybe brought her back up the stairs, too," he added, "because there were no tracks from your father's shoes that went below that third step."

"Did you tell Rebecca this?"

He nodded.

"What did she say?"

"She said he must have changed before he went downstairs," Swenson answered.

"Is that possible?"

"Well, we found his bloody shoes and clothes in the bathroom upstairs," Swenson said. "And there was that small amount of time between the second shot and the last one."

"Was that long enough for him to have changed

his clothes, then walked down to the basement and killed my mother?" I asked.

Swenson looked at me solemnly. "Rebecca thought so."

"Do you?"

For a moment, he seemed to review the whole terrible choreography of my family's murder, his head lifting slightly, as the mask dropped into his lap.

"No," he said finally, "I think there was some . . ."

A quick breath left him, and he leaned back into the pillows, brought the plastic mask to his mouth, and drew in a tortured, wracking breath. "Someone else," he said, on what seemed like his final breath, the mask returning quickly to his mouth, his eyes peering motionlessly over its rounded, plastic rim, watching me, animal-like, as if his green, amphibian eyes were poised just above the surface of a murky pool.

Someone else.

As I drove back toward my hotel room that afternoon, I thought of nothing but those words. I remembered that Nellie Grimes had used the same words in her interview with Swenson. She had insisted on my father's innocence, then ascribed the blame simply and mysteriously to "someone else."

My lips parted in the only answer I could offer at the time. "The other woman," I whispered.

But who?

It was nearly night when I arrived back at the hotel. As I headed across its dank, cluttered lobby, the little bald desk clerk who'd regarded me so suspiciously over my long stay unexpectedly motioned me toward the reception desk.

"There's a package for you," he said, then reached beneath the desk and handed me a small, rectangular box.

It had been sent first to my house in Old Salsbury, then to the offices of Simpson and Lowe, and finally forwarded to me here. For a single, surreal instant, I sensed that it had come from my father, some macabre remembrance he'd sent to mock and torment me, a blood-encrusted strand, perhaps, of my mother's hair. I tucked the package quickly under my arm, took the stairs up to my third-floor room, and tossed it, unopened, on the bed.

It lay there for a long time while I sat beside the window, staring out at the deserted street, still trying to reason out the identity of the unknown woman who, in the end, had helped my father destroy not only one, but both my families. Step by step, I once again walked the paces of my father's crime, following the bloody tracks Swenson had followed, a trail that led from Jamie's room to Laura's, and finally down the basement stairs to where two women had waited for him, one crouched behind a cardboard box, the other standing over her, waiting in an awesome silence for the shotgun to be passed.

I drew my eyes away from the window and let them come to rest on the small, brown box that had arrived at my hotel that day. I went to the bed, picked it up, and began to open it slowly, ritualistically, as if I were uncovering a treasure of vast renown, some relic from an ancient faith.

It was no such awesome thing, of course. It was nothing more than Rebecca's book.

I stared at it, disappointed, exhausted, barely engaged enough to keep my eyes upon it. Still, it had its own dark allure. The jacket was rather melodramatically illustrated with the face of a sinister-looking paternal figure, but the title seemed as cool and academic as its author: *THESE MEN: Studies in Family Murder,* by Rebecca Soltero.

For the rest of the night, I sat at the window of my room and read Rebecca's study of "these men." One by one, she explored and exposed them, moving through those elements of character and background which united them, closing in on that single element which joined them together in a dark, exclusive brotherhood, the fact that they were, above all, deeply romantic men. So much so, that each of them had found a kind of talisman, an emblem for his extreme and irreducible yearning. "Creatures of a visceral male romanticism," Rebecca wrote, "each of these men had found a symbol for what was missing in his life."

True to her method, she then ticked these emblems off. Crude and childish, they would normally have seemed no more than the physical representations of men who had become locked in boyish fantasies. But under Rebecca's transforming eye, they took on an occult and totemic symbolism: Fuller's baseball bat, Parks's simple curl, Townsend's foreign stamps, Stringer's safari hat, and last, as Rebecca described them, "the sleek racing bikes of William Patrick Farris."

"By clinging to these symbols," Rebecca wrote, "these men made one last effort to control a level of violent romantic despair which women almost never reach."

With the exception of my father, each of them had even gone so far as to take these totemic objects with them in their efforts to escape. Fuller had thrown the bloody bat into the back seat of his car;

Stringer had worn his safari hat onto the plane he'd hoped to take to Africa; Townsend had stuffed his briefcase full of foreign stamps beneath the seat he'd purchased on an eastbound train; and Herbert Parks, though trying to disguise himself in other ways, had stubbornly maintained his enigmatic curl.

The tenacious hold of these symbols upon the imaginations of the men she'd studied led Rebecca unerringly to the final conclusion of her book:

> In the minds of these men, the most immediate need became the elimination of whatever it was that blocked their way to a mythically romantic life. That is to say, their families. Essentially, they could not bear the normal limits of a life lived communally, domestically, and grounded in the sanctity of enduring human relations. Instead, they yearned for a life based, as it were, on male orgasmic principles, one which rose toward thrilling, yet infinitely renewable, heights of romantic trial and achievement. In time, they came to hold any other form of life in what can only be described as a murderous contempt.

But even as I read this final passage, I wondered if it could actually be applied to my father. For where, in all the descriptions of vast romantic torment which dotted Rebecca's book, was the man who'd puttered with a bicycle in the basement and played Chinese checkers with a little girl, and who'd said of these simple, normal, intensely humble things, "This is all I want."

Once more, I read the section of Rebecca's book

which dealt with my father. She'd written elegantly and well of my family's life, and even given my father an exalted place among her other subjects by suggesting that his particular totem, the Rodger and Windsor bikes, provided the most fitting symbol for the destructive male romanticism she had studied and at last condemned, "a thing of high mobility and speed, self-propelled and guided, capable of supporting only one lone rider at a time."

Only one?

Then to whom had he passed the shotgun that rainy afternoon?

Once more I imagined the "someone else" with whom he might have joined in such murderous conspiracy, but even here, I found that there was still something missing, something that didn't fit.

And so, at last, I returned to the small stack of crime-scene photographs Rebecca had sent to me. Slowly, one by one, as the early morning light built outside my hotel window, I peered at each picture, my mother's body behind the floral curtains, her blood-encrusted house shoes on the floor beside her bed; Jamie, faceless, beneath the wide window, his biology book opened to the picture of a gutted frog; Laura, her body wrapped in a white terry-cloth robe, her bare feet stretched toward the camera as if trying to block its view.

By the time I'd returned the last of the pictures to the envelope that had contained them, I still was no closer to knowing if Rebecca had been right about my father. At least for me, she had not yet solved the mystery of his murderousness, but she had doubtless offered the only clue as to where and how it might be solved.

FIFTEEN

Rodger and Windsor.

Rebecca had made an immensely persuasive case that the men she'd studied had been unable to live without their private romantic totems. In my desperate need to find him, it struck me at last that my father might have been no less obsessed than the rest of them, that the sleek red racing bikes he'd imported from England had perhaps made the same romantic claim upon his mind as foreign stamps and safari hats had made upon the other men in Rebecca's book.

It was a wet, fall day when I reached Rodger and Windsor's offices in New York City. The cold drizzle I'd walked through had given me an even more desolate appearance than usual, and because of that, the neat young man who came out to the front desk to greet me seemed hesitant to come too close.

"May I help you?" he said.

"I'm looking for my father," I told him.

"Your father?" he asked me, puzzled. "Does he work here?"

"No," I answered.

Then, in all its appalling detail, I told him the

story of my father's crime. One by one I showed him the crime-scene photographs of my mother, Laura, and Jamie. At each picture, he flinched a little.

"Your father did all that?" he asked finally.

I nodded, then took out Rebecca's book and read him the relevant passage. He listened with a rapt intensity.

"My father was obsessed with these bikes," I told him, "he wouldn't be able to live without getting one." I waited, then added, "And I'm sure it would be red."

From the look on his face, I could tell that the young man in the starched white shirt and plain gray tie had decided to do everything he could to help me. Something exciting had unexpectedly come into his life, and as I looked at the eagerness I could see building in his eyes, I wondered if I had been like him on that day Rebecca had first arrived at the offices of Simpson and Lowe. Had I been nothing more than a clerk with a clerk's long day looming before him? Was that the secret of my fall? Was it no more than the flight from boredom that had killed my wife and son?

I thought of my father, too, the way he'd trudged up the narrow aisles of his hardware store day after day. I saw the listlessness in his eyes, the weary rhythm of his gait, and it struck me more powerfully than ever before just how dangerous a man may become when he suddenly feels no compelling reason any longer to live as he has always lived.

The clerk nodded. "And you want me to help you find him?"

"Yes," I said, then added, "I have reason to believe that my father crossed the border into Mexico."

The clerk smiled. "Then let's start in Mexico," he said.

And so we began there, going back through the stacks of sales invoices that stretched toward the present from the distant year of 1959. With a continually deepening level of engagement, we stalked the passing years. It was the clerk who found the first hint of my father's new abode. He pulled a single sheet of paper from the file. "Could it be this?" he asked.

I took the paper and looked at it. The order was dated March 17, 1962, and it was for a single red Rodger and Windsor bike. It had been received from a bicycle shop located in a small town on the western coast of Mexico. The man who'd signed the order had used the name Antonio Dias. There had been other orders from other places, of course, but this was the only bicycle shop that had ordered only one Rodger and Windsor, and that had specifically stipulated that its color must be red.

During the next twenty years, as the clerk discovered, this same Antonio Dias had ordered thirty-two red Rodger and Windsor bikes. The shipping invoices showed that during that same time he'd moved to nine different towns, each time farther south until he'd finally reached the border of Honduras.

In 1982, the orders had abruptly stopped. For the next three years there were no orders from Antonio Dias. Then, in November of 1985, one appeared again. This time, however, it had not come from Mexico, but from far more distant Spain, from a town about the size of Somerset, but located on the Mediterranean, and which bore the exotic and romantic name of Alicante. At the rate of nearly two a year, the orders had continued to arrive over the next seven years. The last one had been received only two months before.

The clerk looked at me significantly. "If this Antonio Dias is your father," he said, "then my guess is, he's still in Alicante."

And so I made my plans to go. I renewed my passport, then waited in my hotel room for it to arrive. During that time I watched no television nor read a book. I wrote no letters nor read any that I received. I didn't want to be distracted. As the days passed, I sank deeper into my own closed world. I no longer nodded to people on the street. I didn't answer when they spoke to me. The days passed, and my world grew smaller. At last, I shrank into a small, dark seed.

The passport arrived, and I bought a ticket to Madrid. From there, I took a bus to Alicante.

It was nearly midnight when I arrived. A foreigner, with no knowledge of the language, I took the first hotel room I could find and stretched out on the small, narrow bed to await the morning. Through the night, I thought of my father, of how near I sensed he was. I tried to imagine his face webbed in dark wrinkles, the sound of his voice as it spoke in a foreign language. But he remained as elusive as always, still as remote and towering as he had been the day he'd stood on the veranda and silenced all of us with nothing more commanding than his gaze.

I awoke very early, just after first light. Across from my bed, I could see a small sink, a wrinkled towel that hung limply from its bare metal rack, and a battered armoire. They didn't look the same as in my escapist dream, however. Nothing was the same. Outside my window, where light blue, rather than white, curtains lifted languidly in the warm morning breeze, there were no tiled roofs or dark spires. There was only a sprawling modern town gathered around a much older one.

It was still early when I left the hotel. Across the street was a large market, decked with bright-colored vegetables and row upon row of sleek, silvery fish. Pointing first to one thing, then another, I bought a piece of bread and a cup of coffee, eating as I continued on my way.

I'd written the address to which the last Rodger and Windsor had been sent on a piece of paper, and for nearly an hour after leaving the market, I moved from person to person, showing each the address, then following an array of hand signals, since I could not understand what was said to me. Block by block, turn by turn, I closed in on my father, moving deeper and deeper into the old Moorish quarter of the city. Perched on a high hill, a huge fortress loomed above me, its massive yellow walls glowing in the sun.

At last I found the street I'd been looking for. Madre de Dios it was called, Mother of God. It curled near the center of a warren of other narrow, nearly identical streets, and at its far end, half hidden in the shadows, I saw a sign. It was carelessly painted, and hung at an angle, the way I knew he would have painted and hung it. It read BICICLETAS.

I approached the store slowly, with a sensation of shrinking, of returning to the size of a little boy. I felt as I had felt that night I'd gone down the basement stairs, hesitant, unsure, eerily afraid of the man who stood behind the large black wheel.

And so, once I reached the shop, I found that I couldn't go in. Through a single, dusty window, I could see a figure moving in its dim interior, moving as he had moved, haphazardly from place to place, but I could not approach it. Each time my hand moved toward the door, it was seized by a terrible trembling, as if I expected the shotgun still to be cradled in his arms.

After a moment, I turned abruptly and walked across the street, standing rigidly, unable to move, while a stream of men and women, some with children at their sides, casually went in and out, ringing the little bell he'd hung above the door.

There was a small, dusty plaza just up from the store, a place of scrubby trees and cement benches. I went there and continued to watch the entrance of the shop. As the hours passed, I remained in place, my back pressed up against the spindly gray trunk of an olive tree. To the right, a gathering of women, their faces hung in black scarves, talked idly while young children scrambled playfully at their feet. At the far end of the square, old men in black berets tossed wooden balls across a dusty court, their faces shaded beneath a canopy of palms.

Time crawled by, minute by minute. The sun rose, then began to lower.

While I waited, I imagined it again.

I imagined following him as he made his way out of the little bicycle shop. Using the landscape that now surrounded me, I saw him trudge along the deserted street, winding uphill toward the ancient fortress, its gigantic walls glowing yellow above him, striking and unreal. I imagined stalking him steadily as he crossed the little plaza, his feet shuffling cautiously over the rubble of its broken walkway. I saw myself close in upon him as he turned into a narrow, nearly unlighted alleyway, passed under a low, crumbling balcony, and disappeared behind its veil of hanging flowers. It was there I saw myself sweep in behind him, rushing beneath the balcony, the two of us suddenly gathered together behind the dense curtain. I heard myself say, "Father," then watch as he turned toward me. I knew that I would give him time to turn, time for him to see me, time for his body to stiffen as the word continued to echo in his mind, as he wondered hopelessly, and with a wrenching sense of terror, if it could be true.

Then and only then, I would strike, raising the blade above his trembling, horror-stricken face. "This is for Laura," I would tell him as I delivered the first blow. "And this is for Peter and Marie."

For the next hour or so, I continued to luxuriate in my father's murder, reliving it again and again, rejoicing in his agony, while the sun sank farther toward the sea, and still, he did not come out. By then the other shops had closed, their owners marching off to the nearest tavern to while away the remainder of the afternoon, while my father remained inside his shop. I'd seen the door of my father's shop close, as well, then a hand draw down a curtain, but nothing more. At first, I imagined him still inside, perhaps piddling with his latest Rodger and Windsor. But as the hours passed, a graver thought occurred to me. Perhaps he had escaped again. In my mind, I saw him crawling out a dusty window, then trotting down a narrow alley to where a small boat waited for him, bobbing lightly in a peaceful sea.

For a moment, I felt a great terror sweep over me, the fear not only that he'd escaped again, but that he'd escaped from me, as if, from the beginning, from that first flight into the rain, that had been his one true aim.

I stood up and peered out toward the shop, my

eyes squinting against the still-bright sun, and almost at that instant the hand appeared again, and the curtain rose.

With the afternoon siesta over, customers began to come and go again. There were not many of them, as I noticed, but then my father had never been one to attract a steady clientele.

The light began to change with the final waning of the afternoon, darkening steadily until the first blue haze of evening descended upon the street. At last, the first lights began to shine from the shop windows that lined the narrow, winding route of Madre de Dios.

It was already full night when those lights began to blink off again. The one that shined beneath the tilted sign for BICICLETAS finally blinked off, too.

Seconds later, I saw him back out of the shop, pulling the door closed behind him, then turn slowly to face the plaza. A streetlight cast a silver veil over him, and in its light I could see that he was dressed like the other old men of the region, in a dark suit, with a faded white shirt that looked slightly frayed at the collar, and no tie.

He turned up the street, and then I saw his yellow cane as it hung limply from his hand. He placed it firmly on the ground and began to walk slowly up the hill, the cane tapping lightly in the nearly deserted street.

As he moved toward me, I could see that he was still tall, though bent now, his shoulders slightly rounded. His hair was white, and his face was brown and leathery, drier than I remembered it, parched by his long years in the sun. The only thing that remained the same was his piercingly blue eyes.

They didn't glance in my direction as he headed

across the street, then into the little plaza, finally going by me at a distance of no more than ten or fifteen feet. A woman nodded toward him as she passed and an old man waved from the other end of the square, but my father didn't stop to talk to either of them.

He continued on, his feet plowing unsteadily across the dusty plaza. When he was near the middle of it, I stood up and watched him closely, as if expecting him to vanish magically into the air. In the distance, I could see him moving past the old men tossing balls in the courtyard, the women with their children, his feet raising a little cloud of dust behind him.

He was almost at the end of the plaza before I fell in behind him, trailing him at a distance, the eyes of the people in the square following me almost as intently as I followed my father.

Slowly, with an old man's gait, he made his way up a narrow street, then, to my surprise, turned abruptly to the right and entered a small tavern.

He'd already taken a seat behind a round, wooden table when I entered the same tavern seconds later. There were other men around him, men at other tables, old men who looked as weathered as he, their eyes deep-set and encircled by spidery webs of dark lines, their skin deeply furrowed. But they were shorter and rounder than my father, who still retained something of the tall, lean figure I remembered from my youth. It was clear that they knew him, perhaps even associated him with the American cowboys they'd seen in movies and on television, the silent, solitary, lethal men whose brave adventures made their dull, familial lives seem small and cowardly and of little worth.

I took a seat across the room and watched as my

father ordered his first drink. When it came, I saw that it was sherry, a drink that struck me as quite bland for a man who on a rainy November day had, with the help of "someone else," taken a shotgun to his family.

Sherry, I thought, *my father drinks sherry,* and suddenly I saw him as a man of tastes and appetites, an old man who walked slowly through the dusty streets, his shadow moving jaggedly along the flat stone walls. The specter of my youth, the gray figure in the basement, the slaughterer of my family, there he was before me, drinking sherry and wiping his wet lips with a soiled handkerchief.

There he was, but still I found that I couldn't approach him. And so I watched from a distant corner, my fingers tapping rhythmically against my knees, my eyes moving toward him, then away, as if fleeing a flash of brutal light.

The night deepened hour by hour, but my father didn't leave his chair. One sherry, sipped slowly, was followed by another. He ordered a plate of sliced ham and a piece of bread smeared with tomato, eating his dinner at a leisurely pace, his blue eyes closing from time to time as he leaned back tiredly against the tiled wall.

From time to time, other men would sit down with him and chat awhile, but my father seemed to greet them distantly, talk to them absently, pay them little mind. As each one left, he merely nodded slowly and said, "Adios," in a tone that seemed faintly sorrowful, so that even in the grip of my hatred I sensed that there had been a loneliness to his exile, things he had endured, losses he had silently absorbed. For a moment, I was able to imagine the long night of his escape, the flight to a distant land, the constant shifting from town to town, the years of fear and dread. *What at 417 McDonald Drive,* I wondered, *could have been worth such a deep and endless sacrifice?*

At around ten, as he continued to sit alone and unmolested, an African trader in black trousers and a billowy purple shirt approached his table. A lavender turban was wound loosely around his head. He smiled at my father and drew several carved figures from a cloth bag, elephants of various sizes, a giraffe. He arranged them on my father's table. My father glanced at them, then shook his head.

The trader remained in place, persistent, trying to make a sale. My father shook his head again, then turned away, his eyes settling on one of the tile paintings that adorned the opposite wall, the head of a woman wreathed in luscious purple grapes. His eyes lingered on it, the eyelids slightly drooped, the skin wrinkled, but the eyes themselves still luminously blue, the way they'd looked that night as I'd stood, facing him from the third step.

The trader drew a wooden mask from the dark sack. It was crudely carved and sloppily lacquered, a work done without interest and for little pay. He placed it on my father's table, edging one of the elephants away.

My father didn't look at the mask, but only waved his hand languidly, refusing once again.

The trader returned the carvings to his bag, then glanced about the tavern, his eyes large and bulging, his black skin nearly blue in the dimly lighted room. He saw no other likely customers and headed for the door.

My father watched him as he walked away, the lavender turban weaving gently through a cloud of thick white smoke. A woman at the adjoining table gave my father a knowing glance, but my father only shrugged and lifted his glass in a faint, half-hearted toast.

As I sat only a few yards from him, I wondered to what it was he might still offer even so weak a toast. Was it to life? To death? Could he toast others, or were they only doll-sized figures on a featureless landscape, things like a wife and children, things he could do without?

It was nearly midnight when he rose suddenly, startling me far more than I had thought possible. I saw him rise and come toward me from the choking, smoke-filled depths of the tavern. He was upon me almost instantly, his shadow moving in a dark gray wave across my table. As he passed, I felt him brush my shoulder. I looked up and saw him glance down at me, nodding quickly, as if in apology, before he suddenly stopped dead and peered at me frozenly. For an instant, I thought he might have recognized me, and I quickly turned away. By the time I looked around again, he'd disappeared.

But he didn't go far, only a little way down the same narrow street, and into another tavern. It was emptier than the first, and he took a table at the back. I took a table not far away, and watched him more closely, as if afraid that he might vanish once again.

Under the light which hung above him, I could see the dust that had settled upon the shoulders of his jacket. There was dust on his sleeves, as well, and dust on his shoes. As I sat, watching him, I imagined dust in great brown lumps pressing in upon his guts, his lungs, his brain. I imagined his veins thick with dust, a brown mud clogging the valves of his heart. I could even envision a thick, dusty blood pouring from him as I jerked the blade upward, gutting him in one swift thrust.

He leaned back against the wall of the tavern and closed his eyes. I wondered if, at such a moment, he'd ever allowed his mind to return to McDonald Drive. Or did he go there only in a nightmare in which he watched helplessly as a little boy came down the basement stairs, stopped on the third step, and grimly leveled a shotgun at his panicked and unblinking eyes?

His eyes opened suddenly, and I saw that they were aimed at me. He glanced away and didn't look at me again. His hand lifted to his mouth, brushed against his lips, then drifted back down to his lap.

I could see a torpor in his movements, a languidness which seemed to pull even at the sharp, sudden darting of his eyes. Moments later, when a dark-haired beauty strolled past his table, he didn't follow her appreciatively, but simply let his eyes drop toward the glass he cradled gently in his right hand. At that moment he seemed quite shy, captured in shyness, almost shrunken, made of straw, himself a weightless miniature.

And yet I was still afraid of him, afraid of the scenes within his mind, the long walk up the stairs, the look on Jamie's still-living face, the backward plunge my sister's ruptured body must have made as the volley struck her, the plaintive, begging eyes of my mother as she'd crouched behind the cardboard box. I knew that there was a hideous gallery of such pictures in his brain, though the fact that he'd lived with them for so long seemed unimaginable to me.

Time passed, but my fear did not.

I could feel my hand tremble each time I thought of approaching him, and it struck me as unseemly to be so afraid of such a spiritless old man. What could he possibly do to me at this point in our lives? His physical force entirely diminished, his moral force long ago destroyed, he was nothing but an empty shell, a shadow.

And yet, I was afraid.

I was afraid because, for all his weakness and frailty, he was still my father, and the line that connected us was still a line that he somehow controlled. In his presence, I felt myself become the little boy who'd moved down the stairs, felt his gaze stop me dead.

I was afraid, and I knew why. I watched his eyes and knew exactly what I feared.

After all these months of hating him, I was afraid that when we met at last, and after I'd confronted him with everything he'd done, rubbed his face in the blood of those he'd murdered, that after all that excruciating pain had been unearthed again, and he sat, stunned, stricken, his blue eyes resting upon mine, that at that moment I would see again, know again, only this time with perfect clarity, that he had never loved me.

It was that which made me hate him again with a fierce, blinding passion. I hated him because he had not loved me enough to take me with him in his flight.

I felt my body rise suddenly, as if called to duty by an overwhelming need. I felt it move forward smoothly, righteously, with an angelic, missionary grace.

His eyes lifted toward me as I approached his table. Once I reached it, I started to speak, but to my amazement, he spoke first.

"Stevie," he said.

Stunned at the sound of his voice, thrown entirely off track by the fact that he had spoken first, I didn't answer him.

"Stevie," he repeated softly, "sit down."

Still, I couldn't speak. And so I snatched the envelope from my pocket instead, took out the three photographs, and arranged them quickly on the table before him. There, beneath the weaving candle, he could see them in a dreadful line, my mother in her bed, Jamie on his back, Laura sprawled across the floor of her room.

Then, at last, a voice leaped out at him. "Why did you do this?"

He watched me, utterly calm. He seemed beyond fear or regret, beyond anything but the long travail of his seclusion. His eyes regarded me coolly. His hands didn't tremble. The ancient power of his fatherhood surrounded him like a fortress wall.

"We had happy times," he said at last. "You remember them, don't you, Stevie?" He leaned back, the broad shoulders pressed firmly against the tile wall. His eyes dropped toward the photographs, then leaped back up at me. "Happy times," he said again.

The face that watched me seemed hardly recognizable, the "happy times" little more than sparkling shards thrown up by a blasted family. I remembered other things, instead, the icy immobility of his face as he'd stared out at "poor Dottie" from the smoky interior of the old brown van.

"You didn't love my mother, did you?" I asked.

He looked surprised by the question, but unwilling to lie.

"No," he said.

"She was dying."

Again the surprise, followed by the admission. "Yes, she was, Stevie."

"But you killed her anyway."

He started to speak, but I rushed ahead. "Why did you clean her up after that? Why did you put her in the bed that way?"

He shook his head slowly. "Respect, maybe, I don't know." He shrugged. "Pity."

I could feel my mouth curl down in a cruel rebuke. "Respect? Pity? That's why you laid her out like that?"

"Yes, it is," he answered firmly, as if it were a source of pride. "She was a very modest woman. I didn't want her to be seen like that."

"What about Jamie?" I shot back. "You didn't care how he was seen, did you?"

"What do you mean?"

"Leaving him in his room the way you did," I told him brutally, "lying on his back like that, with his face blown off."

He turned away, flinching slightly. It was the first emotion he had shown, and I felt a cruel delight in its suggestion that I had at least some small power to wound him.

"And what about Laura?" I asked tauntingly. "What about her?"

He didn't answer.

I tapped the photograph that showed her on her back, her chest blown open, her bare, soiled feet pressing toward the lens.

"You left her like Jamie," I said, "lying in her blood."

He nodded, almost curtly. "Yes, I did."

My legs dissolved beneath me as if I were being pressed down by the sudden weight of his complete admission. I sank down into the chair opposite him and released a long, exhausted breath.

"Why did you kill Laura?" I asked.

The light blue eyes squeezed together. "Because I had to," he said sharply, "because I had no choice."

It was a flat, factual response, with no hint of apology within it.

I scoffed at the notion of his being forced to carry out such a crime. "You had to kill Laura?"

"Yes."

"Why?"

The old rigidity returned to his face. He stared at me stonily. "Once it started, I had to finish it."

"Once it started?"

He shifted slightly and drew his hands back slowly until they finally dropped over the edge of the table. "The killing." His eyes darted away, then returned. "It wasn't what I wanted, Stevie."

Suddenly Swenson's words rushed toward me. *Someone else. Someone else was in that house.* I stared at him evenly. "Who made you do it then?" I demanded. "Who did you do it for?"

For the first time he seemed reluctant to answer.

I looked at him determinedly. "Who wanted us all dead?"

His face tensed. I could see that he was going back now, that I was forcing him back.

I glared at him lethally. "Tell me what happened that day."

He looked at me as if I knew nothing, as if I'd just been born, something marvelous in its innocence, but which had to be despoiled.

"That's not when it began, that day," he said. "It didn't just happen, you know."

"Of course not," I told him. "You'd planned it for a long time."

"What do you mean?"

"Those two tickets, remember?" I said. Then, so that he could have no doubt as to just how much I already knew, I added, "Those two tickets to Mexico City, the ones you bought in June."

His face tightened. "You knew about that?"

"Yes."

"How did you know?"

"The police found out," I said.

He looked strangely relieved. "Oh," he said, "the police."

"They found out everything," I told him.

He leaned forward slowly, his hands clasped together on the table. "No, they didn't," he said.

"Everything except who helped you kill them," I said.

"Helped me?"

"Yes."

"No one helped me, Stevie," he said. "What I did, I did alone."

I stared at him doubtfully. "Two tickets," I repeated, "one for you, and one for someone else." I paused a moment. "Who was she?" I demanded, my voice almost a hiss, visions of Yolanda Dawes circling in my mind.

His face softened, his eyes resting almost gently upon me. "Do you remember that morning when we were all having breakfast and Laura was talking about a report she'd done in school, and Jamie kept attacking her, belittling her?"

"Yes."

He shook his head. "Jamie was always at

Laura," he said, "always trying to humiliate her, to take away her dreams."

He was right, of course, and it was easy for me to see everything that had happened that morning, the terrible hatred my brother had shown for my sister, the delight he'd taken in chipping away at her vibrant, striving character. That morning he'd been even worse than usual, his small eyes focused upon her with a deadly earnest: *You're not going anywhere.*

My father turned away for a moment, drew in a deep breath, then looked back toward me. "I couldn't take it that morning," he said quietly. "I couldn't stand to see what he was doing to your sister." He smiled. "I knew how much she wanted out of life, you see," he went on, "how much she wanted her life to be different."

"Different from what?" I asked.

"Different from my life, Stevie," he said. "Different from your mother's life, and what Jamie's life would probably have been." He stopped, as if remembering her again in the full glory of her extravagant desire. "She talked to me about it, you know," he added after a moment. "About all she wanted to do in her life, all the places she wanted to go." He smiled softly. "She would come down in the basement where I was, and she would talk to me about it." His eyes drifted away slightly. "Always barefoot, remember?" he said, almost wistfully. "I used to tell her to put on her shoes, but she never would. She was like that, untamed. She'd always go back up with her feet covered with that grit from the basement floor." He grew silent for a moment, then shrugged. "Anyway," he said, "that morning after Jamie had acted the way he did, I went out and sat down in that little room we had, the one with the vines." He stopped, his voice a little harder when he spoke again. "That's when I decided that it couldn't go on like it was, Stevie," he said. "That something had to be done about it."

"You mean, something had to be done about Jamie?"

"About what he was doing to your sister," my father answered. "Something had to be done about that."

I remembered the look on his face as he'd sat alone in the solarium that morning. It was a grim, determined face, all doubt removed. It was then that he'd decided that "something had to be done," I supposed, not while he'd sat gazing at my mother as she stooped over the flower garden, but that spring morning when Jamie had launched his attack upon the daughter that my father loved.

My father's hands drew back, each of them finally drifting over the edge of the table. "I told Laura about it a week later," he said. "She came down to the solarium one night. It must have been toward the middle of that last summer." He drew in a deep breath. "I told her what I wanted to do."

I looked at him, astonished. "Kill us," I muttered.

His eyes widened, staring at me unbelievingly. "What?"

"That you were going to kill us," I said, "you told Laura that?"

He shook his head. "No, Stevie," he said, "not that." He paused a moment, watching me brokenly. "Never that."

"What then?"

"I told her that I'd decided to take her away,"

my father said, "that I'd looked through a lot of travel brochures, and that I'd already decided on the place." He looked at me solemnly. "I told her that I'd already bought two tickets to Mexico, and that I was going to take her there."

"And leave the rest of us?" I asked.

"Jamie wouldn't have cared," my father said. "And your mother, she'd always wanted to move back to Maine, where she'd grown up." His face took on the look of a mournful revelation. "There was someone there, Stevie. Waiting for her, you might say. Someone from way back. Someone she'd never forgotten."

It was the phantom lover, of course, Jamie's real father, a man in a mountain cabin, as I imagined him at that moment, writing letters to my mother on soft blue paper.

"Jamie and your mother would both have been better off in another place," my father said.

"And me?"

"You're what made it hard, Stevie," my father said. "I hadn't really decided about you."

I stared at him bitterly. "At the time you killed them, you mean?" I asked brutally.

My father did not so much as flinch. "I chose to save my daughter," he said with a grave resignation.

A strange pride gathered in his voice, and suddenly I recognized that at that moment when he'd told Laura of his plan to take her away, at that precise moment in his life, and perhaps for the only time, his love had taken on a fabled sweep, had become a thing of knights on horseback and maidens in dire distress, a romantic mission of preservation and defense, one far different from the type undertaken by those other men with whom Rebecca had already forever linked his name.

"I never saw Laura more happy when I told her about Mexico," my father said.

In my mind, I saw them together in the little solarium with its windows draped in vines, my father in the white wicker chair, Laura below him, her face resting peacefully, as if she were still a little girl.

"Why didn't you go then?" I asked. "Why didn't you just take her and go away?"

"Because toward the end of the summer I found out your mother was dying," my father said. "I couldn't leave her in a situation like that. So I canceled the tickets." He shook his head helplessly. "I didn't tell Laura right away, and when I did, she looked as if her whole world had collapsed." He seemed to bring her back into his mind, fully, in all her furious need. "Laura wasn't like me," he said again, "there was something great in her." He stopped, then added, "But there was something wrong, too, something out of control."

"When did you tell Laura that you'd canceled the tickets?"

"Around the middle of October."

"Did you tell her why?"

"I'd already told her that your mother was very sick," he answered, "but I'm not sure she realized that it had made me change our plans until I actually told her that I'd canceled the tickets, that we wouldn't be going to Mexico together."

I stared at him evenly, remembering the sudden, wrenching illness that had gripped my mother the night of the fireworks. I remembered how Laura had prepared her a glass of milk after we'd returned.

"Laura tried to kill her, didn't she?" I asked coolly.

He nodded. "Yes, she did," he said. "I thought it was over, after that. She'd done something terrible, but I thought that would be the end of it." He looked at me pointedly. "Until that day."

That day.

"It was raining," I said softly, "that's almost all I remember."

He drew in a quick breath. "Yes, it was raining," he said. He waited a moment, as if deciding whether or not to go on. "I was at the store downtown like always," he began finally. "I was alone. There was so much rain. No one was on the streets." The old mournfulness swept into his eyes. "Then the phone rang," he said. "It was Laura. She said that your mother had gotten sick, and she told me to come home."

"When was this?"

"Around a quarter after three, I guess," my father said. "I went home right away."

I could feel a silence gather around us as we sat facing each other in the small tavern, vast and empty, as if ours were the only voices that had survived a holocaust.

"Laura met me in the kitchen," my father said. "She'd made me a ham sandwich, and for a minute, I thought that the long time she'd been so angry with me, that it was finally over."

"Where was my mother?"

"Laura said that she was upstairs," my father answered, "that she was a little better, that she was taking a nap."

And so, suspecting nothing, my father had sat down at the kitchen table, and taken a few bites of the ham sandwich Laura had made for him. She had disappeared upstairs almost immediately, and after a time my father had wandered out to the solarium and slumped down in one of its white wicker chairs.

"I wasn't there very long," he said, "when I heard someone coming down the stairs. It was your mother."

Perhaps more fully than I had ever thought possible, I now saw my mother in all her lost and loveless beauty. I saw her move softly down the carpeted stairs in her fluffy house shoes, her hand clutching the throat of her blouse, a woman perhaps less foolish than any of us had thought, her mind already wondering which of her children would try to kill her next.

"From where I was sitting, I just saw her go by," my father said. "Then I heard the basement door open, and I knew she was going down there."

He heard her feet move down the wooden stairs, then went back to the little book he'd found in the solarium, reading it slowly, as he always did, his eyes moving lethargically across the slender columns.

"Jamie came in after that," he said.

Encased in a vast solitude, rudderless and without direction, my brother came through the kitchen door, trails of rainwater dripping from his hair. He glanced coldly toward my father, but didn't speak. Instead he simply bounded up the stairs.

"I heard him close the door to his room," my father said. "He made a point of slamming it."

After that, but for only a few, precious moments, a silence had descended upon 417 McDonald Drive. For a time, as he read in the solarium, my father had heard nothing but the rain.

Then a blast of incredible magnitude rocked the house.

"I thought it was a gas explosion," my father said, "something like that. I couldn't imagine what else it might be."

He jumped to his feet, the book sliding to the floor of the solarium. He stared around a moment, not knowing where to go. In a blur of speed, he saw Laura fly past the open space that divided the living room from the downstairs corridor.

"The way she was running, I thought something must have happened upstairs," my father said, "so I ran up there, thinking that Jamie might be hurt, that things might be on fire."

And so he rushed up the stairs, taking them in broad leaps, plummeting down the corridor where he could see a blue smoke coming through the open door of Jamie's room.

"I ran into his room, thinking that he must be hurt, that I had to pull him out," my father said.

What he saw was a boy without a face.

"And I still didn't know what had happened," my father said, breathless, already exhausted, as if he had only now made that dreadful run. "I still didn't realize at that point that Jamie had been shot," he said wonderingly, as if, through all the years, this was the strangest thing of all.

He ran to him, picked him up slightly, his shoes already soaking up Jamie's rich, red blood. Still stunned, dazed, unable to think, he heard a roar from down below.

"Then I knew, I think," he said, "but even then . . . even then . . ."

Even then, he didn't know for sure that his family was being slaughtered.

"And so I just stood there, in the middle of Jamie's room," my father said.

Just stood there, his eyes darting about wildly until he finally bolted toward the basement.

"From out of nowhere, I thought that it must be someone else," he said, "that some killer had broken into the house somehow." He looked at me, the astonishment still visible in his face. "I thought that it was this killer who must have chased Laura down the stairs, that she'd been running from someone else when I'd seen her fly past me that time before."

And so he began to run again, into the bedroom across the hall, then down the stairs, taking long, desperate strides as he searched for "someone else" in the living room, the dining room, the kitchen, his bloody tracks leading everywhere until, at last, they led down the basement stairs.

He stopped on the third step, stricken by what he saw.

"Your mother was behind a big cardboard box," my father said. "Laura was standing just a few feet away. My old shotgun was in her hands. The barrel was still smoking." He looked at me unbelievingly. "She was barefoot, like always."

Barefoot, yes. Like she was in the photograph that should have told me everything, her bare feet stretched toward the camera, their upturned soles covered with the dark grit she'd picked up from the basement floor as she'd stood and aimed the shotgun at my mother.

Swenson's words came rushing back to me: "Someone else. Someone in the house. Someone helping."

Laura.

My father shook his head slowly. "She just

looked at me, and she said, 'Now we *have* to go!' " He stared at me pointedly. "She meant Mexico," he said, "that now, after what she'd done, that I had no choice but to take her there."

After that, they'd gone back up to the kitchen together, my father shaken, lost, unable to register the events that had just swept over him.

"I knew she'd done something to your mother a month before," he said, "but I'd never dreamed that she would do the same to Jamie or to . . ." He stopped and looked at me emptily.

"To me?" I said.

He leaned forward, his eyes very gentle. "She wanted me to do it, Stevie," he said. "She said she couldn't."

Then she had gone upstairs to her room, walking briskly up the stairs, like someone who'd just been released from prison.

"I stayed in the kitchen," my father told me. "I thought about it all for a while."

For a while, but not for long. Only for that short interval which Mrs. Hamilton had noticed between the second shot and the final one.

"I knew Laura had to die," my father said, "and I knew that if I killed her, they would blame all of it on me, that you would never know what she'd done to them."

Or had planned to do to me.

"So I wiped her fingerprints off the gun," my father said. "Then I walked upstairs and . . ." He stopped, his eyes glancing away for a moment, then returning to me. "It was instant," he whispered.

I saw my sister turn, saw her eyes widen in disbelief, her hand lift futilely as he pulled the trigger.

"That left you," my father said.

That left me, yes.

To live on, though alone, remembering the love of my sister.

My father watched me a moment, leaning back, as if to get a better view. He seemed infinitely relieved, though carrying the same, ancient burden he'd carried through it all.

"I hadn't really had time to think about anything," my father said. "But after Laura, I went downstairs and thought about what I should do. Later I went back upstairs to change my clothes."

And so the bloody shoes had never gone below the third step, though by then I knew that my father had.

"But I decided to clean things up a little," my father said. "I knew you'd be coming home any minute, and I didn't want you to see . . ." He shrugged, the sentence trailing off into a brief silence before he began again. "After I'd finished with your mother," he said, "I decided that maybe I should take you with me." The blue eyes softened. "So I waited for you, Stevie. I didn't do anything about Laura or Jamie. I just left them where they were and waited for you to come home." He looked at me plaintively, as if in apology. "But you never came," he said. "The phone kept ringing. I thought it might be you, but I was afraid to pick it up."

And so, at last, he'd walked out into the rain.

"I went to the store and got what money I could," he told me. "Then I drove to Oscar's and bought a few things." He looked at me tenderly. "The last thing I did was call the house. I thought you might be there. Just come in, maybe. Not seen anything. I didn't think it was possible, but I wanted to give it one last chance."

One last chance, to take me with him.

"But you still weren't there," he said.

I looked away from him, stared at the wall. I felt my hand rise and press down upon my lips. I didn't speak.

"I did see you one more time, though," he said. "After I left the house that day, I drove up to a place near my parents' farm. I knew there was a cabin in the woods. You may remember it yourself. We all went up there one time."

"I remember it," I answered softly.

"I stayed there for over a month," my father told me, "then I decided to head south." He paused a moment, his eyes settling gently on my face. "On the way down, I drove by Somerset and took some flowers to the graves. I'd just finished putting some on Jamie's grave when I saw you and Edna coming up the hill." His voice seemed about to break as he continued. "I ran off into the woods. I could see you at the graves." He fell silent for a time, then added, "I've lived alone since then. I never married. Never had more children." He watched me, as if not sure he had the right to inquire into my life.

"How about you, Stevie?" he asked finally, tentatively.

"Yes, I got married," I told him quietly.

He seemed pleased, though he didn't smile. "Any kids?" he asked.

"A son."

"Where's your family now?"

I shrugged, but not indifferently.

"Gone," I told him.

I saw a terrible bleakness come into his face, a father's grief for the losses of his son. "Sorry," was all he said.

Once again, we sat silently for a time, then walked out of the tavern together. It was very dark, and so my father guided me through the twisting, ebony streets, past the olives and the palms, through what was left of the labyrinth, until we reached the unlighted beach.

"Stevie?" my father began, then stopped, as if brought to a halt by the look he'd glimpsed upon my face.

I didn't answer.

Far in the distance, through the immense stillness, I could see a ship in the darkness, sailing blindly, it seemed to me, toward its nightbound home.

ABOUT THE AUTHOR

Thomas H. Cook is the author of eleven novels, including *Sacrificial Ground* and *Blood Innocents,* both Edgar Award nominees; *Flesh and Blood, The Orchids, Elena, Tabernacle, Night Secrets, Streets of Fire, The City When It Rains,* and *Evidence of Blood;* and two works about true crime, *Early Graves* and *Blood Echoes,* which was also nominated for an Edgar Award. He lives in New York City.